THE CRAFTER'S SON

Book One of
The Crafter Chronicles

By
Matthew B. Berg

Woodfall Press
P.O. Box #6011
Holliston, MA 01746

eBook ISBN: 0-9785791-2-7
Paperback ISBN: 978-1-70-708826-3
Hardcover ISBN: 978-0-9785791-3-5

10 9 8 7 6 5 4 3 2

Join the Crafter's Guild!

Become a member and become part of the story.

- Members of the guild are always the first to hear about Matthew's new books and publications.
- Members will receive access to free behind-the-scenes content, such as maps, character sheets, and other Crafter artifacts—as we create them.
- Finally, some lucky guild members will have the opportunity to become beta readers for book two (and beyond!).

Check out the back of the book for information on how to become a guild member.

To my mother and father.
For their endless support and enthusiasm!

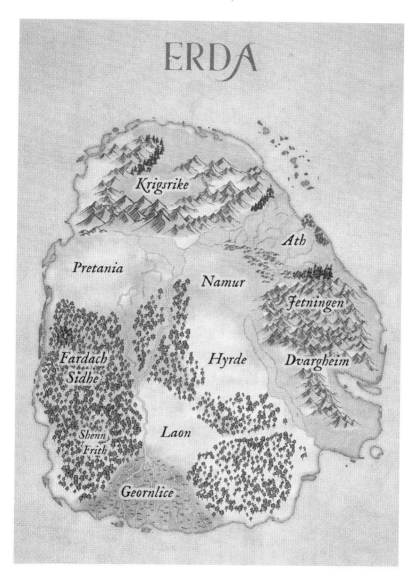

1

THE RUN

Breeden's small hands worked the net carefully as the sunrise unfolded in fiery arcs across the sky. To his sixteen-year-old sensibility, it was the most incredible sunrise he had ever seen: deep reds and purples bled in broad streaks into burnt oranges and yellows above the floodplain to the east. Fully half the world was ablaze in a riot of colors overhead. Rich, earthy smells rose from the lake. And the crispness of early spring cleared the last wisps of lingering sleep he bore from rising so early.

With difficulty, he tore himself away from the sky's majesty. He had no time for sunrises right now. He shifted his seat closer to the balance point of his small rowboat and adjusted his grip once again. The net's rough hemp was clammy and pricked the skin of his calloused hands unpredictably as he maintained a steady draw against the weight of the water. Then Breeden noticed the roiling of the water above his net. He was startled at first, the churning mass looking like a thing tentacled and evil. But he quickly realized he could pick out the forms of individual fish sliding over, under, and around each other like a dark, wet fistful of arm-thick worms. Relief from the brief stab

I

of fear, and joy at the arrival of the anticipated fish, swelled in his chest. The running of the herring had begun!

His father had set Breeden upon the course he now followed in the hopes he would beat the rush of townsfolk who would soon scramble onto the water in anything that floated. The harvest of nearly limitless quantities of fish from these waters over the next two weeks would provide food for months to come for many, and a windfall commodity to be distributed by boat and wagon for others.

For Breeden and his parents, all the fish from today's catch would be salted and smoked dry for storage. Breeden would catch additional fish during the summer months, which they would eat fresh, but today's bounty, once properly prepared, would last them through the winter—perhaps even until next year's run.

It was all Breeden could do to muscle the first haul over the side of his father's rowboat. And the pair of bushel baskets he had brought with him proved woefully inadequate to contain even the first net's catch. But he cast the net two more times and landed two more hauls, each somewhat smaller than the last, before he collapsed at the bow of the sturdy little boat.

Only then did Breeden take the time to rest and to admire the sky and the now visible orb of the sun rising above the distant tree line. His boat sat in the middle of the River Woodfall's narrow mouth at the southernmost end of Long Lake. The broad and treeless expanse of the river's floodplain afforded him a wide and unobstructed view of the sun's rise for miles to the east and southeast. A low mist clung to the lake's surface against the far banks, where shade offered it a few more minutes' protection, but the water around him was clear and smooth, reflecting the sky's now fading colors.

As he swept his gaze from the south through the east, he caught sight of a will-o-wisp. The halo-shrouded mass of blue and blue-green lights moved through the air like an erratic school of fish. He watched it for a few more moments before it disappeared. Even the brief sighting made Breeden's heart race. He had seen will-o-wisps before, though usually at night. But they weren't common by any means, and most people Breeden knew were superstitious of them. Many thought wisps were ill omens, but others, as Breeden, thought they were bits of magic that, should you be able to lay your hands on one, would grant you any wish. He waited to see if it would reappear, and when it didn't, he sighed and looked about once more.

Gazing north, Breeden could see several small fishing vessels. Some had sails furled and were engaged in landing the salmon, which lived in the deeper waters of the lake. Others were done with their morning's work on the water and were returning to shore to begin the sorting and cleaning of their catch. Beyond the boats and beyond the range of his eyesight, Breeden knew the lake continued north for many leagues. A small vessel like the ones before him would take as long as two or even three days to make the trip to the northernmost tip of the aptly named Long Lake.

After several minutes of reflection, Breeden reluctantly retrieved the oars and set off for shore.

2

ENCOUNTER

It wasn't until he arrived at the pier that Breeden realized he would have a hard time bringing his bounty home without assistance, but he loaded a single bushel basket as full as he could manage and set off anyway. The basket was somewhat more than half full, but it still presented a daunting challenge to Breeden's young frame, and he had to stop at the landward end of the pier and set the basket down to catch his wind. When he straightened once again to pick up his burden, he discovered an old man standing where he'd have sworn none had stood moments earlier.

The old man had a thick head of long hair, more white than grey, and long mustaches that ran trimly down below his jaw. His features were strong and firm, and his skin bore the leathery appearance of a man who had spent his life at sea. He wore a half-smile, and his furrowed brow made him look as though he were waiting for someone.

Breeden recovered from his surprise and bid the old man good morning.

"Good morning, my son. You bear a heavy burden for one so young."

"Yes, sir. It's the run, finally here."

"I can see that." His half smile broadened, and his eyes crinkled up. "And it appears as though you've no intention of sharing with anyone else!"

Breeden could tell the man was joking, but felt abashed nonetheless. "I've been out each morning for nine days. My father would say I've earned the early bird's share."

The old man's smile softened as he looked beneath the sandy mop of hair and into the hazel eyes of the young man before him. He could see the obvious sincerity behind his words. "As you have, my son. Nine days? You are a persistent one. By your father's bidding, or on your own?"

"A bit of both, sir. My father asked me if I needed him this year. Other springs we would go out together, but this time he asked. And when he asked, I got the feeling the right answer was to say no, so I did. He seemed happy, so I figure I made the right decision."

The old man nodded sagely. "It sounds like your father has raised you well. I'm sure you make him proud."

Breeden smiled, feeling embarrassed, and a bit proud, from the comment. Too, there was something about the old man and the way he spoke that made the exchange feel particularly genuine. Then he remembered the challenge that remained before him. "He may not be so proud of me if it takes me ten trips back and forth to the house to bring home all the fish I've caught. I didn't think how I'd get the fish back without him."

The old man furrowed his brow once again as he pondered the boy's predicament, but before he could speak, Breeden continued. "I suppose it's okay to leave the rest of the fish in our boat and go get him to help me. I won't be long—just a handful of minutes each way. And even though I wanted to do this all by myself, I suppose I don't really have a choice, right?"

"I'm sure the fish will be fine," the old man chuckled softly.

"The morning is cool yet. And there don't appear to be any thieves about. Perhaps a wheelbarrow?"

Breeden considered briefly and then laughed. "What a great idea! I could probably manage without my father if I brought back the wheel-barrel. And the fish won't be alone as long either!"

"By all means, then, you must hurry along. Don't let a foolish old man hold you up on your errand."

"Thank you, sir! Good morning!"

The smile faded ever so slightly from the old man's eyes as Breeden turned and jogged up the road.

3

OLD FRIENDS

Since Breeden's family lived but a short walk away, only a handful of minutes passed before he returned. When he stepped back onto the pier, he noticed that the old man was gone. For some reason, this didn't surprise him. There was something sad about the entire encounter, though he couldn't understand why.

He shook off the hollow feeling and began loading his fish into the wheelbarrow.

HALF AN HOUR LATER, Breeden arrived at home with a two-wheeled cart filled to the top with fat black-and-silver herring.

He leaned the handle of his cart against the wall and walked over to a rain barrel at the corner of his house, grabbing the small pail from a hook hung well under the eave and scooping out some water to wash the scales and slime from his arms and hands. He would need his father's assistance to unload and prepare the herring for storage, but he would need to be clean before entering his home to ask for help.

The two-story house before him had a narrow front that

faced the main road, which followed the River Woodfall's bend. Their home was built on the bank of the river, and the rear of the house, his father's workshop, overhung the river by several feet. Above the simple wooden door that served as his home's entrance were the words "Holt Andehar, Boatwright," and extending from the doorjamb was a double-sided craftsman's placard displaying a picture of a carved sailboat, the hull painted cobalt blue, and the sail painted white. The front stoop was swept clear of debris, and the plaster-and-timber exterior appeared freshly whitewashed.

Breeden gave one last glance to the load of fish and opened the front door to enter his house.

Upon stepping inside, Breeden took care in wiping his feet on a mat of bristles and then walked toward the kitchen. He could hear his father in animated conversation down the length of the hallway. Then his mother's laugh rang out. Breeden was surprised at the unusual energy he sensed. *That's odd*, he thought. They were happy people, but he just didn't think of them as people who laughed all the time. And he couldn't remember the last time he'd heard such genuine mirth in their voices. Then a deep rumbling sound, as of a boat rubbing against a submerged rock, issued from the kitchen. Breeden couldn't be sure, but he thought the sound might have contained words. He picked up his pace and approached the kitchen doorway.

And then he saw the giant.

He was seated on a workbench that had been pulled into the kitchen from his father's shop at the back of the house—likely because no chair in the home would have been large enough to accommodate his massive frame. Even seated as he was, his tremendous head brushed the ceiling as he shifted in his seat. His features were like those of a human, though not in the same proportion. His nose, for example, was much broader than even a ten-foot human's would have been. His ears were massive and pointed at the top, like an elf's. Too, his brownish-orange skin was rough and craggy, like the shell of a walnut. And his deeply recessed eyes looked very small, and even smaller for being so heavily shadowed by a prominent brow. His hair was black and curly, and his springlike locks hung loosely about his head.

By contrast, Breeden's mother and father looked like children, seated as they were in the presence of this enormous figure. Breeden's father had sandy-blond hair that was quietly and almost unnoticeably transitioning to grey and white by turns. He had a roundish head, red cheeks more often than not, and bright, intelligent blue eyes. He shared with Breeden a smile that turned up at only one side. His mother had brown hair, hazel-green eyes, like Breeden's, and a warm and beautiful face that had weathered the years well enough that she looked far younger than her husband—despite the fact that she was his senior by almost two years.

After Breeden stood gaping in the doorway for a few timeless moments, his mother finally noticed his arrival and rose to free him from his frozen state.

"Aegir," she introduced, "this is our son, Breeden. When was the last time you visited us? I don't believe you've ever had a chance to meet him. Breeden, say hello to our dear friend Aegir."

Breeden looked the giant in the eye and found he could not speak. Without standing, Aegir smiled at the young man and inclined his head slightly, rumbling so low that Breeden could feel the words in his chest. "Greetings, Breeden. It is an honor to meet you as a young man."

Breeden didn't register the greeting, and even allowing for his youth, his stupor was becoming awkward. His father rose then and guided him to a chair. "I am sorry, friend. My son is young still and hasn't seen your kind before. But I suppose that's pretty obvious, eh?"

Aegir waved his hand to dismiss Breeden's father's concerns. "No worry, Holt Andehar. A day will come, I hope, when the two of us will sail Long Lake together as friends. But the boy is young, as you say, and I have come unannounced." With these words, the giant rose slowly, hunching as he did so as to ensure he didn't strike his head on the high ceiling.

"Don't go." The words, from Breeden, were hardly audible. When all eyes in the room had turned to hear him better, he managed a bit louder. "Stay at least until I've brought the fish in."

Breeden's father laughed softly. "Fish indeed! The boy's wits have returned, and he is his father's practical son! The herring run must have begun, Aegir. We must help Breeden with his catch."

In no time at all, and with Aegir's assistance—despite the protest from Breeden's mother—they had the fish in three large barrels, soaking in brine. They could store the fish in this way for many weeks and could take their time in drying the fish and wrapping them for more durable storage. All agreed that Breeden's haul was unexpectedly large and would certainly last through to next year's run.

Breeden had loosened up while they worked and had begun to ask questions of Aegir. They were innocuous questions at first. "Where do you live? . . . Do your mountains truly reach the clouds?" And they became bolder as the morning progressed. By the time they were finished cleaning up and were once again seated in the kitchen, Breeden was asking more of the types of questions you might expect from a sixteen-year-old boy: "How many stones can you lift? . . . Are the giant women as big as the giant men? . . . Do they breathe fire? . . . How about giant babies? Are they as big as I am now? . . . How many apples can you eat in one sitting? . . . Can you swim, or do you sink if you fall in the water?"

Giants were known, as a race, for their patience, and Aegir

was no exception. He amused himself and Breeden's parents by displaying his dry wit in responding to the less tactful questions Breeden posed.

To the question about giant women breathing fire, he responded, "Upon occasion, and far too often for my comfort." And to the question about whether or not he could swim, he responded, "I sink slower than a stone but faster than I care for." In most cases, Breeden was already thinking of the next question, hardly registering each answer given, and before long Breeden's parents were laughing openly, unable to contain themselves while observing the back-and-forth.

Eventually, Breeden tired of asking questions in such rapid succession, and without being conscious of it, he began to ask ones that required more thought and time on Aegir's part to respond. "What do you do for fun?" spawned a lengthy monologue by Aegir about his favorite hobbies: walking and sailing —both of which he claimed were made more pleasant by the company of his pipe. Aegir became more at ease as he spoke of home. When he talked of walking in the mountains, he painted a vivid picture of pastoral serenity: high and vast slopes of green pastures overlooking a rocky coastline and the lapis waters crashing into pure white foam at the land's edge. His deep and sonorous voice projected the scale and sweep of the mountains and the might of the ocean better than Breeden thought a human's possibly could. He felt the images come together in his mind as the giant spoke until he must surely have the sight captured just as the giant saw it himself.

When he spoke of the sea, Aegir changed the timbre of his voice, and his words became an endless horizon, reefing sails and clanging tackle, and the hollow booming of a ship's hull slapping against the waves. He lowered it once again, and a storm swept in from leagues away, darkening the sky and bringing with it stinging drops of heavy rain. The laughter of Breeden's parents was forgotten, and his mother's mouth hung open along with those of Breeden and his father. Breeden looked in his mother's eyes and could see the enchantment being wrought by the seafaring giant's voice.

When Aegir finally did stop talking, the entire family remained silent for a long moment, allowing the images in their minds to dissipate at their own pace. It would be weeks before Breeden would find that the images had faded beyond his ability to recall them in such detail. And he would never forget the emotions left behind by the giant's view of his home: devotion to the land, awe at the world's beauty, and respect for the dwarfing and unknowable power of nature. In a sudden and surprising revelation, Breeden realized that he wanted to accompany Aegir when the giant left for home the next day.

4
_____

A DIVERSION

The next morning, Breeden allowed himself the rare opportunity to sleep in. Along with the fact that he'd been up so very early for the past week and a half, he'd also worked harder than normal the day before, and his whole family had stayed up late talking with the giant Aegir. When he had finally gone to sleep, he slept deeply and awoke somewhat stiff but otherwise well recovered.

His father and Aegir were sitting at the kitchen table when he found his way down the stairs, a few small pieces of sausage, cheese, and bread remaining on a board between them. He supposed they hadn't been there all night but had gone to bed after him and risen before him. But then, they looked somewhat tired, so he couldn't be sure.

They appeared to be involved in a much more serious conversation than the ones from the night before, and Breeden caught repeated references to "the boy." He understood quickly enough they were talking about him.

"Good morning." Breeden projected the words to make his father and the giant aware of his arrival. He'd been told many times before not to "sneak up on people"—usually when his father was alone in his workshop and Breeden's sudden arrival might cause a startled mishap in carving or the careful alignment of delicate pieces.

Breeden's mother had boiled some eggs for him, and she brought them to the table as he moved to sit down. "Good morning, sleepyhead," she said playfully.

"Good morning, young Breeden!" the giant boomed.

"Good morning, son!" His father wore an odd half smirk as he spoke the words, and Breeden became suspicious.

Breeden paused in the act of sliding his chair back from the table and couldn't help himself. "What is it?"

His father beamed at him and seemed to discard his first and even second response before continuing. "Well, after such a demanding day yesterday, I thought that perhaps you could forgo your chores today."

Breeden became immediately excited but didn't dare show it until he understood the smirk. He decided not to respond, to see if there was more that his father would share. It didn't take long.

"Our giant friend here has not come strictly for a social visit but has placed an order as well. And the material and equipment I have at hand will not be sufficient for the job. It seems we will need to journey to the market to purchase what we can and to arrange for the rest."

Now Breeden was excited. And he decided the smirk might not hold a nasty surprise after all but could be a cousin to the smirk his father wore at Beltide or on Breeden's birthday. His smile broke wide at the prospect of visiting the market with his father. It was something his family rarely felt the need to do, since they were mostly self-sufficient for their day-to-day tools and supplies. His mother would head into town for "womanly things" every so often—dresses and such, he supposed—but that was pretty much the extent of it.

When Breeden did go to market, it was most often for

something specific—a "there and back again" affair, so to speak. But something about the way his father spoke, or about his smile, made this trip sound somehow more expansive, as if the list were a long and difficult one, and they might have to spend a good amount of time seeking among the wares of the various merchants. Or at least Breeden allowed himself to imagine the trip as such.

Breeden's father continued. "We'll be seeing off Aegir at the deepwater piers before we leave for the market—as soon as you have a chance to wash your face and eat your breakfast!"

In minutes they were ready to go.

BREEDEN WAS sad to see the giant go, despite having met him only the day before. In that single evening, the giant had brought a rare and sweet joy to the lives of his mother and father, and had become as natural a presence in their home as another member of the family.

The walk to the deepwater piers was more than twice as far as the pier Breeden had used the day before, but the distance passed quickly. Aegir and Breeden's father filled the time discussing the details of his order, his father plying him with more questions about the design and construction. Aegir answered most of these with "I trust your work, Holt Andehar."

His mother having said her goodbyes at their home, Breeden and his father stood on the pier as the giant maneuvered his boat away from them. The boat was of a size that Aegir could just manage to sail it by himself, with a tiller, four sheets, and a knotted line to raise the keel should he need to.

The fin-shaped "keel" was unusual to say the least. Breeden had seen only a few like it before on Long Lake—the need for a keel of any depth was less critical when navigating lakes and rivers than sailing the open ocean. Common wisdom held that seagoing vessels needed a sturdy and fixed keel to weather the forces at work beyond the coastline. But Aegir appeared to manage just fine with a more flexible alternative to both extremes.

The giant's craft was fast disappearing from view to the north. Breeden thought of the long journey that lay ahead for him. It would be several days before he reached his home. Then it occurred to him, as he considered the relaxed and powerful ease with which Aegir controlled the vessel, that the giant was already there.

With a final wave of his arms above his head, Breeden's father decided it was time to head over to the Ridderzaal market.

5

TALENTS REVEALED

The market was a frantic place, and it always took Breeden a few minutes to acclimate himself to it. The hawkers would yell loudly in competition for the handful of buyers. The animals would bleat, or neigh, or crow. The pungent aromas of a local favorite, satje, marinated meat or fish sold on sticks, would compete with the manure, the tanning chemicals, and the perfumes. The cloth merchants' wares would strike a garish contrast in their rainbow hues to the dull duns and browns of most of the other booths. It was a mad and unpredictable scene, even on a calm day, and even in such a small city as Ridderzaal. And it was even madder to Breeden for the fact that his days usually consisted of helping his mother and father around the house and workshop. As an only child, with no close friends his own age, Breeden led a very isolated and uneventful life. The market was anything but uneventful.

The giant's project called for ironwood, which would quickly dull a blade made of poor-quality steel. Breeden's father explained that the blacksmiths in town would not have forges capable of producing a high enough heat to achieve the hardness required for the giant's job. But perhaps the traders at market might have some workable tools among their wares. He reminded Breeden, too, that the chisels and saw blades he sought would need to be larger than average due to the scale of the project.

They started by looking for any sign of tools at all among the tables and stalls of the merchants, and then they scouted each stall that did to see if chisels, saws, or drawknives might be among them. In front of a garishly painted tinker's wagon, they spotted a large spread of woodworking tools of all sorts and in all types of condition. The tools were spread out in a fan surrounding a battered wooden toolbox that looked as if it would contain the entire collection. Breeden spotted a flat box at one side, opened to reveal a gorgeous set of six silver chisels filigreed with creeping vines and flowers along the tops of the blades.

"I see them too." Breeden's father had followed his son's widening eyes and also appeared impressed with the set's beauty.

The tinker saw their interest and reacted. "You won't find a finer set of chisels this side of the Eastern Sea. Handcrafted by the dwarven smith Bertil, these chisels have no rival in all the land."

Breeden's father smirked good-naturedly at the man. "You don't say." He lifted one chisel delicately from the velvet-padded box, noting the obvious quality of even the box itself.

Breeden wriggled himself between his father and the table, and he picked up one of the chisels, turning it over in his hands. He seemed to become lost for a moment as he did so. But his father was too busy to notice the intensity of his son's examination as he began the dance of determining a fair price for the chisels.

"I should say these chisels are a bit too fine for the kind of work I intend to put them to. Do you have anything sturdier about?"

The tinker didn't miss a beat. "Indeed, I have other chisels, sir, but none compare in beauty *and function* to these dwarven-made blades. They are a special dwarven alloy that polishes as brightly as silver but cuts as the finest steel. I offer you a blow or two with one of my mallets, if you'd like. I'm sure I could produce a scrap of wood for you to test their edge."

"Thanks for that, but I'm sure those tools are far beyond my humble means. Could I see some of your others?"

The tinker realized Breeden's father would not be an easy dupe and shifted to a more straightforward approach. "Indeed, sir. I believe I have an odd assortment of bits and ends in my wagon. Allow me a moment."

When the tinker had disappeared into his wagon, Breeden's father spoke. "Here is where he plans to take his time so we can examine the fine silver chisels more closely. And he will watch us from a window to see that we do. So we won't give him the satisfaction. Go ahead and put your chisel back."

Breeden grudgingly set down the chisel and commented, "They are not as fine as he thinks, anyway. The metal is cheap and ill-formed beneath the silver. They wouldn't hold up under real use and won't serve for what we need."

His father was puzzled at the certainty with which Breeden had made the statement, and he wondered where Breeden's imagination had come up with such a firm and reasonable-sounding assertion. He gave his son an odd look. "They look fine enough to me. Why do you say that?"

Breeden couldn't explain, thinking it as obvious as rain, and was surprised at his father's question. "Can't you tell by looking at them? On the surface, they look pretty enough, but underneath the silver, the metal is weak." Breeden felt his response was weak, but he didn't have the words to better describe what he meant.

His father thought back to a similar conversation they'd had a handful of months ago. The handle on one of his mauls had split, and he had asked Breeden to choose a piece of replacement stock. He knew that among the scraps of wood, there was a likely piece close to the right proportions for the job, which would require minimal whittling. When Breeden had come back with a much longer piece of wood with a fat knot at one end, he had asked his son if there were none better shaped for the purpose. Breeden's response had stuck with him. He didn't remember the exact words necessarily, but the intention was clear: "You'll only have to carve this one later anyway, since that other piece is bound to split."

As now, he had asked Breeden why he believed that to be the case, and Breeden had given him roughly the same response: "Can't you see that it's going to break?" At the time, he'd chalked it up to youthful imagination and had made use of the wood Breeden had brought to him. As it turned out, the knot served as a perfect knurl at the butt of the handle to keep the heavy and long-handled maul in hand during strenuous use. And he had to admit that the grain and density of the wood was excellent for the job.

What stuck with him was a sense of wonder at how the boy had made such a judgment. He considered himself a good judge of wood, and knew the skill to be a combination of art—or more accurately, practiced intuition—and simple experience. But despite Breeden's growing up in a household where working wood was practiced with great care and, all modesty aside, great skill, there was something special about his boy.

The tinker appeared from within his wagon, carrying a large burlap bag that clinked dully in his left hand as he approached. He unceremoniously dumped the contents on the table. It was full of chisels. Breeden's father thought the tinker might have been gathering the tools together after all, and not watching them from the window, as he'd told his son. Or perhaps the tinkers were a more organized lot than he gave them credit for.

Breeden scanned the tools and mentally discarded almost all of them. His father pretended to examine them himself, but he was suddenly more interested in watching his son. The tinker caught the exchange and didn't appear to know what to make of it, but his face revealed that he thought he was somehow being conned.

Breeden had already decided upon four of the larger and wider chisels, two of which appeared to be mated with each other, but he waited for his father before saying anything. He seemed to have finished with whatever sort of evaluation he intended when Breeden's father spoke up. "Well, before I consider any of these rustic blades, why don't we discuss your best price on the dwarven set."

The tinker's eyes narrowed. He hadn't expected the question. But he recovered. "I couldn't let them go for less than one and a half crowns."

Breeden's father blanched at the price. He had expected the tinker to aim high, but never would have expected him to go that high. But the price was on the table, and Breeden's father resumed the dance. "I should say that that's more than I make in a season, sir! I would need to borrow some copper for half that price. The best I could manage with the coins on my person is twenty-five commons."

Twenty-five commons being twelve-and-a-half less than one quarter the starting price, the tinker feigned insult. "Surely you can't be serious. Why, at ten silvers, I would sell them at a loss, never mind less than three!"

Breeden's father feigned being deflated by the assertion. "I suppose they're out of my league, then. I truly can't afford more than twenty-five commons. How about these lesser-quality blades? How much are you charging for each of these?"

The tinker responded without thought. "Make me your best offer, and I will consider it."

His father turned casually to Breeden. "Do any of these

blades strike your fancy, son? It's okay to say no if none are to your liking."

"Yes, sir. There are a few of passing quality."

"How many?"

"Four."

The tinker's frown grew deeper as his suspicion he was being conned became more pronounced. He appeared help-less, watching the father and son exchange words.

"I'll give you five commons apiece for any four my son chooses—not including the silver ones, of course. That's twenty commons—nearly the same price I offered you for the dwarven set."

Now the tinker looked truly surprised. His face had become angrier, and he had seemed prepared to lash out at Breeden and his father, and then, in a moment—so fast that Breeden wasn't sure he'd read the man's growing anger correctly—the man smiled. "Twenty coppers it is. Go ahead and pick your chisels, son."

Breeden looked at his father first, to make sure it was okay, and at his nod, he picked up the four chisels he'd already selected. The tinker paid little attention to which chisels Breeden had chosen, but watched his father extract the twenty copper commons he had been promised from a leather case attached to his belt. When the transaction was complete and they were walking away from the man's stall, Breeden observed that the tinker's smile was gone, and he looked as if he was trying to figure out whether he'd been had. Breeden guessed the man thought the transaction far too easy. Breeden's father glanced back and saw the look. "Good. May he always wonder whether he got the better of us this day."

They turned a corner and were well out of sight of the tinker's booth when his father stopped walking and asked Breeden to pass him the chisels so he could examine them more carefully. His father looked around almost nervously and then pulled one out of the bag and gave it a once-over. The chisel looked serviceable, and the metal was free of rust. And it felt good in his hand. But there was nothing about it that struck him as remarkably different from many of the other blades the tinker had offered for sale.

"So, what made you choose these four from among all those dozens of tools?"

Breeden shrugged his shoulders. "They are aligned better than the others." He struggled for a moment before continuing. "Like straight rows of barley versus crooked ones, I suppose. And there are no obvious weak spots in the metal. Like missing stalks of barley in a field."

"Do you mean to say that you can see inside them?"

"Not exactly, but I can feel the flaws. Like when you rap a cracked stick against a wall and you feel it vibrate. Only I don't need to hit the wall."

His father shook his head and spun the chisel about in his hand in a practiced motion as he tried to come to grips with the situation. "Well, unfortunately, I don't believe we'll find any answers out here. Let's talk about this more when we get home. And we've got one more stop to make before that."

"Where are we going?"

His father smiled. "We're going to see about getting you into school!"

Breeden was not expecting this response and literally stopped in his tracks.

"School?"

But his father had nothing more to offer than a wink and a "Come along, then!" And he grabbed his son by the shoulder and started him moving again.

6

DEBTS AND PROMISES

As long as it had been, and as infrequently as they went to the market, they went inside the castle's inner bailey even less often. Breeden had been to mass at the monastery only a handful of times in his short life. And he was excited at the prospect of visiting once again. "Schooling," on the other hand, wasn't something he'd ever thought about before. He knew that his father had studied with the monks for a short period in his youth, but for some reason, Breeden hadn't thought he'd be afforded the same opportunity.

He wasn't sure what it would mean for him, didn't know what he didn't know. But he was excited anyway. If nothing else, he'd be seeing a lot more of the castle.

By virtue of the route they took, they were already well into Riderzaal Castle's outer bailey when they left the market. The market was to the right of the main thoroughfare leading into the inner bailey. The main approach to the castle was from the north and west—the land route from Arlon. And the road forked in front of the outer bailey into a short road down to the deepwater docks, where Long Lake formed a sheltered cove west of the River Woodfall's mouth.

When Breeden and his father joined up with the main road, there were few people about. Commoners were the norm: people dressed in homespun, albeit well-made and clean. And the occasional noble or wealthy merchant could be seen entering or leaving their carriages. But the nobility of Ridderzaal were small in number and quiet in their comings and goings. Breeden had heard tales of Arlon's grandeur and the arrogance of nobles who lived in the city, but he had a hard time picturing it. His parents had taught him that all people are good at heart and that even the occasional rude customer or pompous noble might well have their own problems and he shouldn't presume to judge them based upon one bad day.

Today they encountered no nobles, rude or otherwise, and they proceeded south along the beautifully maintained road—one of the very few cobbled roads in the area—admiring the budding trees and beautiful homes that lined the roadway. The houses, as elsewhere in the city, were spaced close together, leaving enough room for two or three to pass abreast. More often than not, the top floors extended out over the first floors and overhung the sidewalk. As Breeden and his father approached the inner gate to the castle grounds, the crowds diminished further, and only a handful of people could be found walking about outside.

The monastery was a massive and prominent structure, and of all the buildings within the inner bailey, it was second in size only to the keep itself. The building of the One God's religion had a tall square tower with large round stained glass windows on each face. The windows were high enough that they could be seen above the keep's battlements—which were themselves the height of ten men. The entire complex consisted of the cathedral itself and numerous connected outbuildings.

At some point in the past, the builders of the castle, or perhaps an overly bold monarch, had decided that the keep's two baileys would be more than enough defense against an attack and that the comfort of the nobility in traversing the courtyard via a covered walkway in foul weather was more important than maintaining the integrity of the castle's defenses. The covered walkway extended from the western face of the monastery to a postern gate at the left rear corner of the castle. To the left of a large double-doored entrance on the northeastern face of the monastery was a small footpath leading to one of the outbuildings and its much smaller and humbler door. It was to this door that Breeden's father directed their steps.

Breeden didn't know what to expect and glanced at his father for reassurance. But his father wore an unusual expression. He'd have called it nervousness if he'd ever seen his father wear it before. Was his father intimidated at the thought of entering the monastery? Or was it the person or people they were going to meet who caused him to be unsure of himself? In any event, Breeden became much less confident himself. His father was a rock. If his father had reason to worry, then surely he did as well.

But his father didn't appear to notice the concern he had caused in his focus on the task at hand. He knocked on the door firmly three times using the heavy iron ring that served as a knocker.

The wait felt endless to Breeden, but within about a minute, he thought he detected footsteps beyond the door, and shortly thereafter it opened, revealing a middle-aged cleric in a simple robe of undyed homespun wool.

Brother Cedric had answered the door himself. He was a sturdy man, looking to Breeden to be about his father's age, perhaps a bit older. His hair was cut as if a bowl had been placed on his head and everything showing beneath the bowl's rim had been removed down to the pale skin of his skull. He had black hair heavily peppered with grey and white, a prominent round nose, and simply enormous hands, which enveloped Breeden's own when they greeted each other. He smiled warmly upon recognizing Breeden's father.

"Welcome, Holt Andehar! It is a pleasure to see you, and all the more so for it not being a church holy day!"

"Good day, Brother Cedric." He smiled as he spoke, and some of his nervous tension seemed to leave him at Cedric's words—despite the small jab about his church attendance. "I'd like you to meet my son, Breeden."

"It is a pleasure, my son. Truly, it is a pleasure, and he is a blessing upon you, Holt."

"Thank you, brother. He is a good boy."

"How is Marlene?"

"She is well, brother. She asked that I give you her best wishes."

"I'm certain she did. Quite certain." His face became more serious for a moment, as if to assure Breeden and his father that his respect for the mother and wife was a given. And with the more businesslike air still in place, he continued. "So, what is it that brings you to the monastery on a day of work, and with your son in tow no less? Do you wish to submit him to me for punishment of some mortal sin?"

Fortunately, Breeden was accustomed to sarcasm and caught the glint in Brother Cedric's eye.

"Close, Brother Cedric. I wish to submit him to you, but not for punishment. I would ask that you take him in and teach him as you did me."

Cedric responded encouragingly. "I would be honored, Holt! You came to me a bit too old to teach all I wanted to you. But your son is young enough to have a full course of subjects —not just numbers and writing, as you had!"

Breeden's father smiled, obviously relieved at such an immediate and heartfelt response.

Cedric continued. "I have a few students already and recently took on two more, due to start in a few months, but I don't see why I couldn't take on another. Six students might make things a bit hectic at times, but I believe that any child of Holt Andehar will be far more boon than burden to my little group."

As his father and the cleric exchanged further pleasantries, Breeden considered the fact that Cedric had also taught his father, and it dawned on him that he'd always known this, and yet he hadn't thought to consider Brother Cedric's age. He must be a good deal older than he looked to have taught his father so many years ago. And yet he really did look no older than his father.

The conversation waned a bit after the business at hand and accompanying small talk were completed, and Cedric appeared to sense an unaccustomed awkwardness in his former charge.

"We will commence as autumn begins—the day after the equinox—and we will make allowance for any who need leave for the harvest. But you look as though poised for another question, Holt. Was there anything else?"

Breeden's father seemed to screw up his courage to respond. "I wish to make a donation, Brother Cedric. To what degree may I contribute to the good work of this monastery? Will ten crowns do for now?"

Breeden perked up at mention of more money than he'd ever seen in one place at the same time. And Brother Cedric looked suddenly pained, seeing a good man struggle over a discussion involving what must be to him a considerable sum of gold. "Sir, I will gladly accept your donation, now or at any other time—especially one so generous as yours—but you are not committed or required to donate. It is the work of God to educate youth, and all who wish to be so educated may do so here in His house."

A strange look came over Breeden's father, and he responded slowly, carefully. "When I was a boy, Hugh Robinet told me that a noble had taken pity on me and provided my guarantee in gold, and that this was how I was able to sit in on your lessons with the children of nobility, such as him. He held it over my head until my final days of studying with you." It was obvious that he wished to go further, that there was underlying pain associated with the memories he now confronted. "Do you mean to tell me that this was not the case? That all these years, I have labored under the burden of my own unworthiness, believing myself indebted to a man who does not exist, and it was nothing more than the spiteful fabrication of a spoiled child?"

Cedric's expression became quite serious. "It would appear so. Robinet? Hmph. I always did have difficulty with that troublesome boy—now doubtless risen to a troublesome duke. This is not an excuse, believe me, but to undo the influence of parents is hard work, and from his father, he had a mean streak in him from the very first. I am sorry, Holt."

Breeden's father shook his head, his shaken confidence gone and replaced with a new determination. He stepped forward and placed the heavy pouch in Cedric's hands. "Take the coin, brother. I saved my earnings against this day so that my son would never have to suffer the humiliation I did at Robinet's hands, and so he would be assured of—or so I hoped my meager coin would cover the cost of—schooling under your tutelage. And now I find that it was all a lie. I should have expected it, I suppose. He always was a cruel and cunning boy. But I took his words as truth because I did feel unworthy. It was too easy to do, I guess, being the only commoner among your students. And to be honest, that feeling has followed me ever since . . ."

Cedric pondered a moment and offered, "Do not be so hard on yourself, Holt. It would seem that the lie—though cruelly intended—bore a beautiful harvest. You have done as the scrolls of the prophet Usen would have had you do, and taken a grain of sand—a painful and distracting irritant to you, as to the oyster—and made of it a pearl. You should consider that, at least to some extent, Robinet's lie may have driven you harder to achieve success in business and emboldened you to the task of raising such an honorable and respectful boy.

"I will not be so coy as to argue that you should be grateful to Robinet, but I hope you can come to realize now that you have proven yourself more than worthy enough to have learned beside members of nobility—a secular construction with which, I daresay to you, I wholly disagree, incidentally. You are a better man than Robinet, Holt Andehar. And your son being your son will undoubtedly become a great and worthy man himself."

Cedric held out the pouch solemnly, trying one more time to get Breeden's father to reconsider. At the shake of Holt Andehar's head, Cedric nodded and smiled, and tied the pouch to the rope belt about his waist.

Cedric then turned to Breeden, took his hand in his own, and offered, "I ask you to remember this day, Breeden Andehar. Your determination will be tested in the months and years ahead. But you should always remember this day. Do not forget that we are all equal under God's eyes. And we are judged not by our birth but by our words and deeds. Your father has proven himself the equal of any man today, and you should not let the Hugh Robinets of the world try to convince you otherwise."

7

QUESTIONS RAISED

After dinner that night, his father excused himself and excused Breeden as well, telling his wife they were going to go for a walk. She appeared not to know the purpose for the walk and seemed curious about it but indicated her approval readily enough in the way mothers so often do: "Don't be too late now."

They walked out the front door together, and his father turned right, toward the pier. It was another beautiful day turning into a beautiful, though somewhat pleasantly cooler, night, and his father commented idly, "Should have brought my pipe. Beautiful night. It's been so hot of late I haven't wanted to smoke." He wasn't as passionate about it as his giant friend Aegir, but when he had a night like tonight to enjoy his pipe, Breeden knew his father hated to miss the chance.

The moments passed as they walked, and although Breeden assumed he knew his father's purpose, he still felt nervous and had a hard time enjoying the night the way his father appeared to be.

"So, can you try again to explain to me what it is you see, exactly?" His father's question came out in a natural, almost casual tone, and Breeden checked his face to see if he was as calm as he appeared. He couldn't really tell, but he was relieved, in any event, that the question was out. Though he wasn't sure he could do a better job of explaining himself than he had earlier.

He thought for a moment before responding. "I'll try."

And then Breeden had a moment of insight, and thought of a way that his father of all people should be able to understand him. "It's like the grain in a piece of wood. In fact, I think with wood it is the grain. Only instead of seeing just what you can see on the surface of a board or timber, I can see the grain all the way through the wood. And, not so much on the surface, but inside the wood, there is . . . something inside the grain, something that almost feels alive. And it's this thing that gives the wood its strength. This thing and the grain itself, that is. Sometimes with wood I can see that there is something wrong with the grain, some kind of flaw. And the stuff that's inside isn't as strong at those points either. It's like the flaw in the grain keeps the stuff inside from working right. I'm sorry, this probably doesn't even make any sense. I'm having a hard time with this."

"Don't worry. I can see you're struggling with it. And I do think I'm coming to better understand what you see. Let's talk about the wood some more. It sounds like you're describing the sap running through a tree's veins. Is that what you see?"

"No, it's not sap—at least I don't think so. It's not really liquid. And it appears to be alive. I can't say it better. It's as if the stuff is waiting to move, waiting to flow. It's like water, and it's kind of like sap, but it's as if it's alive and almost trapped within the wood. I'm sorry, I just can't seem to explain it better."

Breeden looked at his father then, their walk having taken them all the way to the base of the pier, where Breeden had seen the old man. In his father's eyes, there was pity and curiosity and perhaps confusion. He stopped walking.

"That's enough for now, Breeden. If you find that the words come to you and you want to talk about it more, please let me know. But I want you to make me a promise. I want you to promise me that you will not talk with your mother about this, or anyone else for that matter. People might think you possessed of demons or worse. Talk to me. But talk with no one else. Perhaps your schooling will reveal some answers to you."

They both stood at the pier's landward end and looked out over the water. Steam rose from the water as night's cooling air rolled in, and Breeden thought about summer approaching. Then his father put his arm around Breeden's shoulders, squeezed him, and turned him around for home.

8

QUESTIONS ANSWERED

That night, Holt Andehar had trouble falling sleep. He tossed about long after his wife had drifted off. When he could take no more, he threw back the covers and headed downstairs to his workshop. The light from the moon was enough for him to see by, but he found a tinderbox and lit a taper anyway, placing the taper in a wooden holder and releasing a heavy, pent-up sigh. He was almost furtive in his movements as he untied the burlap bag he had brought home from the market.

He reached into the bag and drew out the chisels his son had selected. They appeared well enough made, as he'd commented to his son earlier, and were in fair condition. They had the extra-wide blades he would need to work on the giant's project and were crafted with a full tang—all from one piece of metal that ran from the tip of the blade through the entire length of the handle.

One of them was exceptionally dull and seemed to have been subjected to very heavy use. The others had sharper edges and must have been better cared for—though even the sharpest blade would require a good turn at the stone before it would be useful for his needs. But he set down the ostensibly better blades on the workbench and put the bag down beside it.

His sharpening stone—one of the most valuable of all of his possessions, particularly in his line of work—was a small wheel, about two handspans across, that was mounted on an axle in a metal-and-wood frame he had built himself. Attached at the axle, on the right, was a handle. And attached at the left side of the wheel was a thin metal arm that extended around to the front of the stone. Where the arm would have contacted the face of the stone, there was a small wooden clamp.

He placed the most heavily used and battered of the tinker's chisels in the clamp and adjusted the angle of the blade as it contacted the stone, by maneuvering the metal arm in small, precise adjustments. Placing the chisel and adjusting the clamp took him a few minutes before he was satisfied the angle was correct and the blade was held firmly against the stone. The clamp also had a small handle attached to it, which would allow him to adjust the contact point of the chisel as he worked —to ensure that the entire face of the cutting blade was uniformly ground. The handle would also permit him to push the chisel more firmly against the stone than the clamp would do on its own. He tested both of these movements until he was comfortable everything was operating smoothly.

And then he began to turn the handle, spinning the wheel away from himself. He started slowly, and leaned forward to watch the blade's contact with the smooth, spinning stone. Whatever he saw pleased him, and he accelerated his spinning. The steady hissing sound of the grinding metal became almost soothing after a while. He kept the wheel turning for a handful of minutes, continually raising and lowering the clamp as he did so. Then he released his grip on the handle and allowed the wheel to slow itself to a stop. He removed the chisel from the clamp and was surprised to see that the blade still needed more sharpening. He'd thought for sure he had spun the wheel more than long enough to sharpen it. The metal must be quite hard —harder than most of his own blades even. He smiled and shook his head. Breeden had been right, even about the most ill-used of the blades.

As he placed the chisel back in the clamp and tightened it once more against the stone, he happily considered how well this chisel would work on the exceedingly dense and difficult ironwood required for Aegir's project. And more importantly, he considered his son's remarkable talent. He had always thought the boy was special, and despite a slight anxiety over the mystery of the whole business, he was content for now to know that his son's abilities were real and, as far as he was concerned, proven.

He would sleep tonight after all.

9

NEW FRIENDS

To Breeden, the months crept by in an unbearably slow fashion. When he wasn't doing chores around the house, his mother was expanding on his lessons in table etiquette, on forms of address, and on manners in general. She had always been careful about instructing him to be polite but had never been one to care for the devilish details required by noble society. But Breeden had gotten the sense she didn't want him to be an embarrassment to her in front of the nobles, and so she now worked on him whenever she had the chance.

He spent less time on the water than he usually did, his fishing excursions with and without his father having tapered off. And despite his father having long ago taught Breeden to read, all of a sudden he wanted to cram in more lessons before the fall. As a consequence, Breeden had been reading and rereading *The Prophecies*—the only book his family owned. One of the few opportunities Breeden had to himself came on Saturdays or after the church services the whole family now regularly attended on Sunday mornings. But he seldom had the time or energy to wander too far during these intervals. Along with everything else, his father's business had picked up.

Besides the boat Aegir the giant had requested, his father had received an order for two launches for one of the deepwater fishing vessels anchored north of the castle, and for a small but ornate sailboat for a wealthy glass merchant.

When four months had finally passed, the morning after the autumn equinox found Breeden walking the back roads of Woodfall toward Ridderzaal by himself. He was pretty sure this was the first time he had ever been allowed to walk the city streets alone, and he was very excited and a touch nervous, he had to admit. But the walk was mostly uneventful.

He walked a similar route to the one he and his father had walked the day they had bought the chisels from the tinker at market and had spoken with Brother Cedric about Breeden's schooling. But instead of walking so far west, he bypassed much of the main road leading into Ridderzaal by cutting through the wealthy Merchants' Quarter.

He was coming out of a side street that merged with the main road when a young girl about his age came barreling out of a home to his right. She would be pretty, he thought immediately, if she weren't wearing such a stern and unfriendly face. And when she almost bowled him over in her haste, he became even less certain of her beauty. But she was gone in a flash and without apology, and so he dismissed her carelessness with little in the way of a second thought.

As it was so early, the main roadway was nearly empty. Two men in the white-aproned garb of bakers set up their carts close by one another, chatting idly. A produce merchant carried a heavy crate overstacked with cabbages toward a booth already half-full with neatly arrayed fruits and vegetables. And a young man in a guard's uniform appeared at a half run from the street opposite Breeden, headed toward the castle and trying without success to primp his rumpled uniform.

Breeden took it all in as if he were watching one of his sunrises, capturing every detail in his mind. The sights of the city in the morning were ones he was unaccustomed to, and as he was alone, they were somewhat disconcertingly invigorating. He felt small stabs of fear when something unexpected presented itself, or whenever a voice was revealed from behind the corner of a building. He found he could literally feel the pumping of his blood through his veins for most of the trip. And when he spotted the arch to the inner bailey, and the cathedral's tower beyond, his heart caught in his throat.

The morning sun was rising in the east, and the first rays had reached the top of the cathedral's tower. The sky above was indigo, fading downward in an imperceptible transition to a dark robin's-egg blue. His pace slowed as the sun's rays reached lower and lower, and finally hit one of the tower's enormous stained glass windows. The entire window was suddenly aglow with a riot of colors so bright Breeden found he could neither look at the window any longer nor tear his eyes away. After a moment of staring, he realized he had stopped moving. He resumed walking with effort, lowering his eyes and shielding them with his hand to allow them to adjust back to a normal level of light.

Unaware of exactly how much time had passed while he stared at the cathedral tower, he considered that he might be running late, and picked up his pace to a brisk walk. He was through the arch in a moment. As he approached, he could see a gaggle of children standing outside the same door to the monastery he and his father had used months before. Two boys stood to one side, talking together in low voices. One was massively tall and broad of chest. He held himself erect, and from a distance, Breeden had thought he was an adult. The other was shorter than Breeden, slighter of build, and leaning casually against a low railing at the base of the few short steps before the door. There were two other boys and a girl as well, each looking awkward and uncomfortable, and each maintaining their own space a few feet away from each other.

One of the two remaining boys had brown hair and was somewhat shorter than Breeden but was stockier and had a sour look on his face. He glanced periodically at the first two boys and seemed to renew his scowl in that way whenever it was in danger of fading away. The fourth boy was tall and somewhat narrow of shoulder, though not nearly as tall as the first boy. He had high cheekbones and blond hair cut in a rough fashion and worn just above his shoulders. His clothes were plainer than those of the others, and he appeared, if not the most nervous, certainly the most out of place. And last of all, there was a girl with long brown hair. Breeden was amused to discover that it was the same girl who had brushed by him with hardly more than an "Excuse me" earlier that morning. When he met her eyes, she made the same recognition and frowned slightly. Breeden couldn't help himself as he approached, and observed, "Looks like you made it on time."

She paused for a moment as if to gauge his words and scowled when she saw the corner of his mouth twitch upward in amusement. It was at this point that Breeden realized any chance he'd had at receiving a well-intentioned apology from her was likely dwindling.

After recognizing his failure to get off on the right foot with the girl, he moved on to the others, making eye contact with each one and saying a short "Hello" in greeting. The slight fellow was the only one who responded with more than a grunt or imperceptible mutter.

"And hello to you as well," he responded. "My name is Kestrel Starkad. This big oaf at my side is Laudan Marchant. The short one is Derek, but he can speak for himself. As for the other two, I believe they may be mute."

Breeden laughed at that and walked over to shake Kestrel's hand. "I'm Breeden Andehar. And I'm glad to meet you. Do you know when we're going to get started?"

"I'm not quite sure, but I expect Cedric may be giving us

time to get to know each other. He's probably watching us from a window somewhere." He raised his voice and projected, "ISN'T THAT RIGHT, BROTHER CEDRIC?" Then he cocked his head to one side as if awaiting a response from the absent monk.

The big fellow at his side, Laudan, by Kestrel's introduction, flinched slightly but somehow seemed familiar with, and prepared to be surprised by, Kestrel's behavior. "Don't scare them off, Kestrel. I'm sorry about him, Breeden. He's crazy. But he's mostly harmless. As he said, my name is Laudan. It's good to meet you." He extended his hand, and they shook firmly, Breeden's strong grip not overpowered by the larger boy's, as he'd feared.

"I'm Oskar."

"I'm Janelle."

The tall blond boy and the girl both spoke at once, overcoming their self-imposed isolation at precisely the same time. They smiled at each other, and both laughed at their timing.

Breeden turned from shaking Laudan's hand and shook first the girl's and then the lanky boy's. "It's a pleasure to meet you as well."

"Oh, a real pleasure all around, I'm sure. What a load of road apples." These words were spoken by the boy Kestrel had identified as Derek. "You bloody commoners are so pitiful with your 'airs'! Where did you come from, Oskar? Straight from the streets or via an orphanage? Perhaps you're the get of some worm-ridden prostitute. And, Breeden, I'd guess from your calluses and the sawdust on your pants that you're a carpenter's son. And the pretty little girl in last Beltide's best dress? Hmm. A spoiled merchant's daughter, as sure as I'm the son of the Duke of Chavenay."

Oskar's expression grew flat and serious, but he didn't say anything and didn't make a move. Breeden was torn between being surprised at how observant Derek had been to notice the sawdust—he'd been careful to clean himself, after all—and being angry at the comments he'd made about the blond boy's background.

But Kestrel became visibly angry. "You're such an arrogant jerk, Derek. That's a great way to make them feel welcome."

"Who says they're welcome?"

"Shut up, Derek!"

"You shut up, Kestrel. Are you suddenly the defender of peasants and whores' get?"

Kestrel walked over to Derek and looked him levelly in the eye. With the two standing that close, Breeden thought that Derek would have the edge in a fight. He was much thicker of torso and limb.

But Kestrel had a fire in his eyes. "So what? So what if they weren't lucky enough to have been born a son of Duke Robinet, like you? If they had, they'd probably be just as big a jerk as you are."

"Robinet . . . ?" The word left Breeden's mouth before he could catch it.

But Derek had heard it, and he turned on Breeden. "You stay out of this, peasant. And don't you speak my father's name again. It's been dirtied from you uttering it even once."

Breeden decided he didn't like this boy, and he couldn't help himself. "Your father, the duke, is the dirty one. He's a dirty liar and a pig."

The girl squeaked. Even Kestrel gasped. And Derek bordered on apoplectic. "Why, you bloody uppity peasant! I'll kill you for that!" And he rushed at Breeden, who was standing about two yards away.

Kestrel appeared stunned by the turn of events and realized too late that he had missed his chance to grab Derek and hold him in check.

Breeden, although perfectly average in height and build, was larger than Derek, being about the same build but a few inches taller. But Derek had gathered speed in his short run, and he struck Breeden solidly in the area between his stomach and his chest. They hit the ground hard, Derek landing on top of him. But he lost this briefly held advantage when Breeden rolled him off with a shove. And then Breeden was somehow on top of Derek, sitting astride his chest. Breeden felt his father's humiliation at the hands of this boy's father. And he could see that the boy was on track to do the same to him. But Breeden wasn't about to stand by and let that happen. Before he realized what he was doing, Breeden found that his vision had narrowed and darkened, he had grabbed Derek by the hair, and he was slamming the boy's head backward repeatedly against the cobblestones.

Laudan, until now an innocent bystander, responded by lifting Breeden by the back of his shirt off Derek and then grabbing both of his arms to restrain him. Derek scrambled groggily to his feet and went after Breeden, swinging his fist at the immobilized Breeden's face. All Breeden could do was turn his head sideways to avoid the brunt of the attack, but it was enough. Derek's punch hit him on the top and side of his head instead of in the face. It still hurt, but it hurt Derek at least as much.

Derek recoiled from the pain and immediately cradled his wrist in his off hand. Laudan released Breeden with care, making sure he wasn't going to lunge after Derek when he did so. But the rage had left Breeden as quickly as it had come, and he simply shook his head and touched a small but rising bump on his skull. It hurt, he thought, but it wasn't that big a deal.

It was at that moment, of course, that the door opened and a smiling Brother Cedric appeared. "Good morning, children! Have you introduced yourselves?" His eyes narrowed as he realized that something important had happened and saw Derek favoring his wrist. He looked in the eyes of first Oskar, then Kestrel, then Breeden, and finally Laudan to try to determine who had been involved in the tussle with the duke's son. "Is everything all right? Derek, what's wrong with your wrist?"

Kestrel replied before Derek or anyone else had a chance. "Oh, yes, sir. We've all become acquainted, sir. And I must say that it's going to be a very interesting year!"

But Kestrel's sarcasm aside, Cedric received no response. And when his questions went unanswered, he grudgingly desisted and led his students into the monastery. To Breeden's surprise, Derek hadn't turned him in—as he had been sure would be the case. It wouldn't occur to Breeden until much later that he shouldn't give Derek too much credit, and that the boy likely failed to speak out of embarrassment rather than through some noble sense of honor.

10

FIRST CLASS

The morning of the first day of schooling with Cedric involved a tour of the monastery and grounds. He said that he was doing it to familiarize everyone with some important landmarks in case they became turned around in the maze of hallways, but Breeden got the sense he was proud of what he was showing them as well. As the morning progressed, the brother seemed to relax and forget the caution he had exhibited upon first greeting the children. His enthusiasm leaked out here and there when relating the history of a monk featured in a certain painting, or when showing them a library of antique books, scrolls, and scraps of parchment.

He concluded the tour on a rooftop terrace overlooking the west grounds of the monastery, adjacent to the keep. The terrace was an immaculately maintained garden of flowering plants, evergreen bushes, and even some herbs and vegetables Breeden recognized. Its view was spectacular, enabling them to see the main roadway all the way back to the gate of the outer bailey and nearly the whole approach up to the main gate. The view was almost panoramic, and were it not for the keep itself, they would have had a sweeping view of the entire city and the countryside that fell away from the city's walls, down to the lake and river below. The rooftop garden was the true highlight of the tour. Breeden had never seen or experienced a view like it.

Cedric gave them all plenty of time to admire the plants and the view, and encouraged them to sit down on one of the many benches or garden seats placed throughout. "But please keep your attention on me, if you will. I'd like to begin the first lesson up here. It is such a beautiful retreat that I think it serves well the purpose of hosting my first homily."

He composed himself for a moment and allowed time for Laudan to join the others on one of the benches. When Laudan remained where he was and didn't appear inclined to sit, Cedric began anyway, "Today's homily is on the gods. The first, or 'old,' gods. And the true God.

"Many of you have parents or nurses or friends who say prayers to the old gods. If they are wishing for luck, they might choose the Pretani god Mungo. If strength in battle, Götar, the dwarfish god of war. If fertility, the Shenn Frith goddess Mikele.

"Some do so without thought, and even out of habit—not necessarily believing the god will answer their prayer, or even necessarily believing in the god himself. Well, I am here to tell you that the old gods are real."

There were stunned faces and suppressed gasps all around. Breeden got the feeling that Cedric was joking or had something up his sleeve, so he didn't take the words too seriously. And Cedric looked awfully pleased with himself, so to Breeden, this merely confirmed his suspicion.

"How do I know the old gods exist? you might ask. Well, I know because I have met them."

At this even Breeden was surprised. He looked around at the others, and the only one who looked unfazed was Kestrel. Derek and Laudan grew angry. And Janelle and Oskar appeared shocked. But they didn't have too much time to dwell on the monk's words before he continued.

"It's true. And from what I have been able to determine, these gods are no godlier than a troll or a dragon or a pixie. They are not human, certainly. And they have abilities that we cannot comprehend or duplicate. But just because a troll will grow a new arm when one is severed, does that make the troll better than we are, or more than we are? And because a dragon can live for more than twenty times the lifespan of a man, does that make it immortal? No, it does not.

"It is my belief that the 'gods' we humans worship were once men. And if not men, and something else altogether, like a troll or dragon, then they are certainly not gods in the sense, and with the powers, people have ascribed to them. In speaking with these gods—those who have allowed me to do so—and in reading the accounts of those who have also spoken with the gods, I have discerned one fact that weighs heavily against the immortality and superiority of these gods. And it is this: they each have a collective memory that begins at roughly the same point in the past.

While it is true that this memory begins thousands of years ago, it is also true that because of this limit to their memory, their existence can be argued to have been finite. And since their existence is finite, it is safe to assume that these gods are no more creators of the world in which we live than the elves or the giants. Were they influential in the development of our cultures and our societies? Yes. Were they responsible for bettering or worsening our condition, as was their wont? Yes. But these facts do not mean that the old gods are true gods in the way that the one true creator God is.

"Laudan, what can you tell me about the one true God?"

Laudan seemed surprised at the question and had to compose himself for a moment before answering. "God is all-knowing and all-powerful. He judges men for their evil thoughts as well as their deeds. He is righteous and holds the wicked accountable for their wrongdoings and sets aside a place in paradise for those who follow His path. He—"

Laudan appeared willing to continue, but Cedric interrupted him. "You have said what God does but not talked about what He is. Can you describe His nature?"

Laudan wasn't daunted by the interruption or the question. "We were made in His image, so we know that He looks like us. Or rather, that we look like Him. And He is everywhere at once, so He is manifestly vast. He is—"

"Is He flesh?" The question was sharp and firm.

"No. He is not made of flesh. He is immortal."

"That which is flesh cannot live forever?"

"No."

"So if not of flesh, then what is God?"

At this, Laudan was silent. Cedric allowed the moment to linger, until Breeden felt himself growing increasingly uncomfortable. Breeden was wondering why a priest of the One God's church would call his own god's existence into question. The moment lingered longer. Breeden glanced around the table and saw expressions of fear, anger, and confusion on the faces of his peers. Laudan was pensive. Then finally Cedric broke the silence. "I will answer my own question, Laudan. He is in all things. He is the stuff of life. He is that which leaves a man's body when he dies. He is spirit, and He is everything that is not Him.

"Ask rather, what is *not* God? For you were right when you said He was everywhere. He is not merely everywhere; He is everything.

"Are the old gods immortal?" As he asked the question, he turned to face Breeden, looking him directly in the eye.

Breeden had no response. He had no opinion. He had frankly not thought about it before, and had a hard time even trying to figure out how he could provide his teacher with any kind of satisfactory answer at all.

But Cedric wouldn't relent. "Breeden Andehar, are the old gods immortal?"

Breeden still had no clue why Brother Cedric was picking on him, and had no idea what kind of answer he was looking for. But a thought occurred to him, and he found himself asking a question rather than answering Cedric's. "Since you met them, can you tell me, are the old gods made of flesh?"

Now it was Cedric who appeared caught off guard. His somewhat stern and knowing look, his penetrating eyes, his dramatic and pregnant poise, were replaced with a look of delight. Then, as quickly as it came, he took control of himself once again, and he answered quietly, almost without thought. "They may not be. I cannot say."

At that, Breeden had an answer. "Well, I would say that if they are not made of flesh, then perhaps they are made of the same stuff God is, and I suppose they could be immortal after all, even if they were born thousands of years ago."

Cedric considered Breeden's words, and his expression changed again. His scholar's face returned, but with a scholar's curiosity instead of conviction. "Your words have provoked a memory, Breeden. I once read a scroll where a priest argued that the old gods were made of the essence of magic, that they had no flesh but were creatures who not only wielded magic but were wholly of magic. But this just proves the point I set out to demonstrate, and that is this: there is no such thing as magic."

The stern face of Laudan cracked, and he almost sneered at his teacher. "First you say that the old gods are real, and now you are saying that there is no such thing as magic. Are you testing us or simply making sport of us?"

Cedric smiled. "Your salvation is the one test that really matters. As to how you arrive at the truth, the path is yours to choose. I merely wish to make your way clear of the obstacles of superstition, tradition, and simple habit.

"Is there magic in the world? Well, it is too simple to say yes or no without proof. Are there mysteries and powers beyond our ken? Most certainly. Could man's or elf's or dwarf's magic, as possessed and used by wizards and enchanters, be the manifestation of God's presence in the world? That is what I believe. And to call this powerful essence, present in all things, magic is to admit that you don't understand its nature any more than you can understand the nature of God.

"I have heard wizards try to describe the nature of magic and fail. And I am talking about those who are born gifted in its use, as well as those who have come to understand better the rules of magic only through long years of practice and dedication. The great wizards of magic could no more explain to me what magic is than I could explain the nature of God. But just as you have all witnessed real magic practiced in your short lives, so do I see the work of God revealed before me each day I rise.

"The existence of God is as obvious to me as the water that fills Long Lake. And just as you can reach your hand into the waters of that lake and feel water—even without being able to tell me exactly what water is—so do I feel the presence of God each day during the exercise of my duties. Like a hand that enters the lake dry and leaves the lake wet, I am changed by coming into the presence of my god. But unlike the water on such a hand, the presence of God lingers long in me while I do His work.

"What are the rules of water?" Cedric posed the question but hardly gave anyone a chance to answer before he continued. "You cannot hold it in your hands, but need a bucket to carry it from one place to another. Even the smallest, most invisible hole will provide water a means of escaping. When the weather gets cold enough, water freezes and becomes ice. When thrown on a fire, water will extinguish it. And a properly built boat can travel across water faster than a horse can run on land.

"Are there other rules of water? Assuredly. Each of us has learned the rules I have mentioned without conscious thought, by regular interaction with it. Do we try to catalog these rules in order to better understand water's nature? Most of us have not, or wouldn't think to take the time. But many sailors do just that, because water is so very important to their livelihood and their very lives. The sailors know, too, which rules are immutable, unchangeable, and which rules are dependent upon circumstances or conditions. Well, just as with the sailor's understanding of water and the wizard's understanding of magic, there are rules to understanding the true God.

"It is my hope that over the course of the time we spend together, you will come to understand what I consider to be some of the most important rules, the rules of the world and of life. It is further my hope that you will someday recognize that it is only through God that all these rules exist. God made the world a place of rules, a place of logic, so that we could better come to grips with the world around us. It is God who made water. It is God who made what we commonly call magic. And it is only through the grace of God that we even exist, are able to understand these rules, and are able to live our lives as we do.

"The ultimate lesson for today, therefore, is that the world operates on logic, operates on rules. In the most extreme case for myself, or more clearly stated, where my knowledge is most limited, I understand that even magic follows a finite and strictly understandable set of rules. And the true God, the one and only creator God, has created it to be this way. There are things in this world we haven't yet explained and that aren't tangible in ways we understand, but that is merely because we haven't yet come to understand them, not because we cannot do so. God, in his great wisdom and generosity, has granted us the power to discern for ourselves the nature of our world. And He has left it to us to determine for ourselves, each of us, what exactly that means."

He looked around the class and saw pensive looks on every face. He appeared satisfied.

"Okay, that is enough for now. Your first lesson is given. Let's eat."

11

LESSONS

For the first few weeks of class, Cedric moved them around the monastery quite a bit and held class in many different places. They would study in one of the many libraries, outside on the garden terrace, as they had that first day, and in various rooms of the keep itself. When discussing religion, he once held class in the sanctuary of the cathedral.

At the beginning, his lessons focused almost entirely on history and religion. Unsurprisingly, Kestrel, Laudan, and Derek, as the noble-born members of the group, had a better sense of history than the others, albeit a version of history skewed by the stories passed down from their respective ancestors. During many discussions, the noble boys would interject their own interpretations or understandings of the events, sometimes even arguing heatedly with each other. Cedric patiently assured them that where there were disagreements among the scholars, he would let them know, but where all sources were in agreement on a given subject, he believed it was safe to assume he was presenting an accurate picture.

Breeden found the whole thing fascinating, as his sense of history was limited to his own homeland of Hyrde. Further, he remembered hearing stories from his father about the gnome wars, particularly the most recent, which was fought from Ridderzaal Castle. Breeden recalled that in this war, the humans had united under the great Hyrden king Wilham, but he was sure he couldn't recall hearing any tales of conflict between the humans.

The new perspective he received at the hands of Brother Cedric was a human civilization constantly at odds with itself. The nations of the Krigares, the Laonese, the Gaidheal, the Mahjars, the Pretani, and the Hyrdens were continually making war with one another. And despite the objective nature with which Cedric taught his lessons, it was clear that the motives behind much of this warfare were less than noble: expanding a nation's borders, capturing wealth or resources, enslaving other peoples, or a simple lust for power. Breeden was shocked there could be such self-interest in the world. And he had an even harder time believing that humans could be responsible for so much that was so wrong, and even evil.

When his father had told him tales of warfare, he had talked about the wars with the gnomes and trolls, which, to Breeden, had felt very primal. They were black and white. They were about the survival of the human race. But Cedric's story of warfare between humans was not so cut and dried.

Gnomes and trolls were one thing, he told himself, but his parents had plainly sheltered him from the darker side of the human race. They weren't so naive as to tell him he could trust everyone, of course. And they made sure that when he traveled in the city, he was careful to watch where he went. But then, until recently he hadn't been allowed into the city on his own, so he supposed he might be more sheltered than he realized.

This day, they were in the second-tallest tower of the keep, in a small private library. The few narrow windows present provided some light, but even on such a sunny afternoon as it was, the light had to be supplemented by a pair of lanterns in order for everyone to see and read the fragile texts Cedric passed around as he spoke.

Breeden was trying his best to read the words on the page before him, but it was hopeless. Over the years, the ink had been fading from black to a very pale brown, and at the same time, the vellum upon which it was written was darkening toward an all-too-similar brown. To make matters more difficult, the writing contained many words he'd never learned and was written in a dialect he could barely decipher as it was. Breeden raised his head from the tedious and impossible task and passed the scroll to Janelle, seated immediately to his left at the huge study table. She accepted the text without a word, and Breeden turned his eyes and attention to Cedric.

". . . but the clan chief Keir had fortunately gathered together all the highland clans under a war pact.

"At Keir's enjoinment, the clans had united in a moot upon the Hyrden victory over the Laonese, concerned—correctly, I probably don't need to add—that the Hyrden king would next turn his eyes to their fat herds of cattle and vast croplands. Had Keir not acted with such decisiveness and forethought, it is possible our friend Kestrel here would never have been born. For it was King Wilham's way to defeat utterly, even to the last man, any force that confronted his—if he thought that his victory was assured, that is. But when the small vanguard of his army—about two hundred men, himself included—reached the foothills of southern Pretania, he was met by a fearsome host of well over one thousand fighting hillmen and highlanders. And even though he, and most of his force, were on horseback, enough of the Pretani before him had ponies that he might not have succeeded in getting away—had he made the attempt.

"But he was a bold king. And he raised his checkered flag of parlay and rode forward, his van following behind. That day, with one-fifth the number of men he faced at his immediate command, the Hyrden king won an oath of fealty from the collected clansmen of the Pretani. No blood was shed. There were those among the clans who wanted to attack, despite the fact that their outlying scouts had reported a massive host of more than ten times their strength approaching behind the greedy king. And it is very likely true that his vanguard could have been overtaken by the Pretani before the rest of his forces arrived.

"But at the moot, Keir had been made war chief, and he knew that killing the Hyrden king would have brought down the wrath of the unstoppable army behind him. And he knew too, or at least suspected, that swearing fealty to the Hyrden king was the only way to save the lives of the clans' armies. An army of the size assembled against the Pretani could not be defeated in the field. We can't say for sure, but many believe Keir was plotting even then, that he planned to wait until the considerable army before him was dispersed. Perhaps he thought, 'What price is a year of fealty for the lives of my people?'

"How long did that year last, Kestrel?"

Kestrel wasn't glancing out the window or fidgeting as he typically would but had been paying unusually close attention to the story, since it involved his own homeland. He had a ready answer to Cedric's query. "Two hundred years and counting, sir."

Breeden was amused by the fact that Cedric couldn't stifle a small chuckle. Kestrel's remarks were generally somewhat flippant but always incisive. Cedric continued. "Kestrel knows better than anyone. The great king Wilham knew just exactly what Keir must have been thinking. But if Keir was nobody's fool, King Wilham was nobody, for he changed the nature of warfare forever after. I know I've made it somewhat obvious to those among the nobility, but could you tell me what innovation King Wilham brought about that so effectively kept Keir and the rest of the clans from reclaiming their sovereignty? Janelle?"

Janelle had been paying attention, but her face was a cloud of anxiety as she answered. "I'm not sure, Father."

"Brother, my child. I am not the Abbot."

"I'm sorry, Brother Cedric. But I don't know. Did you already tell us the answer? I don't recall hearing you say it."

Cedric smiled. "Don't worry, dear child. It will come. And we each bring with us our own strengths. You shone brightly enough when we discussed courtly etiquette last week. Why, you made the noble boys look like bowing and scraping farm boys in comparison. Anyone else, besides Kestrel?" Kestrel had already begun to speak when Cedric excluded him from the question.

Derek spoke up abruptly. "He didn't dismiss his army. Or not all of it, anyway."

Cedric smiled again. "Thank you, Derek. That is absolutely correct. He chose to maintain an army even during times of peace. As Derek implied, the army was greatly reduced from the days of its greatness, but especially at the beginning, he maintained a considerable number of knights and—this is where he was truly being original—foot soldiers. He had decided to conscript peasants for a permanent force, which he maintained in housing outside of his keep, this keep, in the first royal city of the kingdom.

"As I said, warfare would never be the same again. Immediately after the war, King Wilham did something else, this definitely not original but proven effective throughout the ages: he built a network of spies whom he placed in high positions in the lands he had conquered. With these spies in place, he could find out about any attempts to rebel against him, or even to gather troops. And when the Duke of Laval first tried to assemble troops at his keep, near the western forest, they were met by a highly trained unit of professional soldiers who arrived in a matter of weeks.

"The next innovation in maintaining a kingdom came from Wilham the Second, Wilham's eldest son. It was his idea not to outlaw the assemblage of troops by the outlying nations, but rather to control personally their assembly. Further, he extended the conscription of peasants and the permanent stationing of knights to Laon and Pretania—to be placed under *his* control. Now the sons of most nobles were in his court. So along with having a large share of the soldier conscripts of his potential enemies, he had also arranged to have noble 'hostages' available from every country represented in his court. Brilliant. Almost genius levels of forethought, really."

Oskar was squirming in his seat and couldn't seem to control himself. Cedric noticed, and called on him. "Oskar, you look as though you have something to offer."

Oskar froze. But then he appeared to relax a bit before responding. "Brilliant, my arse. Street-smart is what it is. That's a gang move. Nothing but kidnapping and blackmail. Doesn't require a monk to come up with something like that."

Cedric laughed. "Yes, Oskar. It surely is. They use fancy names for it among the nobility. But you're absolutely right. It's a practice that isn't significantly different from what you likely saw on the streets of Arlon growing up."

But Breeden was still thinking about the underlying lesson. He had heard the names of these countries before, but he hadn't had a good sense of their geographic relationship to one another until that very morning, when Cedric had begun their lessons by unrolling an enormous map of the land. He recalled from the map that there were three human nations Cedric had yet to mention in the lesson. And because it seemed Cedric had no intention to do so, Breeden couldn't help it and spoke up. "What about the Mahjars and Gaidheal, or the Krigares for that matter? Didn't King Wilham try to conquer them as well?"

Cedric smiled. "And I can always count on you for your timing, Breeden. We weren't going to discuss these nations just yet, but mentioning them in the context of the larger war does make sense. Derek, what of the Gaidheal?"

"They were protected by the elves."

Cedric nodded. "That's true—in part and in effect, if not in fact. Most scholars agree that King Wilham believed the elves to hold the Gaidheal's best interests at heart. But whether or not the elves would have engaged a human army—particularly one the size of Wilham's—to defend other humans is a matter of some debate.

"Any other reasons? Derek again."

Derek thought a moment before responding. "Shenn Frith doesn't have anything worth plundering?"

"The Gaidheal's home actually does have quite a fortune in precious metals and jewels, though perhaps, as you indicate, it is not worth the risk of incurring the wrath of the elves. They may appear a primitive people, but they love shiny things as much as any other humans, and that the gemstones and metal coins are originally from their 'mother', the land itself, gives them a justification they can safely defend within the confines of their religion. So I'll give you some credit for that answer. Can you think of any other reasons?"

Derek thought longer this time and shook his head. "Sorry. But no. I can't think of anything else."

Cedric replied, "Don't feel you've missed the mark, Derek. Your first response was likely the most important and undoubtedly does account for King Wilham's reluctance. If I were to add anything, it would be that Shenn Frith, the land occupied by the Gaidheal, does not provide any distinct strategic advantages. Possessing that parcel of land would give King Wilham no improved position over his enemies—no control of critical waterways, or mountain passes, for example—nor, due to the fact that the Gaidheal are gatherers and eat solely what they can obtain from the land itself, any critical matériel or resources that could benefit his campaign, i.e., grain or cattle. Add to these facts the very daunting specter of the elves, and I think you have a fairly clear assessment, as the Hyrden king would have made.

"And the Mahjars? Kestrel?"

Kestrel, as he often did when he had something to offer, looked to be on the edge of his seat. But upon hearing his name, he relaxed visibly. The tone of his response was casual but confident. "The Mahjars are fierce fighters, but their homeland, Namur, doesn't really have any cities to speak of. And they don't hoard wealth the way the Laonese and Hyrden do."

Derek interrupted at this. "Laonese and Hyrden, my arse! As if the Pretani are so noble and above such things! You—"

Cedric raised his eyebrows at Derek and interrupted, barely elevating the volume of his lecturing voice. "That will be enough, Derek. Though your point is well taken. We should seek to identify cultures that are not concerned with hoarding wealth, rather than singling out the Laonese and Hyrden. Kestrel?"

Kestrel continued. "As I was saying, the Laonese had richer plunder and easier pickings than the Mahjars. And yes, I suppose the Pretani did too. But the Mahjars are nomads and shepherds, and have almost nothing in the way of treasure. And their land is dry and harsh. In the northeast, they do have a fertile valley, but they leave that place as it is and don't harvest their own food or grain from it, because they leave that piece of land free for the wild horses, their breeding stock. And I hear they harvest the wild horses in this valley only sparingly, leaving the strongest males and females to mate and strengthen the lines. For King Wilham to reach these horses, he would have to fight his way through an unforgiving, dry grassland and battle Mahjars intent on protecting the valley—the key to their way of life.

"So my answer is maybe longer than you wanted, but the long and short of it is that the Mahjars had nothing to offer King Wilham, and what they did have of value, their horses, would have been too dearly won."

Cedric was impressed. "Well said, and very thorough, Kestrel. Those are excellent reasons and could very well explain King Wilham's decision to leave the people of Namur alone. And that leaves the Krigares for . . ."

Breeden cleared his throat and, in so doing, drew Brother Cedric's attention and another raised eyebrow, this one a question rather than an admonition. Breeden did have something to contribute, but he also had second thoughts. But Cedric was looking at him, and he was drawn into continuing. He began roughly.

"I have heard stories about the Krigares . . . I can't say as to their truth, but if they are true, I know I wouldn't want to attack them. They are supposed to be fiercer than any other opponent. They show no mercy to their enemies and fight to their own deaths before they surrender themselves. They are savages. Barely civilized. Though my father says that in their way they are also men of honor."

Cedric was nodding as Breeden spoke, and interjected when he paused. "What you say is true, Breeden. They are an uncivilized people by our standards, but they are also not so simply classified. In many ways—their treatment of travelers in their lands, for example—they behave more admirably than we do. As you say, they are men of honor—in their way. They have a primitive code of behavior in the Krigsrike and adhere strictly to its tenets. Those who do not adhere are shunned, cast out, or killed. Forgiveness is not among their teachings.

"But I digress, and I am answering your question. I apologize. Please continue."

Breeden was still a bit unsure of himself but continued nonetheless, not just addressing the monk in his response but looking around the room and taking in all of his peers as well. "And along with their fierceness and their unforgiving nature, as Cedric said, the other reason is that they live on the other side of impassable mountains. To attack them without going over the mountains or through the passes, he would have had to do it by ship, since the mountains are so high and are always covered in ice. And to attack them by ship would be crazy, since the Krigares are the best sailors and rowers in all the lands. So even though the Krigares probably have all kinds of treasure stored away up there from their raids, I think King Wilham probably couldn't figure out how to beat the Krigares to get it."

Cedric replied warmly. "Very true, Breeden. Very true. And because King Wilham actually feared the Krigares militarily, he felt it was necessary to formulate a treaty with them, lest they interfere with his plans for the Pretani, or just harass or raid his army for sport. Another thing about Krigares: they have made warfare their hobby, their calling, and their passion. As you say, they are fierce, but they are also a nation of warriors. And the Hyrden king knew this, so he knew he would need to bribe them in some manner to keep them out of the conflict.

"He decided to promise them access to some of the Pretani land in the northwest, including a warm-water port—warm for them, anyway, at least in comparison to the rest of the Krigares' ports. Once he had defeated the Pretani, of course. The Krigares' 'king,' who controlled the coastline immediately north of the proposed parcel of land, agreed to the plan. Wilham didn't know it at the time of the treaty, but the man claiming to act as king of the Krigares was really more the equivalent of one of Kestrel's clan chiefs. But that he didn't speak for all the Krigares is really academic, as he did control the most important piece of land as far as Wilham was concerned: the southern access to plunder along the western coast of the land. Only a few small raids by other Krigares from farther north and east ultimately interfered with Wilham's efforts. So in the end, his treaty, limited though it was, probably did prove to be helpful."

Breeden felt good. His answer had seemed to satisfy Brother Cedric, and for perhaps the first time since he'd begun his lessons, he had not felt as though he didn't belong.

12

HEROICS

K estrel had awoken early that morning to prepare for the day's hunt with the castle's hunt master, a half-elf and former scout of the elf queen's famed legion. His name was Aelric, and it was not often enough Kestrel had the opportunity to hunt or train with him, especially considering it was his favorite part of the training he received as a squire and future knight of the king's court.

While Kestrel had encountered elves in his homeland on a handful of occasions, they had always been isolated meetings that involved his father and some political discussion or another. He had never spent enough time with any of them to appreciate their culture or to truly get to know them. They had always came across as cold, laughed rarely, and when they did, it seemed to Kestrel they did so at inappropriate times. But something about the elvish people fascinated him despite the fact that he found them so detached, and difficult to understand. Their uncanny abilities in hunting, scouting, archery, and moving silently and invisibly through the trees had been a common daydream of his when he was a child. He had imagined he was one of them, moving so silently he could sneak up on a hart and slap it on the flank. He had imagined himself shooting a bird from the sky with a bow and arrow, and leaping from the branches of one tall tree to another as nimbly as a squirrel.

His childhood imaginings had finally found confirmation in Aelric, the castle's half-human, half-elven hunt master. Aelric ran as swiftly as a hound. He had the endurance of a horse. He could literally stalk a rabbit and catch it in his bare hands. And most impressively, he could outshoot any man Kestrel had ever seen with a bow and arrow. He was unerring in his accuracy. Aelric knew so well the limits of his own abilities that he would not even raise the bow to his eye if he thought the range were too great, or the obstacles too much of an impedance to his chances of a successful shot. Literally without fail—as Kestrel heard it reported—if he raised the bow to his eye and he let go the string, his arrow would strike its intended target.

Kestrel was in awe of Aelric's ability. He was in awe, too, of his talent as a tracker and stalker while hunting. And so it was that Kestrel took extreme care in preparing himself on the days when he was told he would accompany the half-elf on a day or weekend trip to add deer and boar to the castle's larder and to train the young squires of the court in the skills of the huntsman. For most of the squires, the training was fairly basic, but with Kestrel and a few of the more promising and talented boys, they would also learn skills needed to succeed in the more advanced arts of forest craft.

Kestrel rechecked his pack one last time to ensure he had brought an extra bowstring. He had, of course, as he had determined for the third time already that morning. He'd also brought his bedroll, a long, slightly curved hunting knife he had meticulously sharpened the night before, a length of stout cord to hang game beyond the reach of wolves and bears, and a bag of salt and herbs he would have used in his homeland to apply to a field-dressed deer to keep the meat from spoiling.

He refastened the straps of his pack to ensure nothing would fall out, and swung it up over his shoulder, heading out of the barracks and toward the makeshift mess in the room adjacent to the one where he slept. He smiled at the other squires still eating their breakfast, grabbed a full loaf of the warm, hard-crusted bread that arrived from the baker minutes earlier, and saluted them by placing the loaf against his forehead. "Good day, gentle squires! Ye shall be eating venison when I return on the morrow!"

The other squires were obviously accustomed to Kestrel's antics, and a couple even threw heels of bread at him as he walked out of the room. Kestrel smiled even more deeply, finally satisfied that he was ready to join Aelric, and excited about the prospects the day held for him to demonstrate to Aelric how much he had learned since their last expedition.

THE GROUP that would be going on the hunting trip today was small. And the two younger boys had little to no experience as far as Kestrel knew. Besides these two were Derek—no mean woodsman by any standard and, Kestrel thought with no false modesty, second only to himself among the squires—and Tavish Ranald. Tavish knew the basics of hunting—what to do and what not to do—and he was a fine shot, but he just didn't have the knack for tracking that Derek and Kestrel demonstrated, and he stalked so loudly he couldn't sneak up on a tree. But he was a hell of a swordsman—and a good egg. Kestrel liked him a lot, and he thought Tavish liked him just fine too.

The day was bright and the sky blue as Kestrel left the barracks and headed for the mustering point near the keep's east gate. Fall was treating them to a day that felt more like summer, and there were only the wispiest of high clouds in the lightening sky.

Derek's always unpredictable moodiness aside, the question of the day remained the personalities and abilities of the two untested young squires, whom Kestrel didn't know all that well.

As Kestrel approached the gate, he saw that Aelric had not yet arrived, so he decided to have fun with the two younger boys to test their mettle somewhat.

"Good day, lads! Where do you think you're going today, then?"

The boys exchanged glances and then looked at Derek questioningly—who, it appeared to Kestrel, was making a show of ignoring them as much as possible. Kestrel loved this. They were playing right into his hands.

"Are you mute? How is it that they've let mutes join the ranks of squiredom? Derek, is it not still a requirement that all potential knights be able to speak?"

Derek hadn't been listening, and turned at hearing his name but then turned away again, seeming to guess that Kestrel was trying to provoke the younger boys.

"Ah, well, it must be my day to work with the unfortunates of the world. I have three mutes on my hands, after all! You two, over there, do you have some kind of document to prove you are supposed to be here? Or do you await the baker on his morning rounds? If so, why the daggers and bows? Do you plan to shoot yourself a bannock for breakfast?

"Still nothing, then? Come on, you two! Lighten your loads and smile already, would you? Good grief!" Kestrel saw Tavish coming then, leading five saddled horses with Aelric close behind, and he allowed his joviality to get the better of the reserve he usually demonstrated around the man he respected so much.

"Hunt Master! Can you tell me what to make of these three mute squires? Is this an oath you've had them take to show their loyalty? Should I cut out my own tongue to join them in a vow of eternal silence?"

Unlike the handful of elves he had encountered in his homeland, Kestrel had seen Aelric's eyes express emotion from time to time. And although these occasions were rare, if Kestrel wasn't mistaken, he'd have sworn the half-elf's lip had just twitched ever so slightly. Could it be that Kestrel had made a human joke that had cracked through the hunt master's grim exterior?

Aelric's eyes flashed again and then were flat once more as he responded. "Aye, Kestrel. It is your turn next. Only they did not cut out their own tongues. I cut them out for them. Come here now, so I can be sure to have a quiet trip today." As he spoke, Aelric drew his hunting knife—with a blade a full hand longer than Kestrel's own—and extended his hands forward as if he were preparing to engage Kestrel in hand-to-hand combat.

The twitch in his eye was the tell Kestrel needed, or he'd likely have been more frightened than he was. But it was enough to give him the confidence to stand still as the half-elf approached and remain motionless while he tilted his head back. But he had to admit he became concerned when the half-elf drew close enough that Kestrel could feel his breath, which smelled, he noted absently, of heather, against his face. Kestrel must have shown some movement of discomfort in his face then, because Aelric responded with a rare bark of laughter before withdrawing and snapping his knife back into its sheath in a quick, fluid motion.

"Enough games!" And just like that, the hunt master had returned them all to their purpose. "These boys do not know quick mud from quick bread. And they cannot string a bow, track a rabbit across fresh snow, or start a fire without a tinder-box. They would be as helpless in the eye of Woods Heart as a suckling baby taken from its mother's arms.

"The day's lessons, and tonight's as well, will try to start them on the road to learning what the rest of you already know. If God is merciful, one of these unlikely boys might even surpass you three and become a true woodsman, to match perhaps the meanest elf of Aoilfhionn in ability.

"But while it is unlikely any of you shall ever reach even that mark, you should know that I not only believe it to be possible, but I know it to be so. For there are trackers among the human legends, and even those who walk the green today, who were and are the match for many elves in the skills of which I hope to teach you but a mere fraction.

"Your first lesson is this: time spent in the woods, awareness of one's surroundings, and common sense are the three components necessary to become a master of woodcraft. Lack any of these three elements, and you will never be more than one who travels through the woods at the will of the forest and its inhabitants.

"Let us be off, then. Load up your steed for a few hours' journey. We will take no pack horses, and when we break for our midday meal, we will be tethering the horses and continuing the rest of the trip on foot."

The boys fell to. Each was guided to a horse by Tavish and began to load them as instructed. Kestrel's single pack, bedroll, and bow were secured quickly, and he was done and mounted within moments. He had been closest to Tavish when Aelric gave the order to mount, and he had selected a roan stallion with a rangy look in his eye. He had never ridden this horse before, and he took some time now to get comfortable with him. The horse had been a good choice. He was fiery but well trained, and responded to the slightest pressure from Kestrel's knees. He turned him this way and that, and walked him slowly around the others, weaving between them at close quarters and trying to judge his behavior around other horses.

Finally satisfied, Kestrel took another look at the boys who would be accompanying them on their hunting trip. His initial impressions were good. They were quieter and more subdued than many of their peers, who put on brave fronts to try to impress the older and more experienced squires. He wondered how much of that was being intimidated by Aelric and his words to start the trip. And he wondered whether they would become bolder and brasher as they became comfortable with their surroundings and their traveling companions. Kestrel had witnessed such behavior before. He hated it. He much preferred someone like Tavish, who was quiet and confident without feeling the need to be a bully or brag about his accomplishments.

The last of the three boys had mounted. Aelric, still on foot, began to jog away from them at a steady, league-eating pace, bending southward and then straight west, and keeping the boys on horseback at a trot.

As promised, and nearly four uneventful hours later, Aelric slowed to a walk at the verge of a wall of trees that extended as far as the eye could see to the north and south. They had reached the edge of the great central forest of Hyrde. Kestrel was excited. He had always skirted this forest by traveling north by northwest from Ridderzaal, toward his homeland.

It was an appealing forest to his senses, comprised of old-growth hardwood as far to the north as the forest extended— about halfway to the border of the plains of Namur. To the south, he knew it transitioned to softer, water-loving trees and pines. But that was many, many leagues from here and in an area where the gnomes would still dispute trespassers, and so he had always given it a wide berth.

As the boys came closer to him, Aelric addressed them. "Dismount here. We will lead the horses into the forest a short way, where there will be ample fodder and drink for them. The stallion Kestrel rides will see that they remain where we leave them."

Half an hour later, they were on the move. Each wore on

their backs all the gear the horses had been carrying, and they were eating such cold meals as cheese, hard bread, and satje as they went. The boys had been tasked with bringing their own food, and most had chosen well. Kestrel was partial to the dried, leatherlike beef and, before swallowing it, would chew on a single piece for long minutes until all hint of salt had been extracted. But one of the two new boys had brought a loaf of fresh bread, pears, and soft cheese. And the other had brought a fresh-salted fish wrapped in oilcloth! Their struggle to eat as they hiked through the woods provided Kestrel with a good deal of entertainment. And even Tavish shook his head at the boy trying to take a bite of fish while using his other hand to scramble up a low rise.

Each boy also carried at least one skin of water, and all had taken Tavish's lead when he refilled his at the brook where they left the horses.

When they had walked deeper into the woods for the better part of an hour, Aelric stopped them once again. "For two or three furlongs now, we have pushed ahead of us a doe in heat. Have any of you seen it?"

Kestrel's cheeks turned red. He had not, and he guessed that none of the other boys had either. Always careful to be the first to admit to a failure, as his father had taught him, Kestrel responded out loud. "I did not, though now you've told me, I can find it if you'll let me."

Aelric shook his head. "No. There's no gain in finding her, since we've no intention of bringing her down."

Kestrel was mortified at the comment. He hadn't meant he would shoot the doe! He had only meant as he said: He would find it. He would track it. He scowled at the thoughts he imagined running through the minds of his peers: that he had made a mistake and the hunt master had corrected him before the group.

After a moment longer, Aelric continued. "But . . . I didn't say anything about the hart that noticed her passing and now follows her." The hunt master smiled, clearly enjoying himself.

Kestrel's ears perked up. Hart! He removed the bow from over his shoulder and unwound the string wrapped about its length, stringing the bow with his foot in a fluid, practiced motion. He would not draw an arrow, however. Stalking with a nocked arrow made it harder to clear branches and move stealthily, as Kestrel had learned many years earlier. It had been a lesson he'd learned himself, and it had stayed with him.

He checked the direction of the wind by turning in a slow circle and judging when he felt its gentle pressure against both ears at once. The wind was from just north of east. And the deer would want to remain downwind of any animal that might be following them. So if they were pushing the doe as Aelric had said, the doe would be trying to stay slightly south of where they were headed. He started moving westward, hoping to work his way around the deer, glancing once at Aelric to make sure the half-elf was looking for the boys to make their own decisions, and it was therefore okay to proceed.

Kestrel quickened his pace and began to stalk, stepping carefully as he walked on the balls of his feet. He moved ahead, farther and farther from the rest of the group. He glanced back briefly. Derek, ever the opportunist, was moving around the deer as Kestrel did, but to the south. Tavish, Kestrel was pleased to see, faced in the direction of the deer and was speaking to the new boys gathered before him. He was giving Kestrel and Derek time to get into position before he continued the push. Kestrel knew that Tavish would have the boys line up on either side of him and then walk a broad line straight in the direction the deer would be heading. He looked up once and nodded to Kestrel, confirming his intentions. Kestrel smiled and waved back in a quick thank you. Then he was off.

Kestrel moved even more quickly now, assured that he would be getting more cooperation than competition from his fellow squires. Even Derek, whose motives would be more strictly personal than the others', would be effectively helping the group by his approach and by the fact that Kestrel knew he was apt to act as another "pusher" whether he intended to or not. His stalking skills were not his greatest strength in the area of woodcraft.

Kestrel hunched over as he ran so he could carry his bow parallel to the ground and low enough that he could avoid snagging it on the thickening underbrush into which the deer had moved. Thinking again that Derek would give him an unwilling assist, he cut farther to the right to ensure the deer weren't pushed in his direction too soon—before he'd had a chance to get downwind. He ran farther west for a few more minutes, and then, on some instinctual sense that he'd gone far enough, he bent his way southward and slowed down his pace to ensure he would spot the deer before they spotted him. Even without his scent to aid them, the animals weren't blind.

He moved slowly, turning his head as little as possible and doing most of his scanning with his eyes. He tried not to focus on any one tree or other feature of the terrain, knowing from experience that he'd be better able to catch motion at the edges of his vision if he weren't distracted by wondering for too long whether that storm-overturned root ball was a massive cave bear and that broken branch was a set of antlers.

He had moved another twenty or thirty yards when he caught sight of something slightly to the left of the direction he was heading, and about thirty yards away. He relaxed. It was Derek. But then something else caught his eye, to the right of Derek and moving up behind him quickly. It was a . . . *gnome?* No, he didn't think so. What was it? He couldn't be sure, but the creature closing in on Derek was no human or other creature he'd ever seen before.

It was humanlike, with a sallow cast to its features, almost yellow in the sunlight that filtered through the canopy of trees.

Its mouth jutted forward into something like a flattened snout, and it had pointed ears like a wildcat's. Disconcerting Kestrel was the fact that it wore a leather vest and leather pants, which came down to just past its knees. But it was the way the creature moved that made Kestrel's spine squirm. It ran with a low, loping stride, its arms almost hanging to the ground. And as it closed in on Derek, it pushed off the ground, the saplings, and any other obstacles in its path as smoothly as a wolf or dog might while running down prey.

Kestrel froze as his mind tried to grasp what he was witnessing. Was it a gnome? He didn't know. It didn't look like the painting he had seen in one of the libraries where Cedric held their lessons. But then, some of those paintings weren't nearly as good as Cedric seemed to think they were. His gut told him it wasn't a gnome, but he just didn't know what it was. And he hesitated.

As it came closer to Derek, Kestrel could see that Derek had finally heard it approach and had turned to engage the creature. But his bow and arrow were not at the ready, and somehow Kestrel knew that the creature racing toward Derek would kill him as quickly and efficiently as a wildcat or a bear would. He wasted no more time, pulled an arrow from the quiver at his hip, and nocked and drew the arrow back to his eye. He tracked the creature for a split second and then let fly his arrow, continuing the swing of his bow to the left as he did, to ensure the arrow followed the path the creature was taking.

Kestrel kept his eye on the creature and tried to watch for the arrow, but it moved too quickly for him to track its path through the air. Sometimes he could see them in flight, and other times he could not. He wasn't sure why. While he watched the scene before him, he knew he should draw another arrow from his quiver in case the first one missed. But some part of him knew that if he missed with the first, he would be too late to save Derek. And the logical part of his mind knew that if that were to happen, he would have plenty of time to draw as many more arrows as it took to kill the creature before it could reach him. Then the creature lunged. Or so it looked initially, until Kestrel realized that he had struck it with the arrow after all. The creature fell short of Derek by no more than two or three yards, dead before it hit the ground.

Instinctively Kestrel realized there might be more than one creature about, and he forgot Derek for a moment and spun about in a circle to be sure that none were closing in on him. He saw nothing, shook free the shiver of fear that had taken hold of his body, and then turned about more slowly to be sure he hadn't missed anything. He hadn't. Apparently, there had been just the one.

He looked back to Derek and saw the boy staring at the creature at his feet, seemingly unable to comprehend what had just happened. He had dropped his bow and drawn his sword. But were it not for Kestrel's arrow, he could see that Derek would not have been prepared in time to defend himself. And it would have been Derek who lay dead on the floor of the Hyrden forest.

Kestrel became suddenly conscious of what had occurred, and oddly, he realized that he felt embarrassed. It was as though he'd borne witness to something he never should have seen. That Derek's helplessness was not something he was prepared to acknowledge. That he should let his fellow squire know he was there. That he should tell him he had witnessed the whole thing. But he didn't have the heart to do so. Instead, he stood silent, bow in his left hand, hanging limp at his side, his right hand resting on the lip of the quiver at his hip.

The moments passed, and Kestrel couldn't understand why no one had come running to see what had happened. Then he considered that the creature had made no sound and had been stealthy enough to sneak up on a boy whom Kestrel knew to be an able soldier and an excellent woodsman. And the arrow that had brought the creature down had been silent as well.

Kestrel heard a deep grunt to his left. He drew and nocked another arrow and held his bow ready, not immediately recognizing the sound for what it was: the snort of a hart on sentry, of a male deer asking of the woods before it that any other deer in the area step forward and reveal itself. He turned and saw the hart faintly, among the fallen leaves that made up the forest floor, and against the gathering twilight. Its back was to the east. Kestrel glanced to his right and noticed that Derek had seen the deer as well and was watching it as silently as he was.

Neither boy made a move as the deer took its time, two or three tenuous steps at a time, to walk the twenty yards it took to bring it directly between them. It was then Derek noticed Kestrel for the first time. And as the deer passed on in silence and at its own pace, Kestrel could see that Derek finally understood what had happened. The twilight deepened. The deer moved beyond their range.

And Derek nodded in thanks to Kestrel. He had saved the boy's life.

WHEN AELRIC and the others arrived in response to Kestrel's whistle, Kestrel and Derek were bent over the creature Kestrel had killed. Kestrel noticed that his arrow had passed straight through the creature, right under its armpit. He had given the thing a clean death. The observation made him feel good—regardless of the creature's intent.

Derek flipped the creature over, and Kestrel noticed for the first time that it bore a long dagger, still in a sheath, on its belt. It had not drawn its weapon as it had closed on Derek. A kernel of doubt crept into his mind. He couldn't have mistaken the creature's intent, could he? No. It had been running toward Derek so quickly and in such a predatory way that it had to have intended him harm. But the doubt remained, and Aelric seemed to read it in his eyes as Kestrel allowed the still-sheathed dagger to fall back against the creature's hip.

"Kobolds don't need a dagger to kill, Starkad. Look at its claws."

Ah, a kobold! Kestrel thought. *That makes more sense than a gnome.*

But Kestrel did as he was instructed and looked at the creature more closely. He was shocked to see claws like a cat's sprouting from stubby and almost humanlike hands. He lifted one briefly and turned it over. The skin of the palm was a chalky yellow. And the back of the hand was covered in a sparse tuft of fine dirty-blond hair. Aelric was right: the long claws, like those of a wildcat, were clearly lethal.

Aelric offered more. "Put it out of your head, Starkad. Derek knows, and I know, that you had no choice. Kobolds are not redeemable. Even elves shoot them on sight in the west. And we won't even shoot gnomes until we've established their purpose."

Kestrel nodded. The creature had been intent on harming Derek. He knew that. He guessed he was just having a hard time dealing with the fact that he'd never even seen a kobold before, and now he had killed one. It felt wrong somehow. Maybe it was the tales of kobold merchants and the kobold bartender from his childhood. And from the stories, he'd always thought they were more like dogs and less like humans than this creature had been. It even wore a shirt and pants, and carried a blade with it. The image was a disturbing one, and Kestrel had to fight off another shiver down his spine.

Aelric seemed to understand the thoughts that coursed through Kestrel's mind. "You did well, Starkad. A fine killing shot of a mindless creature that sought Robinet's blood."

At mention of his name, Derek spoke up as well. "Thanks, Kestrel. I really owe you one. I didn't even know you were there, and I never saw him coming after me until it was too late. He'd have had me for sure."

Kestrel couldn't think of an appropriate response, but for some reason, it occurred to him to tell Aelric about the deer. "I had a clear shot at the hart, Hunt Master. And he was a beauty. But I'd just shot the kobold, and I, well, it just didn't feel right to kill the deer. At the time, anyway."

Aelric nodded in approval. "Just as well, Starkad. You'd have had to dress it near this thing." His face showed clear disgust.

Then Aelric, in a rare display of his more human nature, placed his hand on Kestrel's shoulder. "You've shown a clear head and a true eye today. And while a kobold is no man or gnome, it is near enough when you see one lying on the forest floor, is it not?"

Kestrel nodded. Aelric seemed to know what he was feeling.

Aelric continued. "You did well. You'll make a fine scout of the King's Army, Starkad."

Kestrel was torn. He was elated at the hunt master's words, but he still felt sick to his stomach thinking about what he'd done. And long after he took his last look at the form on the ground next to him, his mind's eye saw the half-human face of the kobold lying in the peace of death on the forest floor.

Derek had been picking over the kobold's possessions while Kestrel was engaged with Aelric, and he had laid everything out on top of the kobold's vest, which he had also removed, and had spread out on the ground. There was the dagger, a pouch of poorly struck copper coins, and a necklace comprised of a leather cord and a translucent green stone bound about its middle with a thin copper wire. A small pouch was off to the side, and Kestrel could see mold growing on the open flap, and bits of half-eaten food had spilled out of it. Apparently, there was nothing else of worth.

Derek spoke to Kestrel. "Take whatever you want. They're your spoils to claim."

Kestrel picked up the dagger and drew it from its sheath, noticing as he did so that Derek's eyes had dropped at his selection. But Kestrel took one look at the notched and chipped blade, at the yellowed bone handle that wobbled slightly on its tang, and he gently tossed the dagger back on the pile.

Something of the child in him liked the look of the green stone, but he hesitated in claiming it, feeling morbid at the thought of carrying it around with him. But then it occurred to him that the necklace could be a way to remember the creature from whom he'd taken it, and a symbol of the kobold's spirit rather than simply a trophy of a kill. Maybe if he took it, it would be his way of paying respect to the creature he had killed. These thoughts passed rapidly in his head, and on impulse more than anything, he grabbed the necklace.

Surprising himself then, he bent his head and put the necklace about his neck, tucking the stone into his tunic so that only the leather cord was visible.

Kestrel looked around to see how the others might react to his decision. Aelric wore a quizzical face Kestrel couldn't interpret, but the others didn't appear to deem it as noteworthy as Kestrel did and were already looking back to the pile to see if Kestrel would take anything else. Kestrel understood. "Go ahead. Take whatever you want. I've no interest in anything else."

Derek smiled and grabbed the blade, his face showing an unusually expressive satisfaction. Kestrel suspected the blade would be a prop for telling stories more than a serviceable knife.

The copper coins remained where they were, and no one made a move to claim them. And it was not until Aelric gave the order that they should all head back toward the horses that Tavish Ranald went back to collect them.

13

AN ARRIVAL

Fall was grudgingly holding out against winter one day when Cedric held the day's lesson in the rooftop garden. There were a handful of locations Cedric used more often than others for his lessons, but the garden was far and away Breeden's favorite. Maybe it was because it had been the location of his first class, or maybe it was because of the beauty and peacefulness of the place itself. In any event, it was a magnificent day, and on a day like this one, the garden was exceptionally special. The sun was shining brightly, and there was a pleasant bite to the air. Breeden tried to blow vapor from his mouth. He smiled. Not quite cold enough. But close.

Cedric's lesson was drawing to a close, and even the cleric appeared to have trouble keeping himself interested. He was talking about the political factions in Laon and the rising power of the merchant class there. Breeden had first thought the topic was too advanced for him, but when he looked around the rooftop at his peers, he saw that there were vacant and inattentive faces in surplus. Even Oskar, who was always so alert and eager lest he miss anything important, looked bored.

Cedric was in the middle of a sentence when he suddenly

stopped. "And in an environment where the merchants are permitted to buy royal writs of inheritance, it is but one step away from a system of government where power is derived more from earned wealth than wealth is derived from inherited power. In the waning influence and even disappearance from court of many of the oldest households in the court of Laon, we can see the demise of the latter and the rise of the former. It is only a matter of time before . . . before I bore even myself half to death. I'm sorry, children. But it seems that today's lesson is going to have to undergo an indefinite postponement due to lack of interest and clement weather. Enjoy your lunch hour, and then some. I will see you back at the east wing library immediately following the ringing of the first bell."

The words had no sooner left Cedric's mouth than Kestrel was sprinting for the stairs. But something caught his attention, and he stopped short several feet from his goal. "Well, now. What's that about, then?"

His eyes were facing the front gate of the inner bailey, and everyone, Cedric included, turned to see what he was looking at. By its appearance, it was the carriage of some wealthy noble. The carriage was enormous, completely covered in gilt, and wrought with intricate detail. Breeden had seen nothing even remotely as impressive or gaudy before and guessed that it must be the carriage of someone high in the court.

Derek spoke first. "I think that's the king's carriage. But how could he arrive without our knowing? And why would he come here?"

Breeden didn't like the way Derek said *here* but chose to ignore it in favor of devoting his full attention to the mysterious and captivating carriage, which continued to roll toward the keep. When the carriage was still in sight of the group, and just before it would have passed out of vision beyond the corner of the keep, it stopped. Apparently, there was some sort of honor guard in a formation that extended from the gate to where the carriage had stopped.

Soon everyone had migrated to the low wall at the northwest corner of the garden to watch the spectacle. From this vantage, the carriage and honor guard were close enough that Breeden could see the stern faces worn by the guards. After a handful of moments had passed, the duke's steward arrived from within the castle and approached the carriage in a slow and stately manner. Upon reaching the carriage, he opened the door, held it open with one hand, and offered his other hand to one of the carriage's occupants. Breeden wasn't sure, but he thought he heard the steward say, "My lady."

He mouthed the words in imitation, trying them out and wondering who it could be. "My lady?"

Breeden looked around at the others. Oskar and Janelle were beside themselves with excitement. Derek was interested as well but was trying hard not to show it. Kestrel and Laudan were talking quietly to themselves, Kestrel trying to appear uninterested, and Laudan seemingly genuine in his lack of concern. It was then Breeden noticed that Cedric was not so much interested as amused at the tension in his students. *He must know*, thought Breeden.

"Who is it, Cedric?"

Breeden's words caught the others off guard. And now Oskar and Janelle were torn between hearing what Cedric had to say and watching to see someone emerge from the carriage. But Cedric smiled in response to Breeden's query and would only reply, "One of my new charges. She will not be participating in your group, however. It will be a private-tutoring affair."

"But who is it?"

But this time Breeden's words were lost in a collective gasp as a stunningly beautiful young girl emerged from the carriage. She wore a full-length gown of yellow silk and had radiant blond hair that extended down to her waist and shone like spun and polished gold. Her face was a delicate construction of soft curves and gentle angles. Her nose was small and perfect. Her cheekbones were high. And even from this distance, all the boys were taken aback by her sheer beauty.

Derek was the first to speak, and when he did, his voice was laced with a rare and telling respect. "The princess."

Breeden was stunned and couldn't take his eyes off the young girl, who looked to be—if he had to guess—only a few years older than him. She held herself erect as she stepped down from the carriage, and Breeden was struck by her poise and dignity as she moved. There was a sense of calm and composure about her, as if she were not of the real world but rather a figment of a waking dream. And despite the fact that they were watching her from a rooftop more than ten yards above the courtyard in which she stood, she seemed somehow to float above even them. It felt impossible to believe she was a creature of flesh. She gracefully took hold of the steward's arm, and they proceeded toward the castle at an agonizingly slow but, to Breeden, quite welcome pace. When she finally disappeared from view behind the building, it was a great cruelty she had not lingered longer within his sight.

As if a spell had been broken, Breeden found he was able to move again and look about. Everyone but Cedric and Janelle was gaping at the location where they had lost sight of the princess. Cedric began to chuckle a low laugh of genuine mirth, and Janelle looked like a viper ready to strike out at all of them.

Kestrel snapped out of it next and whistled, low and long. "Well, I swear I've never seen anything so utterly beyond my reach in my life. Did you ever even imagine that there was such beauty in the world, Breeden?"

Breeden shook his head, and Oskar answered for him. "No, I did not. I swear I never would have thought it possible."

Breeden glanced back to Janelle and found she was now

83

looking directly at him. Upon capturing his attention, she squinted her eyes in as baleful a glare as she could muster and stormed off to the stairway.

Breeden watched her leave with a face torn between smirk and confusion. To Oskar he queried, "What do you suppose that was about?"

Oskar shrugged his shoulders. "Jealousy, I'd say, though I'm not sure of what or whom exactly. Perhaps she didn't like seeing our jaws all hit the floor at once!"

Kestrel and Breeden both laughed at that.

When Breeden looked at the other two boys, he noticed that Derek's face was a mask of concentration, while Laudan's was one of utter rapture. Breeden had never seen Laudan demonstrate such open emotion before. He was always quiet and kept to himself. And he never became caught up in the debates and arguments Derek and Kestrel were so fond of stirring up. Now that Breeden thought about it, the boy only seemed truly comfortable talking with Kestrel.

As Breeden watched, Derek broke off from staring at nothing and followed after Janelle, his steps full of purpose. But Laudan was a statue, and it looked as if he still held the image of the departing princess in his mind.

And then Kestrel noticed Laudan's state and laughed out loud, grabbing his friend's arm and giving him as hard a shove as he could muster. Laudan maintained his balance easily but did finally emerge from his trance. He looked confused and asked, "I'm sorry. What was the question?" And he glanced around, noticing first Cedric's amused and still-chuckling face, and then Kestrel's wry look.

Kestrel responded without missing a beat. "The question was about the rise of the merchant class in Laon. Cedric was just saying—"

Laudan picked up on Kestrel's tone, realizing that a joke was being made at his expense, and he punched Kestrel in the shoulder, his long reach more than countering Kestrel's agile attempt to dodge out of the way. The blow struck solidly, and Kestrel grimaced in genuine discomfort. Breeden and Oskar smiled at the exchange, and Cedric grimaced along with Kestrel.

"Words, Laudan. Do not resort to your fist when your mouth can serve." The admonishment was mild and light in tone, but Breeden could tell Cedric was serious at the same time.

Laudan responded with immediate remorse. "But he is as quick with his words as he is with his feet. How am I supposed to best him when I am so slow and clumsy?"

"Exercise your mind, my son. Just as you need to walk about in your armor for a very long time before you can wear it without discomfort and even forget that it is there, you need to practice your words in the same way. Rather than rely on the strength of your arm, which can fail you when sick or tired or wounded, you need to hone your mind to be ready for the times when your strength abandons you. What's more, how many times have the stories been told of the mighty warrior brought down by poison or a stray arrow? Do not forget that in the hour of your greatest need, your strength may not be enough to make the difference.

"And you," he said, turning to face the now thoroughly amused Kestrel, "you need to learn to watch your tongue lest you make pledges from which neither your tongue nor your feet can save you."

Kestrel wiped the smile from his face and assumed a composed expression that Breeden immediately knew was studied. Cedric wasn't convinced either.

"I am quite serious, Kestrel. You may be quicker of mind and defter of foot than most, but there will always be someone quicker. And it is a man's words, even more than his deeds, that too often make his enemies. Lest you think the stories I mentioned to Laudan don't apply to you, reason out, if you will, whether any of those stray arrows may not have been so stray. Those stories are a lesson for both of you. You are, neither one of you, unassailable, and if you are going to be proper knights, you'd best learn, and learn soon, the power that comes from humility. That is enough for now. Go and think on what I have said. I will see you in the east wing library after the first bell."

KESTREL, Laudan, Oskar, and Breeden were quiet as they descended the stairs from the garden. But Cedric had not followed them, so when they reached the bottom of the stairs, Kestrel took the opportunity to jest with Laudan a bit more about the princess.

"So, Laudan, I understand that the princess is here. She apparently arrived this morning. Do you suppose we will get a chance to meet her?"

Breeden thought Laudan looked unsure of himself, and his response was slow in coming. "That was the princess. Of course it was. Why is she here?"

All three of his friends laughed, and Kestrel replied, "Boy, you are a lovesick fool! Cedric just got through telling us that he's going to be tutoring her, and before you ask, no, she isn't going to be part of our group. She'll be a private student of his. But I haven't figured out why Cedric or why here yet."

Breeden couldn't help himself, and even with his limited and romanticized notions about nobility and the royal court at Arlon, he felt comfortable enough with this group to make the suggestion "Maybe there's some sort of scandal the king wants to keep her away from. Or maybe there's more to Cedric than we know."

Kestrel considered the words and didn't dismiss Breeden for being an "uppity peasant," as Derek would have. Instead, he responded with a shrug. "Could be. The royal court is never a safe place to be. And I know that Cedric was a knight under the king's father. So you never know, I suppose. Plus Aelric said something about the Krigares being active right now. Scouts have reported that they may be preparing for war. So more than one reason to send her south?"

Oskar was originally from Arlon and, like Breeden, seemed to be growing more and more comfortable in the company of Laudan and Kestrel. "Cedric supposedly saved the king's father during a terrible battle with the trolls. He's a hero in Arlon for it, and I'm sure the king respects him for it too. I also remember hearing that the old king sent him down here to Ridderzaal on his deathbed. Something about not wanting him to get caught up in politics, I think."

Kestrel nodded. "That could definitely be it, then. Now I'd like to see if we can figure out what the intrigue is all about. Hmm. Anyone up for a run through the cellars tomorrow? I've heard that there are secret passages throughout the castle and that there's even an escape tunnel that comes out on the river somewhere."

Breeden thought it sounded both terrifying and exciting at the same time and couldn't help himself. "I would love to!"

Oskar hesitated but finally agreed. "Sure. Count me in."

Laudan sighed and shook his head, but Breeden somehow knew he would come too. Laudan was very close to Kestrel. In fact, Breeden wasn't sure he'd ever seen Laudan without him. Kestrel would make the occasional appearance on his own without Laudan, but never the other way around.

Kestrel was beaming. "So it's agreed, then! Outstanding! Let's go get something to eat before we have to meet back up with Cedric. Satje?"

AT THE APPOINTED time that afternoon, everyone made their way to the library as Cedric had requested. Janelle still bore a sullen mask and seemed just to tolerate her peers and even Cedric himself. Derek looked unusually relaxed, as if he'd resolved some inner conflict. And the other four boys came noisily clamoring into the room from the hallway, involved in a boisterous, though good-natured, discussion about a merchant they'd encountered on their trip to the market.

Oskar was trying hard to be heard over Kestrel and was comparing the man with someone he knew back in Arlon. "I'm telling you, this guy had a lump on his neck big enough to be a second head."

Breeden laughed, enjoying the back-and-forth between the two and recognizing, not for the first time, the many similarities between Oskar and Kestrel. Oskar was sharp-witted and could launch a comeback to rival anything Kestrel could come up with. And where it was clear Kestrel was much more learned than Oskar, Oskar was easily his match or better in picking up new concepts and in thinking on his feet. Oskar was mentally tough as well, undoubtedly from his upbringing in an orphanage.

But Breeden still gave the edge in confidence to Kestrel. Kestrel was one of the most confident people he knew. Breeden thought that his being raised in a noble household must have made the difference. Breeden suspected that he and Oskar would never feel the same way. During classes with his noble friends, there was always the reality lingering in the back of Breeden's mind that he could never become a knight—that his heritage wouldn't allow it. It didn't bother him though. Well, maybe a little—even as fantastic a notion as the whole thing was.

Breeden's attention returned, and he glanced over at his friends. Laudan was smiling at the continuing conversation between Oskar and Kestrel too but, as always, was also keeping his wall of isolation in place.

Cedric asked them to be seated and gestured to the individual writing desks spread around the room in a rough half circle from where he was standing. The top of each desk was nearly a yard across, the surface tilted upward at the back so the parchment being worked on would be easier to read and work with. Attached at the far-right side of each table, there was a metal basket that contained a small stoppered glass vial full of a thick, dark ink. In front of the ink, in an adjacent metal basket, was a low stone jar full of fine beach sand. The legs of the table were stout and made of a dense wood. And just above the floor, the legs were connected to each other at the sides and back of the table by heavy reinforcing crosspieces of the same wood.

"Since we weren't making much progress with Laonese economics, I thought we could practice the art of treatise writing. Laudan, what can you tell us about the elements of a successful treatise?"

Breeden couldn't help but feel that Cedric was choosing Laudan to start the class in response to the end of the morning's lesson. And Laudan may have been thinking the same thing, because he appeared to visibly steel himself and gather his energy before he spoke, as if he might be in need of reserve breath for a prolonged day of Cedric's personal attention.

While Laudan was answering, at length, the question posed by Cedric, Breeden looked at Janelle, seated immediately to his left, and tried to make eye contact with her. She refused to do so at first, and when she finally did meet his eyes, her glance was hot and cutting. Then she startled him by reaching across the space between their desks and grabbing his writing quill. She placed his quill at the top of her desk and turned her head forward, refusing to look at him. He didn't know why she had done it, and frankly didn't have a clue as to what he should do about it, so he simply smiled and raised his eyebrows at her. Was she mad about the princess?

Lest he draw attention to himself and interrupt the dialogue between Laudan and Cedric, Breeden tried to get her attention quietly. He gestured with his hands and even extended his left leg to kick her chair, but she refused to acknowledge he existed. Breeden glanced back to his right to make sure his teacher was still occupied, and then lunged across the space between them for the quill. But Janelle was expecting him or had seen him out of the corner of her eye. And she snatched the quill before he could reach it and then threw it at him, or rather past him, since it flew by his shoulder and landed on the floor on the far side of his desk. Now it was Breeden's turn to glare, and he did so, but his face was also a mask of confusion. He couldn't understand what her problem was.

"Breeden! What do you think you are doing over there?" It was Cedric. He had finally noticed.

Breeden resumed his seat, and all he could summon was a feeble "I can't seem to lay hands on my quill." And then he pretended to see it on the floor to his right, as if just noticing it for the first time. "Ah, there it is." And he picked up the quill and met Cedric's eyes.

Cedric looked more curious than annoyed and stared at Breeden for a moment, as if expecting the boy to further explain himself. But when Breeden remained silent, Cedric let it go and returned to his discussion with Laudan.

"Laudan, what are the elements of an effective response treatise?"

Laudan was ready with his answer, seeming to know that it would not be his last of the day.

14

ADVENTURE

Winter had finally arrived. And the next day found Breeden, with Kestrel, Laudan, and Oskar, entering the lower rooms of the keep during their morning break. It had been easy enough to find the entrance to the cellars. Kestrel had led the group of four boys into the kitchens below the main hall, and he had asked the nearest scurrying cook's assistant for directions to the cold storage rooms. A breathy response indicated that they were not far, that the dry storage was past the baker's ovens, all the way at the end of the hall. And the cold rooms were below them. The boy looked at Kestrel and Laudan's clothing and, more specifically, their insignia of royalty. He also appeared to consider the clothing of Oskar and Breeden. Whether he thought he faced two young nobles on an errand with their pages, or whatever he may have thought, he didn't even seem to consider the possibility that it might not be appropriate information to share. And he was only too happy when Kestrel dismissed him with a nod and a thank-you.

True to the boy's word, they found a well-used door not far past the baker's suite, and Kestrel descended the narrow and tightly spiraled stone steps beyond with confidence. The others followed quickly. Laudan, bringing up the rear, closed the door behind him, leaving them all in the near darkness of a stairwell lit only by widely spaced torches that guttered as they walked past.

At the bottom of the stairs, a hallway branched in three directions: straight ahead, and directly to the left and right. Kestrel bent to the ground and looked carefully in all three directions. "The kitchen storage has to be to the left. That way bears the marks of the heaviest and most common passage. To the right, the dust is pretty thick. And the middle way is less used than the left but is definitely used on occasion." Apparently without further thought, Kestrel walked straight ahead and grabbed a torch from the wall as he did.

"Why straight, then?" The question was Oskar's.

"We want to find the lower levels—and maybe even the dungeons—so we need to go farther down. If there are stairs somewhere, I would think that the hallway leading to those stairs should be used by someone, at least on occasion. So the hall to the right felt like an unlikely choice, since it appears so seldom used. And as for it not being the hall to the left, I figured, why would the hallway straight ahead be used any more than the one to the right if the hallway to the left leads to both kitchen storage and the stairs down?" Then he shrugged his shoulders. "Seemed to make sense. And if I'm wrong, who cares? We can try the other directions another day."

Oskar laughed. "I was expecting woodcraft. But that sounds like street logic!"

Breeden had a hard time arguing with Kestrel's reasoning, and by the silence of the others, he assumed they felt the same way. The hallway they now traveled was wide and could easily have allowed three men to walk abreast. It was about thirty yards long. There were three doors to the left and two to the right, all made of heavy oak, and all closed, but Kestrel passed them without slowing down. The hallway ended with choices of left and right this time. With a cursory examination of the floor and hardly a hitch in his stride, Kestrel turned right.

A handful of yards later, they came upon a broad stairway on their left, with spacious landings visible heading both up and down from their current floor. Kestrel turned left down the stairs without pausing, and again the others followed without a word.

"This appears to be the main stairwell. What do you say we see how far down they go?" Kestrel tossed the words over his shoulder as he picked up his pace.

They had descended four more sets of stairs by Breeden's count when they finally reached the bottom of the staircase. Upon the discovery that the last two flights of stairs were dark, Oskar, Breeden, and Laudan had each climbed back up to the last lit hallway and retrieved torches for themselves. Breeden wasn't sure about the others, but the hair on the back of his neck had been raised for some time. And the farther they descended, the more his mind wandered into the black corners and unchecked doorways. He knew he had nothing to be afraid of. His father had taught him to use reason to confront his fears. But he couldn't help it. These unused hallways were surely home to ghosts, even if just the memory of former inhabitants.

The hallway at the stair's bottom was dark as well and allowed passage to the left and right. Kestrel held his torch low to the ground and checked for disturbances in the dust and dirt. He examined the ground for a long time, then finally whistled. "Well, I just can't begin to tell how long it's been since someone was down here. Could be a year. Could be more. The dust is as settled as I've ever seen it. Hasn't been disturbed in a long time. But there are old footprints under the dust that head in both directions. Anyone want to flip a coin?"

Laudan spoke up. "I say we go right. I want to start paying

attention, and when I am learning a new place, I always start by going right."

Kestrel laughed. "You want to start paying attention? Guess you're not interested in being a scout, huh? But it doesn't make any difference to me, so . . . let's go right."

They started down the hall with Kestrel in the lead and, again, Laudan bringing up the rear. Breeden suddenly felt self-conscious about the whole thing and wondered if Oskar felt the same. He got the sense Kestrel and Laudan had arranged themselves in this way to protect the two commoners. They didn't have swords on their hips, or anything. But even though all four of the boys carried a knife on their respective belts, he still somehow felt that the two nobles were protecting him. It bothered him a bit, but he had to admit it also felt good, knowing the two boys at least knew the basics of fighting.

As they walked, they passed many closed doors, and a hallway to their left, all of which they ignored. At the end of the hallway, there was a single door and another hallway branching off to the left. Kestrel stopped in front of the door.

"Well, you've gotta start somewhere. How 'bout here?" And he attempted to operate the latch on the door. The latch was quite rusty, though he did manage to lift it. But when he tried to pull open the door, he only managed to move it about an inch. The hinges seemed frozen with rust. Laudan gently pushed his way between Oskar and Breeden, and then not so gently shoved Kestrel to the side.

"Out of my way, puny one, lest thou breakest thy scrawny shoulder." Laudan had deepened his voice and affected a snooty tone, assuming the high form of address still used for certain ceremonies of court.

Oskar and Breeden laughed and stepped back to give Laudan room to try his strength against the hinges. Kestrel grimaced at the gibe but smiled anyway and stepped back beside the other two. Laudan braced his right foot against the wall next to the door and grasped the heavy iron ring with both hands. He gave the ring a quick jerk, trying to pop the hinges free, but the door didn't even budge. Then he leaned back and tried to use his weight and his shoulders to draw steadily against the door, but again the door didn't move so much as a hair.

Breeden was right behind Kestrel as Laudan struggled unsuccessfully time and again, and he finally asked Kestrel if he could take a quick look at the hinges. Kestrel moved out of Breeden's way without comment, and Laudan was focusing so hard on the door, he didn't see or hear Breeden coming up behind him. He was leaning backward again and pulling steadily against the door with all of his weight, and then he tried to rock forward and backward, but still the door wouldn't move.

"Could I take a look at the hinges?"

Laudan heard him this time and acknowledged him with a nod. But there was plenty of room for Breeden to approach the hinges at Laudan's left without interrupting his efforts, and he did so while the larger boy continued to try everything he could against the door.

Breeden extended his right hand to the door's center hinge and touched the built-up rust surrounding it. As he looked more closely at the surface beneath his fingers, he tried to feel the metal the way he had the chisels at the tinker's stall those months ago. His eyes lost focus, and he found he could "see" the patterns in the metal of the hinges, just as he had before. The patterns were quite regular and consisted of densely woven and interlocking strands. Overlaying the patterns in the hinges themselves, there was a separate pattern he could discern from what he intuited must be the rust encasing the hinge. The bonds where the rust patterns met and joined with the hinge patterns were much less dense than either the rust bonds themselves or the hinge's bonds, and much less sturdy.

He tried to focus on a single strand of the bonds and found he could feel something coursing through it. As he had tried to describe to his father months earlier, it was like water, but it wasn't like water. And it felt as though it was waiting to be released.

On a whim, he tried to probe the bonds joining the rust to the iron with his mind, to test them for weakness. To his surprise, he found that the stuff within the bonds responded to his mental probe, and the bonds snapped. He wasn't sure what he'd done, but he felt a small pressure within him release when the bonds broke. At the same time, the center hinge made an audible crack. Everyone jumped, and Laudan took it as a sign to try all the harder to open the door. But it still wouldn't move.

Inspired, Breeden knelt on the floor and tried to duplicate his feat on the bottommost hinge. He didn't know whether he needed to touch the hinge, but he placed his hand on it regardless. More quickly this time, he focused on the rust and found several weak spots. One at a time, he manipulated the stuff inside the bonds, and one at a time, they broke under his ministrations. He broke one more bond, with several more still remaining, and all of a sudden, the bottommost hinge broke free from its encasing rust.

Laudan had been leaning backward with all of his weight and was not prepared when the bottom and then, almost immediately thereafter, the top hinges gave way. He flew backward into Kestrel and Oskar, the three of them sprawling to the floor in a heap. Meanwhile, the heavy oak door came careening around in its arc and slammed into the still-crouching Breeden. In one sweeping motion, he was driven hard against the wall and knocked to the ground.

The others scrambled to their feet, pulled the door away from him, and lifted Breeden off the floor, each asking him if he was okay. Somehow his head remained untouched and he retained his wits, but he knew he would be one giant bruise later that day.

"I feel like a horse just fell on me," he groaned, managing a weak smile.

Oskar was right in his face and sighed when he realized that Breeden was well enough to crack a joke. "You got clobbered! I can't believe you weren't squashed against the wall like a bug!"

Breeden would be sore later, but he really didn't think the accident had been that bad. "You can let go of me now. I think I can stand."

They let go of him and he stood unassisted.

Kestrel watched him for a moment, seemingly concerned about Breeden's health. But instead of asking if he was sure he was all right—which Breeden had been sure would be the next question—Kestrel surprised them all. "What did you do to those hinges?"

Breeden didn't think he had anything to hide, so he just shrugged his shoulders. "I'm not sure. I could tell that the rust wasn't that strong, so I probed at it and somehow got it to break." He didn't have the words to describe what he had done in more detail. "It wasn't really that hard."

Kestrel didn't seem so sure of that and continued to look at Breeden closely. "You didn't appear to be pushing very hard. And you weren't using your knife or any kind of tool, were you?"

"No. I just probed it, and the fibers . . . or strands that held the rust and metal together broke when I did. I'm not sure how I did it exactly, to tell you the truth."

Kestrel wouldn't let it go. "I think I believe you, but I'd really like to know how you managed to do it. What do you mean by *strands*?"

Laudan, surprised by Kestrel's unusual persistence and bored by the exchange, poked his head into the room they had discovered. And what his torch revealed caused him to shout, "By Usen's beard! It's an armory!"

And then even Kestrel's tenacity in his search for answers was exhausted. "What?" He dropped Breeden's gaze, retrieved his torch, and joined Laudan in the unexplored room. Breeden and Oskar were just a few steps behind.

The room was old, as were the arms it contained, but that didn't stop the sixteen- and seventeen-year-old boys from being overwhelmed by the sight. There were rack upon rack of swords, pikes, and maces. There were dummy torsos that bore scale mail and leather armor. There were longbows and cross-bows and slings. There were small round buckler shields and tall rectangular tower shields. There were spears and lances and hooks. The room was enormous and appeared to contain every type of weapon and armor one could think of.

Kestrel was the first to move, after spotting the crossbow rack and releasing a less than knightly "Ooh." Before the others had even decided where to start, he had a light crossbow in his hand. The entire weapon was constructed of metal and looked to be in fair condition, the metal shining by his torchlight. He placed his torch firmly in the U vacated by the crossbow and, using both hands now, tried to draw back the string still attached to both ends of the prod. When the string began to make ominous creaking sounds, he thought better of it. "I'll find a new string for you, don't worry!" By the intensity of his examination, and the fact that he was turning the weapon over and over in his hands, he didn't appear to be in a hurry to see any of the other weapons. One by one his friends left the doorway and spread out around the room.

Oskar moved over to the spears and began checking the heft of each one. Breeden went for the swords, trying the feel of a few of the smaller and narrower-bladed ones. And Laudan stood in front of the armor.

Among the old-fashioned scale mail and the rotting and

scarred suits of leather armor, Laudan had found one suit of leather in remarkable condition. It was a dark brown and had been heavily oiled in the past—so much so it was nearly black. When he wiped away a patch of dust from its surface, the leather underneath reflected back the light of his torch, albeit dully. The armor was covered in heavy bronze discs, evidently designed to provide additional protection in turning away blades that might otherwise penetrate the suit's leather. Each disc was carved with symbols and images of creatures and men. But though the discs looked the same from a distance, close examination revealed that each was unique in design. Perhaps most remarkable of all, however, was the size of the armor: it was enormous. It looked as if he would swim in it, and at sixteen, Laudan was already bigger than many adults. He unfastened the armor from its dummy torso.

Breeden tried to take it all in, but there was too much to see. He still held the broadsword he had found, which had felt *right* in his grasp, and he turned his attention to the activities of his friends. He saw Laudan raising over his head the suit of studded-leather armor that was too big even for him. He saw that Kestrel had moved on from the crossbow and was trying on a pair of intricately carved bronze bracers—too loose, even when properly tightened onto his forearms. And he saw Oskar trying on various helmets, each falling straight to his shoulders.

He realized they all looked like just what they were: boys trying to make the trappings of war fit their unready forms. Laudan wasn't broad enough of shoulder—for the armor he'd found, anyway. Kestrel wasn't thick enough of limb. And he and Oskar were kidding themselves that they would ever be permitted to wear, never mind use, such equipment. At that somewhat disheartening thought, Breeden walked over to the rack where he'd started and placed the sword back where he'd found it.

The afternoon's adventure had been thrilling and even

somewhat terrifying at moments—at least to Breeden. He never would have believed that someday he might be exploring the dark and ancient tunnels beneath a castle. But upon reflecting on the life he knew was in front of him—working in his father's business—the glow of the moment lost its luster for him. This was not his life. This was not his future. He had become friends with boys who would become knights in less than a year, but he would not. Could not. Although he'd never been bothered before by looking closely at his life, he realized that he was now. And building boats with his father could never inspire him the way this room and the images and adventures it conjured could.

"What time is it, do you suppose? How long have we been down here?"

Kestrel looked over at Breeden and saw the look on his face. "Are you all right? Is that fall still bothering you?"

Breeden saw the opportunity and grabbed it. "Yes. Er, ah, no. I'm sure I am all right. But I do ache all over. Do you think we could leave now and come back another time?"

Kestrel was visibly disappointed, and when he looked Breeden in the eye, Breeden thought perhaps he knew it wasn't Breeden's physical discomfort that made him want to leave this place. He held Breeden's gaze a moment and then replied quietly, "As you wish."

And then he was all action, removing his bracers and placing them back where he'd found them. "Laudan! Oskar! Let's leave this place. Now we've gotten it open, it's ours to explore when we want. But I think we've done enough exploring tonight. And not a bad find at all, eh?"

Laudan had noticed the expression on Breeden's face too, and approached him, still wearing the oversize studded-leather armor. "Are you all right, Breeden? That door hit you pretty hard. Are you sure you didn't hit your head?"

"Yes, I'm fine, and no, I didn't hit my head. I'm just feeling a bit worn."

"Well, I'm glad you're okay. But I'm sure tomorrow you won't feel quite so well. I know after a good sparring match, I sometimes have trouble getting up the next morning. Anyway, I'm sure you'll be fine."

While the larger boy was talking, Breeden had found himself drawn to the armor he was wearing. At first he looked at it as he normally would, and then his eyes lost focus. The patterns he saw using his ability both imbued and surrounded the discs themselves and seemed to connect all the discs in a complex web. The weave of the pattern was so intricate that it was dizzying, and a moment later Breeden found he couldn't look at it any longer. His eyes refocused, and he looked Laudan in the eye.

"There is something about that armor . . ."

Laudan hadn't caught Breeden's brief trance, and met his eyes. "What's that?"

"The armor. It's special. It's not just well-made; there's more to it than that. I can't explain it better. I'm sorry."

Laudan didn't appear to register what Breeden was getting at, and grew a concerned look on his face. But he responded to the part he understood. "Thanks, Breeden. I like it a lot too. It's funny, but my eyes just locked onto it when I walked into the room."

"I can see why, Laudan. Are you going to keep it?"

Laudan considered. "I hadn't thought to, since it doesn't fit me, and I may not be allowed to take it, in any event. Maybe I'll ask Cedric about it."

"Oh, no, you won't!" It was Kestrel. "We don't want him knowing we're sneaking around in the cellars. If he knew, and decided we shouldn't be, he could tell us not to, and we'd have to listen. But if he doesn't know, we don't have to take the chance he might not allow it."

Again faultless logic from Kestrel, thought Breeden. He found it hard to argue.

Oskar, finally drawn away from his examination of a pair of scale mail gauntlets, nodded in agreement. "There's a pretty basic rule at the orphanage: sometimes it's easier to ask forgiveness than permission."

Breeden liked the sound of that, but at the same time, he had to admit to himself that it didn't exactly feel honest either.

"Okay, I'm ready." And he was. Breeden had had a long day, and what should have been a fun adventure with his friends had turned somewhat sour in the end.

15

COLORS

A few days later found everyone returning to their classroom of the day, after having taken lunch in one of the handful of empty rooms in the monastery where they didn't risk spilling food on ancient artifacts or priceless vellums. They were passing through a stretch of hallway that had a balcony to one side and overlooked the main rotunda of the keep's entrance. Just as they reached the section of the hallway where the railing began, they heard a commotion below. The huge main doors were being opened, and the horns were being sounded. Breeden wondered why the smaller side door wasn't sufficient—especially when it meant letting in so much cold air —but kept his thoughts to himself.

And then she was before them once again: the princess. This time they were all much closer than the last, and they could see they had not been mistaken about her beauty. Her eyes, now close enough to be clearly visible, were a robin's-egg blue. And her glorious blond hair was tied back in a single thick braid. Her gown was a blue to match a cloudless summer sky, and she wore a fine net of small blue gemstones in her hair. The boys were once again struck immobile.

She stepped into the rotunda delicately. And a young girl no more than eight or nine years old came behind her, holding the train of the long gown the princess wore. But as graceful as the princess made the act of stepping over the threshold, the young girl behind her had no such skill. She stumbled, stepping on the gown as she did so, and just barely remained on her feet.

If the trance the princess had used to capture the boys' hearts had been a dream, what happened next was a nightmare. So quickly Breeden wasn't even sure he'd seen it properly, the princess spun about and struck the hapless girl across the side of the head, shrieking as she did so, "You useless and clumsy girl! I would be better off without you! Leave me! Now!"

The scream was shrill and piercing, and Breeden knew he wouldn't soon forget it. The poor young girl was devastated. She literally cowered before the princess's wrath, and when the princess spoke again, this time with the words "Leave my sight!" the girl bolted out of the keep's entrance and made for the gate to the outer city. From their perch on the balcony, Breeden and the others watched most of her stumbling and sobbing retreat before the massive doors to the keep were finally drawn closed.

When Breeden looked back to the princess, she had already composed herself as if nothing at all had happened. She was perfectly serene, perfectly poised. And she had her hand extended slightly, awaiting the steward's attentions. The whole scene had lasted a matter of seconds. And to Breeden, it was somehow not quite real. He looked around at his friends for some kind of confirmation that they had seen the same thing he had.

"Well, that's one hell of a way to ruin a fantasy, isn't it?" Kestrel was addressing everyone and no one in particular but was careful to keep his voice very low so it didn't bounce off the dome overhead and reach the ears of the princess below.

Janelle looked smugly satisfied. Laudan looked sympathetic. Derek looked troubled. And Oskar had blanched somewhat but didn't appear overly surprised. Breeden wondered if the young orphan had heard tales of her behavior when he was living in Arlon. He would have to remember to ask him when they had passed beyond the balcony and it was safe to speak freely.

The princess and the steward proceeded through the rotunda and passed beyond the view of Breeden and his companions. Looks were shared and eyebrows were raised, but Kestrel's comment had been the only words spoken, and everyone seemed afraid to move from the spot. Finally, at Kestrel's shrugged shoulders and his decision to move off, the rest of the group followed behind.

Not much more than a minute later, they were all gathered in their classroom. Cedric hadn't yet arrived. And when Kestrel closed the door, they all burst into conversation at once.

"What was that?" Breeden bellowed, and Janelle laughed, excited at the prospect that she had regained some of her previous stature from the princess's loss.

"What a little hellcat she is!" chimed in Kestrel. "And I heard from one of the kitchen maids that she has already gone through one train bearer and two ladies-in-waiting! Are you sure you still want to marry her, Laudan?"

Oskar's reply was still excited but a notch or two calmer than the others. "I have heard stories but never would've thought they weren't stretching the truth. But then I don't think I would've believed it myself if I hadn't seen it with my own eyes."

Laudan spoke quietly. "I wonder what happened. I mean, what is she really upset about? There has to be more to what we saw."

Kestrel joked with his friend. "Oh no, you're not going to

make excuses for her, are you? She's a shrew, Laudan—you'd better see that now!"

"I don't know. There has to be more we don't know."

"Oh, there is, Laudan. But I'd guess it's more of the same. Did that girl look like she deserved to have her head bit off?"

Their conversation was interrupted as Cedric arrived. He wore an unusually stern expression on his face and had evidently heard their raised voices and seen their excitement when he entered.

"The princess? The rotunda just now?" Cedric spoke the words mostly as a question, though his tone didn't convey an expectation that their excitement could be over anything else.

Breeden nodded anyway, and Cedric nodded back in response, as if resigning himself to a difficult course of action.

"Hmm. The princess . . . is a fiery one. And she has her own challenges, just as each of us does." He paused then, and Breeden got the impression he was trying hard to choose the right words—not a common occurrence for the very intelligent and well-spoken monk.

"I do not condone her actions of a moment ago, and I don't seek to excuse them, but I would ask each of you to remember a few things. One, she is our heir apparent, and as queen, she will hold power over the entire kingdom. I tell you this as much to remind you to watch your words and criticisms as to try to help you to understand the weight and gravity of that responsibility and how much of a burden it must be for her. Two, her father is a great and well-respected ruler, and well-liked too—which is not always the case with those we hold in respect. And her great-grandfather six generations back was our greatest king in memory. She lives under these two shadows—and the shadows of other fine kings in between—with no brother to take the throne in her place. And therein lies my third point: she needs must be a son to her father, in the absence of a male heir.

"We cannot know what she may have done with her life had

these circumstances not been thrust upon her. Perhaps she would rather have led a quiet life. Perhaps she would have liked to marry for reasons other than political ones. I cannot say, and you should not presume to judge, nor assume that you know her heart.

"One final thing I wish you to know: I am working with her right now. She is my student, as you are my students. And as you know already, or can probably guess, I do not judge success with my students by memorization of rules and dates. I hold myself to a very high standard and am held by my god to one higher still. I will do everything within my power to help the future queen become a ruler to make her father proud."

"That will be enough on this subject for now. Let's get on with our lesson for today." He composed himself for a moment before continuing.

"Oskar, what are Hyrde's top three imports from other provinces or nations?"

16

ENTANGLEMENTS

Winter had lasted forever. Occasional sightings of the princess, disagreements between Derek and, well, most everyone, and, admittedly, some fun times exploring the cellars aside, being cooped up in the monastery for classes all winter had felt a toil. Breeden reflected that he had been learning at least. And he had developed deeper friendships with Kestrel and Oskar especially.

But while it was now technically spring, winter was trying to reclaim its hold, and a late freezing rain had coated the cobbled streets with a thin sheet of ice. Breeden had to use great care to avoid losing his footing on his way to class this morning. That he was cutting it close to making his lessons on time meant he had to fight with himself to be careful but go faster nonetheless.

As he approached the main roadway, Janelle must have been watching for him through the window, because she appeared at the top of her stairs as he passed by. He was staring intently at the ground before his feet as he walked, and her sudden shout startled him. He looked up, caught a glance of her smiling face for a split second, and involuntarily took a staggered step backward. Then he was falling, both of his feet having slipped on the ice and come off the ground at once. He fell backward heavily and hit his head on the paving stones. Darkness surrounded him.

ONLY A FEW MOMENTS must have passed before Breeden came to himself, since Janelle was barely at the bottom of the stairs. He remembered quite well what had happened and was mortified that he should do such a blockheaded thing in front of her. Then she was kneeling at his side, concern evident on her face. "Are you all right?"

At that moment, as the sun's rays filtered through the streets of Ridderzaal and cast the morning's long shadows across the roadway, Janelle's hair became aglow with the sun's soft warmth, and he could see red and gold where normally there was only brown. Suddenly he could think of nothing but how gloriously beautiful she was. He smiled and closed his eyes, wanting never again to open them lest he forget the vision before him.

"Are you all right?" Her voice came to him as if from far away, as if through water or wool. He didn't want to respond. But his head was starting to hurt. And the warmth that had filled him a moment earlier was leaching from his body. Then he remembered that he was lying on his back on an ice-covered road and that he had been on his way to class. Slowly the realization came that he had no choice, but had better open his eyes after all and get to his feet.

When his eyes opened again, Janelle's face showed relief. Breeden couldn't help but groan, and Janelle's concern returned. "You're not all right. I'm sorry I scared you."

"No!" He protested the word. Even then, in his weakness and on the ground at her feet, he wouldn't have her thinking of him in that way. "I wasn't scared. You just distracted me. I wasn't expecting you."

And then she surprised him again by smiling warmly. "You're a fool, Breeden Andehar. But I'm glad you're okay."

He tried to get up then, and she touched his chest gently to hold him down. "Sit. Don't try to stand just yet. Cedric will understand if you're late. I'll tell him what happened."

He laughed softly in spite of himself. He'd been thinking just that—that Cedric would be upset if he was late for class. But he realized that he had to get up despite her protest. "I'm sorry, Janelle. But I have to get to class. This is a very important lesson."

Now it was her turn to laugh. "A very important lesson? On what? The purchasing habits of the merchant class in Laon?" And her smile remained this time, her head still shrouded in the soft caress of the new sun's light.

Again Breeden became caught up in the warmth of her face and smile, and he stopped trying to rise. He told himself he needed to remain where he was for a bit longer to humor her.

They stayed that way for a long moment in silence, Breeden on his back on the icy road, Janelle's hand still resting lightly on his chest. And it felt to Breeden that all was right with the world, despite the seeping cold, his numbing backside, and the pronounced ache at the back of his head.

Janelle broke herself away first, standing up and stepping out of the sunbeam that had enveloped her. She reached for his hand. With some effort, Breeden was kneeling, and after a few seconds more, he was on his feet once again.

Breeden gathered himself for a moment, made sure his balance was intact, and then nodded to Janelle that he was okay. They walked the remainder of the distance to the monastery without incident.

Not knowing where class was being held, Breeden and Janelle looked first in the rooms closest to the monastery's entrance and then worked their way toward the castle. But Cedric hadn't made it too difficult for them, and they found their classroom on the second try.

Cedric had already started class, and though he hardly looked up as Breeden and Janelle found their way to their seats at the back of the classroom, he was clearly displeased with their tardiness.

Derek snickered as the two entered, and received a dirty look from Oskar in response.

As class continued where it had left off, Breeden remembered that Cedric would be discussing a famous naval battle between the great Hyrden king's son, Wilham II, and the Krigares. He was disappointed to realize he had missed the beginning of Cedric's tale, and tried to catch up to the unfolding story as Cedric related it.

Cedric took a moment to compose himself after Breeden and Janelle's disruption, but once he began speaking again, he regained something close to his typical momentum. "And the shipbuilding of the Hyrdens and Laonese under the king's orders was like nothing ever undertaken. Lumber from the great Hyrden forest was floated downriver to Woodfall, past these very walls, and, back when the lower Woodfall was navigable, to the once great open ocean port of Ghent. It was there, at the farthest reach from the Krigares' watchful eyes, that dozens of new ships were constructed. Massive transports, catapult-bearing fast-attack boats, supply ships, and a handful of small and nimble scouts.

"But Wilham the Second was three times a fool. Once for breaking the treaty his father had signed with the Krigares at the close of the battle that saw most of Erda under Hyrden rule. Twice for thinking he could keep a full year of shipbuilding and preparations from being noticed by the seafaring Krigares.

"And when Wilham the Second finally did launch his attack, he was a fool for at least the third time in that campaign, when he chose to split up his forces, directing half to come up and around the west coast, and the other to come up the east coast. Apparently, he felt that he could crush the entirety of the northern tribes between the pincers of his 'armada.' He was quite horribly wrong. And not one of those among his advisers dared to warn him otherwise. Or if they did, there is no record of dissent among the scrolls and books that cover this tragedy.

"All told, thousands of conscripts from among the Hyrdens, Laonese, and Pretani were sent to a watery grave by the nimble fighting ships of the northern raiders. Many hundreds of Krigares lost their lives, it is true—most to the arrows that flew like gadflies between and among the battling ships. But it was only through the bold cowardice of a few officers in the King's Navy that any Hyrden at all survived the battle to tell the tale. Seeing the early rout of the battle, and having prepared for it, in fact, from the beginning, a senior officer of the King's Navy raised the pennant of retreat on his heavily manned transport and ordered his crew to come about. A handful of other ships in the area around him responded in kind. These ships would prove to be the only ones to survive. A little more than a thousand men returned home, a mere fraction of the force that had left Hyrde's waters."

Cedric paused a moment for dramatic effect, scanning the eyes of his pupils, and then he continued once more. "Many lessons are to be learned from this failed campaign. The first lesson was an obvious one that should have escaped no one: never attack the Krigares in a naval battle in their own icy waters, regardless of the size of your force. Among other lessons that I would have you focus on: absolute right doesn't equal absolutely right. As thinking members of the future of our society, you need to know that some orders are meant to be questioned. Would you consider it a sound strategy to attack the Krigares in a pincer maneuver that split your forces, weakening each group effectively by half, and doubling your 'front' as well as the number of your enemy? Had the force attacked from either the east or the west, it would have been united, would have faced a foe of half the number, and would have been able to work its way up the coast, attacking one tribe and village at a time. It is unlikely even that approach would ultimately have resulted in a Hyrden victory. But Hyrde would at least have had a turn at the dice.

"Further, by not considering the tribal nature of the Krigares, Wilham the Second failed to recognize that he was actually attacking two separate enemies at the same time. And he created between these enemies the situation of a temporary peace and a cooperation that may not have been there before. The tribes of Krigsrike do not typically involve themselves in each other's business. It is only in a time of such need as threatens all the Krigares' land—not that of but one or two tribes—where you see such cooperation among them. Each tribe is slow to unite if they don't perceive the threat to themselves. And the uniting is not hastened by the fact that each chief is loath to place his forces under the command, even temporarily, of whichever chief has been chosen as war leader of the forces of Krigsrike.

"At any point during the planning of the campaign, it is certain that wiser heads could have argued against such a rash course of action as that proposed by Wilham the Second. But those involved in planning feared raising his ire. They knew their place.

"Might Wilham have dismissed any disagreement or protest? Certainly. He might have. Might he have had the dissenter executed summarily? Possibly, though Wilham the Second wasn't known for such irrational and spontaneous behavior, the way some other monarchs have been. But even at the risk of losing one's life to protest such a decision, would not the chance be worth taking against the odds that otherwise faced an entire armada doomed to certain defeat?

"The lessons, then: First, consider well your plan and the count of your force if you should decide to challenge the Krigares in their homeland. Second, recognize the risks in executing a two-fronted war, especially when the option to retain a single army at full strength exists and your enemies are not united against you. And third, do not allow a foolish plan or foolish order to come to fruition if you can, through your influence, bring reason to light or effect a change in some other way.

"Learn this last lesson well, my pupils. Many a noble, and even, from time to time, a king, has been known to issue orders that are unworthy, unjust, or even suicidal. It is no more treasonous for you, should you find yourself in such a position, to question that order than it is for me, a teacher of the kingdom's future, to suggest you do so."

AT BREAK, Cedric asked Breeden and Janelle to remain a moment, and after the others had left, he asked them why they were late. They told him the true story, and Cedric was somewhat mollified, though disappointed that Breeden was always cutting things so close. He told Breeden that showing up late for a scheduled engagement showed a lack of respect for Cedric and for his lessons and that he had better get used, in his planning, to the fact that the outside world would sometimes creep in upon him. Further, he instructed Breeden that it was up to him, and not anyone else, to ensure that he was better prepared to meet the challenges the world brought his way. Giving himself a few extra minutes to get to class, against the chance that something unexpected might delay him, was a good start. Breeden was chagrined at the monk's words. And he knew his teacher was right.

Janelle and Breeden made their way to the room where their friends had indicated they were going to take lunch.

The room was on the second floor, in the southeast corner

of the east wing of the monastery. The east wing was the "administrative wing," where all activities unrelated to the actual worship of the One God were held. The room they occupied was a large round one with tall stained glass windows that sent beams of scattered colors across the many small tables and chairs that filled the chamber. It was a comparatively large study and was adjacent to the impressive library of historical and religious texts the monks maintained with such care.

As Breeden and Janelle entered together, Derek was ready with another snicker, and this time he followed it up with a snide remark. "Have you two peasants started breeding yet? If so, my father's farms could always use some more hands."

Breeden, Oskar, and Kestrel all shouted as one, "Shut up, Derek!" Laudan rolled his eyes, and Breeden took a few involuntary steps toward the young noble.

Derek's eyes gleamed at the response, but he wasn't through with his torment yet, and he lunged toward Janelle, grabbing the scarf she was in the process of unwinding from her neck.

"Is this Breeden's leash, Janelle? Do you make him roll over for you? Why is it about your neck? Does he run away from you if you don't tie him up? Or is it just that you fear his mooning will lead him astray if you're not there to guide him?"

And then, seemingly on a whim, Derek threw open a window and tossed the scarf out into the sharply cold wind. "Fetch, boy! Be a good boy and fetch your mistress's scarf!"

Laudan frowned, Oskar cursed, and Kestrel moved to join Breeden, who was now only a few jerking steps away from his tormentor.

Fists balled and knuckles white, Breeden marched up against Derek and thrust his face to within inches of Derek's. "Go get the bloody scarf, Derek!"

Derek laughed. "No, doggy. You fetch your own leash!" And then he shoved Breeden hard, with both hands. Breeden fell awkwardly backward and somehow managed to stay on his feet by grabbing onto a writing desk. Then he charged at Derek in a blind rage. Derek remained composed, and only an ever-so-slight flicker of fear registered in his eyes as he watched Breeden careening toward him. But he held himself still, and just before he went down under Breeden's weight, he managed to lash out with his fist and catch Breeden in the eye. Then he was flattened to the floor.

The impact took the breath out of Breeden as much as Derek, and his momentum carried him over Derek and onto the floor beyond. Derek recovered first and managed to get behind Breeden and catch him in a wrestling hold. But Breeden squirmed and thrashed, and he somehow shook off Derek's grasp. A few seconds of rolling around on the floor and attempted pins and holds by each boy finally ended when Breeden locked his legs in a scissor grip around Derek's waist, effectively immobilizing him. Derek pounded on Breeden's legs with his fists, hard and relentless, but Breeden met each assault by crushing Derek's ribs ever tighter between his legs. Each squeeze earned a grunt from Derek, followed by a gasping curse. "You bloody peasant! . . . You're cheating! . . . Let me go!" Soon the energy of his attack on Breeden's legs trickled down to next to nothing.

"Let me go, Andehar! Let me go . . ." Derek's words faded along with his strength.

Breeden gave him a few more squeezes, releasing more of his slowly ebbing anger in the process. And finally he stopped squeezing altogether. But he would be damned if he would release Derek without some kind of apology or promise or something.

Breeden waited until his breath was somewhat regular, and then he tried to make Derek meet his eyes, but the noble was looking down and refused to do so.

"Tell Janelle you're sorry, and promise you'll get her scarf as soon as I let you go." Breeden's tone was almost conciliatory. He was tired, and as much as he wanted Derek to apologize, he also didn't want to prolong this situation any further.

But there was no response from Derek. No movement at all. He just continued to breathe heavily in low gasps, and to stare at nothing, with his head down.

Breeden squeezed with all of his might, and Derek squealed involuntarily, not expecting more from the boatbuilder's son. He managed to gasp in barely discernable words, "Okay. I'll get the bloody scarf."

It wasn't an apology. But Breeden was relieved nonetheless. He loosened his grip a bit, but the thought occurred to him that Derek might try something when he let him go.

"And tell me that the fight is over. And that you won't attack me when I let you go."

"It's over."

Breeden released his hold and allowed his legs to slump to the floor.

17

TRAINING

Laudan, Kestrel, and Derek would not start their more formal and rigorous military training until they were knighted, at seventeen years old. For Laudan and Kestrel, that meant later this year. And for Derek, it would be the following year, but in the meantime, all three squires participated in regular training exercises once a week to teach them the basics.

Training at their age took the form of drilling in formation, being exposed to different weapons, sparring with swords, and wrestling. Kestrel was small of frame but quick and wiry. He excelled at ranged weapons—longbow, short bow, and crossbow—and was a surprisingly talented wrestler, though he did have a hard time immobilizing many of the boys, all of whom were larger than him to varying extents. At swordplay he was slightly above average. He did well with the short sword and rapier, but had some trouble wielding the heavier and longer bastard and long swords.

Derek was a much more gifted swordsman, even at a year younger than Kestrel. After proving himself during the past several weeks, he had worked himself up to sparring with some of the older squires in Laudan and Kestrel's class. Like Kestrel,

Derek was adept with the shorter and lighter swords, but he was also stout enough to handle even a long sword passably well. Derek was not terribly good with the ranged weapons, but then, most of the boys were not. But he was an above average wrestler and did well against many boys older than himself.

After watching a few of Derek's matches, Breeden felt better about his performance in his own fight with Derek, and how he'd ended up on top—even if he did cheat by using an *illegal* leg lock.

But then there was Laudan. Laudan was strong enough to hold the draw of a longbow and take his time with aiming. He wasn't a great shot, certainly nowhere near Kestrel's abilities, but he was fairly accurate and could sustain a regular rate of fire long after the other squires' arms had dropped numbly to their sides. He was also a bear of a wrestler, dominating anyone he faced, including many of the professional soldiers who had agreed to wrestle him. And he wielded a sword like a young knight. He was not clever with a sword, nor particularly graceful, but he was nearly unbeatable on the sparring field due to a modicum of skill and his dominating strength and endurance.

On this day, Breeden and Oskar were seated on the wooden pavilion that overlooked the jousting lists on one side and the sparring field on the other. While Cedric would normally hold class even absent the three knights in training, he had canceled this afternoon's to spend additional time with the princess. So Breeden and Oskar were afforded a rare opportunity to watch their classmates in training.

They were turned toward the sparring field, watching two squires at work. Each combatant was clad in thick layers of stained and patched padded armor that looked likely to have seen service in the time of their respective fathers, and they were battling with heavily nicked and dented, blunt-edged training broadswords.

Kestrel was nowhere to be seen, but Laudan and Derek were waiting for their chance to fight at the far end of the field.

Breeden returned his attention to the two combatants. The more he watched, the more he realized how good they were, and how evenly matched. They were both using two hands on the respective hilt of what was for a knight typically a one-handed weapon. Each was doing a good job of parrying the other's attack, and both were quick to try a strike when they saw an opening. He watched several attacks, parries, and ripostes, and became caught up in the rhythm. And although they didn't look as though they were taking it easy on one another, the match became almost boring in its back-and-forth nature. Despite their skill, Breeden wanted to see more of a challenge. He wanted to see some of the dominating and heroic swordplay he'd heard about in the tales his father would tell at night: a knight disarming his opponent and allowing him time to retrieve his fallen sword before continuing, a series of relentless attacks that backed the opponent against a wall or a cliff or a river, or a surprising feat of acrobatics that foiled the enemy's lucky blow.

But in all fairness, he could tell that the boys before him were talented. And when he considered that they weren't two years older than he was, he felt more of the same unworthiness he'd felt that day in the armory. He would never be afforded the opportunity these boys had been. He was frankly lucky he had even been permitted to befriend the boys as he had. And Derek would be sure to remind him of his luck, and his unworthiness, should he find himself forgetting.

Breeden looked over to where Laudan and Derek were standing. They were chatting with each other comfortably, and Breeden felt a sudden pang that Laudan even deigned to associate with that *jerk*. Derek had such a cruel sense of humor, and he was so arch and unkind to Janelle, Oskar, and Breeden. He would constantly joke with Laudan and Kestrel so the others couldn't hear—or so they could, but about topics that excluded the others all the same. He never had one kind word to say to any of them. Breeden supposed if he were a noble, he might not despise Derek so much, but he found it a hard bit of imagining.

Immediately in front of the two boys was a sergeant-at-arms watching the combatants carefully. Breeden guessed the man had seen forty years, and probably many of those in combat. His hair was dark, oily, and matted to his head and still bore the impression of his helmet. His skin was pale, where it was exposed, and his face communicated a calm, controlled callousness. After only briefly watching him interact with the boys, Breeden could tell that he had little patience for nonsense. He wore a maroon gambeson under a heavily scarred chain mail shirt that came down to just above his elbows on his arms, and nearly down to his knees at the bottom. And he wore a crisscrossed arrangement of leather straps across his chest, over his shoulder, and attached to a wide belt worn high around his waist. Affixed to the leather straps were numerous metal rings and leather ties.

The sergeant was calling out to the boys as they fought, and commenting frequently on their form. Laudan had once explained to Breeden that the constant testing and the regular changing of weapons was done so the instructors could gauge the squires' natural abilities with different fighting styles and different weapon types. They would also add different types of shields, sword breakers, and dirks to the off hand to expose the boys to the greatest variety of fighting scenarios.

And while some of the instruction was consistent, regardless of a boy's individual abilities—such as using a sword and shield together—later in the training, they would be focused more heavily in the directions of their greatest observed strengths. Breeden had been told that it was typical for the larger boys to gravitate toward the larger and heavier weapons, and for the smaller boys to lean toward the smaller and lighter ones. But preference wasn't always considered, and ability wasn't necessarily so predictable. It wasn't unusual to see a short knight wielding a two-handed sword or a war hammer, nor was it uncommon to see a taller, bulkier knight proving himself particularly skilled with the agile and almost delicate rapier.

With little to show Breeden that one boy had emerged victorious over the other, the sergeant-at-arms came onto the field and called the match. Before walking them off the field, the sergeant took a few minutes with each boy to talk about their strengths and weaknesses, the opportunities they had missed or exploited during the fight, and his judgment of any innate facility with the weapon of the day he might have observed.

When the sergeant had returned to the area where Laudan and Derek were waiting, he pointed at Laudan and then looked around at the prospects before him. He didn't appear to like what he saw. After a moment's more hesitation, he chose a senior squire named Tavish Ranald, who looked and moved more like a young knight. The boy wasn't big; he was about Breeden's size. But he walked onto the field with confidence and a slight swagger to his walk. Breeden was impressed that he seemed undaunted at the prospect of fighting the much larger boy.

Like those who preceded them, Laudan and his opponent were using training broadswords and were instructed to use both hands. For most boys, this requirement was probably beneficial to allow them greater control over the somewhat heavy weapon. But for Laudan, it was a considerable hindrance and slowed his reactions and limited his range, as well as the flexibility of his fighting style.

The sergeant-at-arms gave the signal to begin, and the reason for the confidence of Laudan's opponent soon became apparent. The boy was very, very good. Within a matter of seconds, he had penetrated Laudan's guard with a torso-high feint followed by a low thrust that jabbed Laudan solidly in his thigh. Laudan grimaced in pain and took a few halting steps backward. He looked angry about having been struck. He parried the next two tentative jabs, but when the boy hit him again, this time with the same torso-high feint, followed not by the low jab as before but by a slight dip of his sword tip and then a follow-up thrust back to the torso, his face began to purple with anger. Breeden smiled at the first hit, but after the second, he began to see a transformation in Laudan he'd not seen before. Laudan was normally calm and controlled his emotions well, but right now he looked fit to tear his opponent's head off.

Tavish seemed to sense Laudan's anger as well and backed off the intensity of his attack, moving into a more defensive posture. And it was well he did, for Laudan's eyes were clouding over with rage, and he began to swing the sword like a woodsman's felling axe. Under most circumstances, Breeden would have thought such an attack would be easily defensible, and Tavish appeared to be a capable swordsman. But Laudan's attacks were now coming with ferocity and intensity, and it was all Tavish could do to parry each overhanded swing. The sergeant saw what was happening and yelled out, "Take it down a notch, Marchant! This is a training match!"

But Laudan didn't hear him, or chose to ignore him, and continued his now mindless assault. As the overhanded blows reached a cadence of repetition, Tavish seemed to realize that Laudan wasn't going to stop, and his air of confidence cracked.

The sergeant-at-arms came out on the field and was shouting at Laudan with all of his breath. "STOP THE MATCH! NOW, MARCHANT! STOP THE MATCH!"

Laudan shifted his attack from repeated overhead blows and swung sideways with all of his might, the path of his sword parallel to the ground. Tavish blocked the blow, but he did so at an awkward angle, and Laudan's sword knocked the weapon from his hand. The momentum of Laudan's sword carried it forward into the boy's left arm, just above the elbow. There was a muffled crack, as of a stick broken beneath a blanket. And the boy crumpled to the ground. His face was a mask of agony as Laudan stood over him with his sword half-raised for another blow. Even from this distance, Breeden could see the terror and pain blazing in the eyes of the boy on the ground before him. And then the fight seemed to drain out of Laudan as quickly as it had come. All at once, he appeared to realize what he had done. He lowered his sword and allowed it to slip from his slackened grip and fall to the ground.

The sergeant barked at Laudan as he was bending to examine the fallen boy. "Back to the barracks, Marchant! I'll speak to you later!" And then he was all business, removing a dirk from his broad leather belt and, with surprising care, cutting away the padded armor at Tavish's shoulder. Once he had cut all the way around the fabric, he gently slid the entire sleeve off the boy's arm. He then cut and tore away the linen undergarment the boy was wearing and finally got a good look at the arm. It was clearly broken, a tent of skin jutting out from the otherwise flat and unbroken surface, where a bone was trying to pierce his skin. He shouted for a piece of wood and for the surgeon, clearly looking for something to splint the injury with until the boy could be brought inside the castle. When one of the other boys tried to hand him a training sword, he batted it to the ground.

"Fool! I said wood! Is there no one here with sense in his head?" Instinctively, Breeden looked around him. The spindles of the railing right in front of him. One of those would be perfect. His eyes lost focus as he scanned them to select a likely candidate. There! A few feet away, a spindle wasn't properly fixed in place, its nail loose enough that he should be able to free it. He ran over and jerked it out of its place in a single try. With no time to wonder at what he had done or was doing, he ran down a short flight of stairs to the sparring field and produced the spindle for the waiting sergeant. The sergeant was alone at this point, since the boys who had previously surrounded him had scattered like mice before a farmer's wife when he'd demanded they find him a suitable splint. He saw Breeden coming.

"That'll do. That'll do. Quickly now, boy! Hand me the splint and help me with the binding. It won't go easy as it is, and I don't think I can do it by myself." The sergeant paused for a moment to place the spindle against the boy's arm. "It's a bit long, but it'll serve. Well done, son.

"Now, I need you to cut that sleeve right there into long strips. I'll need at least three or four, and try to get me even more than that if you can. Here's my dagger. It should be sharp enough to make the job go easily."

Breeden dutifully cut the strips from the garment as he was instructed and got five serviceable strips from it. As he glanced up, the sergeant was looking the injured boy in the eye and holding a wad of rolled-up leather in his hand. He was quietly explaining to Tavish that he should bite down on the leather and that his arm would heal properly if he had anything to say about it. The boy looked somewhat calmer from his ministrations and nodded his head briefly to indicate he was ready for what he knew was coming next.

The sergeant waited a moment longer, while still holding Tavish's eyes with his own, and then pulled, a quick but steady movement that straightened out the bones under the skin and put them back in a condition close to proper alignment. As he did so, the boy's body went rigid with pain, and his legs kicked out in an attempt to buck the sergeant off him. Breeden moved to pin down the boy's legs. The sergeant nodded to him in thanks and then continued probing and adjusting the bones into position with the fingers of his free hand.

"I'm going to need help with the binding as well."

He looked around briefly and spotted a young boy trying to watch what was happening from the edge of the field. "Pers! Get over here! Pin Ranald's legs down!"

And then to Breeden: "You. I need you to bind his arm while I hold the bones in place. When Pers takes over the legs, start at the shoulder, right under the armpit, and tie a knot with one of those strips you cut. Then wrap it tight. Not so tight his arm dies and falls off, but pretty bloody tight. And make sure you have enough to wrap down well past the elbow."

As soon as the other boy had taken his position at Tavish's legs, Breeden tied all five strips into one long bandage and then did as the sergeant bade him. While he worked, the sergeant was continually instructing and commenting on his work. "Right, right . . . Good! . . . Watch you don't run out of binding . . . Good knots! . . . A bit farther apart there . . ."

Breeden found himself losing focus once again, and as much as he was beginning to acclimate himself to the sensation, this time he definitely wasn't prepared for what he saw. Within his mind, he found he could perceive the devastation in Tavish's arm. The flesh, sinew, and bone were in disarray, their arrangement and position misaligned. Even with the sergeant's manual placement of the bones, which Breeden noted almost absently was close to perfect, there was too much wrong in the arm. And the complexity of the tissues and their structure was too difficult for Breeden even to contemplate.

He was dimly aware of the fact that part of him was still wrapping the boy's arm, still functioning outside of this separate place where he found his consciousness. As his hands wound the bandage around a troublesome spot in the break, he saw that he needed to open the gap between the bones to allow a fragment of torn flesh to slip out from between the two broken ends. The softer tissue inside his arm had been caught on the sharp edge of the bone and had become trapped in between. He quickly made the adjustment with his hands—to the startled surprise of the sergeant—and then shifted the splint ever so slightly and tightened the wrap to align the opposing bones. As he made the adjustment, Tavish arched his back once more and then went limp. He had blacked out. But Breeden hadn't fully registered the fact, and found he was quite calm and detached from the entire situation. It was as if he were observing himself respond, unwind the bandage one turn, adjust the bones, and carefully rewrap the arm until the part of him that existed in both places was satisfied.

He finished the job with plenty of binding left over and tied his final knot. He stood up awkwardly, not sure what he should do next and disoriented as his full consciousness returned and his focus widened to take in the world around him. He realized that he had been away longer than ever before, and his normal sense of the world took longer to return.

"Where'd you go, boy? For a minute there, I thought you were going to read his future!"

As when Kestrel had asked a similar question of him, Breeden didn't know how to respond, and as he had tried to do with Kestrel, he said nothing.

"And why did you adjust the bones again? I have to admit they might just feel a bit better now than they did after I put them right, but I can't say why, or how you made it so."

If he was expecting an answer, Breeden wasn't prepared to give him one. He was too preoccupied with wondering once again what strange power had been granted to him. Then the sergeant stuck his hand in Breeden's face.

"My name's Hewrey, by the way, Raffe Hewrey."

"I'm Breeden Andehar, sir."

"Don't call me sir. You're no squire any more than I'm a

knight. What's one commoner got any business calling another sir for, eh?"

The words were finally reaching Breeden, and he responded. "True enough."

The sergeant seemed to want Breeden to respond more fully. "Saw you went right to square knots all around. Good to see someone that knows better than to tie an old granny knot. And you were pretty quick with that splint. What was that, by the way?"

Breeden looked the sergeant in the eye, his bewilderment mostly receded by now. "A spindle." He pointed. "From the pavilion railing. It was the first thing I could think of."

The sergeant looked pleased that Breeden was finally responding and answering his questions. Then he appeared to realize that the surgeon hadn't yet arrived, and he glanced down at the boy lying before him. Tavish's eyes were closed. And he had spit out the wad of leather as he passed out. He scanned the area around the sparring field again.

"You!" Now he was addressing Oskar, who had finally found the nerve to approach the injured boy. "Where is that bloody surgeon?"

Oskar jumped. "I'm not sure, Sergeant."

"Well, go find him, you bloody useless statue!"

And then he turned to the small boy still holding down Tavish's legs. "Pers, you can let go now. He's passed out. And by Mungo's beard, you'd better find that bloody surgeon!"

The sergeant spoke again, trying one more time to provoke conversation from Breeden. "Actually, I'm not so much worried about the surgeon at this point. The arm should be fine if he can keep from using it. You did good work today, Breeden. I thank you for your help."

"You're welcome, Sergeant. So, you think he'll be okay? His arm, I mean."

"Sure, sure. He'll be right as rain in two months. Don't you worry about him. Ranald's a tough one. He'll be a fine knight someday. I'm as sure of it as I am of anything else. He's smart, he's confident, he's one hell of a swordsman, and he treats people well. He'll be just fine."

Breeden smiled. He didn't know Tavish, had never spoken with him before, but this grizzled old soldier made him sound like someone he should go out of his way to meet.

A moment later the surgeon arrived, Oskar and two castle boys bearing a litter in tow. The sergeant cursed under his breath, and Breeden couldn't help himself. "What's wrong with the surgeon?"

Raffe looked at him, and uncertainty was reflected in his eyes. "What?"

"You just swore when you saw him coming."

"Oh, no. That wasn't for seeing the surgeon. That was for seeing that it was another bloody commoner that found him."

Breeden looked puzzled, and the sergeant explained. "I had fourteen squires in this field when I sent them to find the surgeon, just as when I sent them in search of wood for a splint. And I've a commoner bringing me the splint, and another commoner finding me the surgeon. What kind of war leaders are we training here? There are lessons aplenty to pass out today, I warrant."

The surgeon reached them then and asked the sergeant and Breeden to clear some space for him. He examined the injury and its binding, probing with his thumbs to determine the extent and nature of the break, and tugging here and there at the bindings. He did this for several minutes and asked a handful of questions as he worked. "Who bound this injury? . . . How long has the boy been out? . . . Describe the incident that caused the injury . . ." After he had finished his probing, he reached into a pouch at his belt and removed a small stoppered bottle, which he uncorked and ran beneath the injured boy's nose. Tavish immediately woke up, and the surgeon placed his hand gently on his chest to hold him still.

The boy calmed at the sight of the surgeon, and the sergeant standing within view at his back. He appeared to remember why he was lying down and spoke. "My arm is broken?"

The surgeon nodded. "Sure is, son. But it's well set. You'll be fine."

Tavish was clearly in pain, but he looked relieved at the man's words. "Laudan . . . ?"

The surgeon returned a quizzical look, and the sergeant responded for him. "He's sorry for what he did. But there is no excuse for such an act. He will be punished, rest assured."

"No!" The act of raising his voice caused Tavish to grimace in pain. And then, softer: "No, he didn't mean it, I'm sure. He's a good kid. He's pretty amazing, actually. I've never faced anyone so strong. But don't be too harsh." He clearly wanted to say more, but the sergeant interrupted him.

"No, Tavish. Save your breath. You will be two months recovering from this wound, and another two months before you are back to where you are today. Don't try to protect him. He needs to understand that his strength is a gift—true, it is an awesome one—but it is a gift not to be carelessly wielded by a thoughtless boy!"

Tavish seemed to understand that Sergeant Hewrey didn't want to hear more excuses, and held his tongue. Breeden was impressed with Tavish and immediately understood why the sergeant spoke so highly of him. And oddly, he found himself agreeing with the sergeant about the punishment as well. What he had seen in Laudan had scared him. Laudan could easily have killed Tavish before he came to his senses. He had seen the look in his friend's eyes. The look was terrifying. The look was death.

The surgeon cleared his throat and ceased his examination.

And when he looked up, he appeared satisfied. "The arm should heal well. The swelling will increase, and we will likely need to loosen the bandages when it does, but the bone is well positioned. Assuming nothing important inside the arm was cut before you managed to put everything back in its proper place, he may regain full use of it. As always, Sergeant, your field dressing is excellent, though I suppose it pays to have so very much experience with such tasks." He had been serious from the first and throughout his examination, but he finally smiled at the last. It was clear to Breeden that the man truly did respect the sergeant-at-arms's work.

The sergeant nodded to the surgeon in thanks for the comment and remained silent, expectant. The surgeon then signaled that the boys who had accompanied him should load Tavish onto the litter. The sergeant dutifully followed the surgeon and the injured boy off the field.

Breeden and Oskar stepped toward each other and nodded in silent recognition that something important had happened to their friend. Or maybe it was a recognition that they now understood something new about Laudan. Breeden couldn't really be sure what he had meant by the nod, nor what Oskar had intended. He was only sure, he supposed, that things had changed, and that Laudan was no longer the respectful, silent, and well-meaning noble he had always thought he was. Breeden found himself humbled by the experience. Laudan was always so composed and so sure of himself. So faithful to his belief in the One God. And he had always shown such patience and restraint when others were so free with their criticisms and their opinions. Like so many other people, Laudan clearly had his own demons.

18

OPPORTUNITY

Breeden was scratching away at a piece of parchment, working on an essay, and wondering how close to midday meal they were. Kestrel, Derek, and Oskar were there too, but Janelle, Laudan, and Cedric were missing. It was an odd feeling not having them there. Their class felt far more than half missing.

Janelle and Cedric were in an audience with the princess. The young merchant's daughter had earned the opportunity thanks to Cedric's confidence in Janelle's composure and her mastery of court etiquette. Janelle had been positively glowing since finding out, but fortunately—as far as Breeden was concerned, anyway—she also had to keep her enthusiasm in check. Breeden had been delighted she had found out about the meeting right on the heels of Laudan's incident with Tavish Ranald. So she hadn't been able to celebrate or show her excitement around the others as she'd have liked. He knew it was eating her up inside and that she normally would have gone on and on.

The price for Janelle's discomfort, however, was that Laudan was still "walking the box," the squires' unofficial name for the punishment of marching around the rectangular-shaped training yard with a heavy spear. Testamentary to how serious the instructors had believed Laudan's offense to be, he had been doing this from sunrise until sunset for two days and was now on his third. He was allowed to stop for a small meal at midmorning, another at midday, and a third during afternoon tea. During these breaks, he wasn't allowed to sit down but could stretch his muscles and set down his spear. He could also eat, of course, and he did so ravenously at each opportunity.

Breeden and the others, even Derek, had stopped by to check on his progress the day before, during their own midday break. They couldn't speak to Laudan, but when he had gone on break, his eyes were free to roam. He had spotted them immediately and nodded his silent thanks for their support. When Laudan's break had ended, he had resumed marching. Their purpose fulfilled, they had been about to leave when the princess appeared from around the corner.

Soldier and squire alike had sprung upright to attention, and Laudan, eyes front and unaware of what had transpired, continued his march. It turned out that the princess was on a midday stroll—unaccompanied—and, curious at the sight of the boy marching all by himself, had stopped a sergeant-at-arms and asked him about Laudan and his punishment. After a brief interaction, she had dismissed the sergeant and watched Laudan for a few moments more before continuing her walk. Once she had gone, Kestrel had talked with the sergeant and discovered the nature of their conversation. The sergeant had told her that Laudan was told to check his blows, that he hadn't done so, and that he was being punished for it. The princess had apparently been unhappy about the answer, but had made no further comment, and then had inexplicably smiled and thanked the sergeant for his courtesy.

As before, Breeden and the others had been captivated by

the unusual and temperamental girl. Completely aside from the fact that she was the princess, she was also breathtakingly beautiful. Then there was the matter of her famous fits of anger, so hard to reconcile with the poised and composed girl they admired from afar.

It was coming up on lunch, and Breeden's essay was, unfortunately, not writing itself. And he was getting hungry. That didn't help matters either. Breeden, Kestrel, and Oskar intended to visit the training yard again today. That is, if Cedric ever came back and told them they were dismissed!

As if the monk had heard Breeden's thoughts, he appeared at the door a moment later, with Janelle in tow. And if Breeden had thought she looked excited before, she was simply beside herself right now.

Breeden, Derek, Kestrel, and Oskar set down their styluses and rose nearly as one when Brother Cedric entered the room. They stood in a relaxed, upright posture and held their hands folded together in front of them. Breeden had learned in one of Cedric's classes on etiquette that one should rise when an elder, or someone of a higher caste, enters the room. As much as Cedric professed to dislike class distinctions, he certainly seemed enthusiastic about teaching manners—even when that involved learning how to behave around one's betters! Such concerns were second nature to the nobles, but Oskar and Breeden had learned solely through repeated exposure, and that they matched Derek's timing today was an indication they had made real progress.

Breeden guessed that this progress may have been at least partly responsible for the pleased look Cedric bore as he came to stand beside the lectern from which he typically directed class in this room. But there was more. "I have an announcement to make." He paused for effect, and his smile grew even broader. "Janelle has been selected by the princess's house matron to become her lady-in-waiting while she remains with us at Ridderzaal!" Breeden had never heard open pride so evident in Cedric's speech. And a quick look at Janelle told Breeden that even Laudan's ongoing punishment would not be enough to dim the flood of self-congratulation and girlish bubbling to which he and his peers would now be subjected by their female classmate.

Cedric continued. "I hope you all appreciate how unique and distinguished an honor this is. There is no precedent of which I am aware for a queen or heir apparent to the throne to select a lady-in-waiting who is not from the noble ranks. But Janelle so impressed Princess Lorelei and her house matron that she has done the unthinkable. It is no mean decision, and I believe it will have lasting impact on future selections. Truly, Janelle has today made history!"

All four of the boys directed mostly genuine smiles at Janelle, a unified display of support that would have been underwhelming to Janelle had she not been riding so high on the excitement of the moment. And when none of the boys made a move to speak or shake her hand, Cedric encouraged them. "Go ahead. No need to stand there like you're cast in bronze. Wish her well!"

They moved from behind their seats then, squeezed her shoulder, took her hand, patted her on the back, and muttered low and jumbled words of congratulations. But the modest display of praise was enough for her, and as Breeden had predicted, it would be days before her mouth would stop flapping with tales of meeting the princess. "She was even more beautiful up close." At that, Breeden raised an eyebrow. "She was so dignified . . . I feared she would think I was sick, I was shaking so badly . . . And she is smart, so very smart!" The boys bore the effusion with moderate grace, and Breeden guessed the others, like him, were really happy for her but just didn't want to hear every gory detail.

Cedric remained apart from them, content to allow Janelle

her moment of glory, and appearing gratified with how every-thing had turned out. He seemed to realize that the boys' patience with the jabbering girl might be wearing thin, and he spoke up. "All right, that's enough for now! What this will mean to our studies together is that Janelle will be late to arrive every morning and wholly absent from us for some of her lessons. But she should still be able to join us for most of what we will do. After all, the princess is under the tutelage of other brothers here as well. I will see that the schedule of their lessons complements our own.

"Go home to tell your mother and father, Janelle. Have your midday meal with your family, and return when you are done. The rest of you should meet me back here at two bells. I will see you then."

Kestrel, Oskar, and Breeden glanced at one another, each seeming to know the others' thoughts, and left the room before Janelle or Derek, heading toward the training yard. Derek, as he did more often than not, went in the opposite direction. And Janelle went home as Cedric had bid her do, to tell her mother and father the good news.

19

BYSTANDERS

The three boys exited the south end of the monastery and cut across the keep's enormous garden, skirting the hedge maze that occupied the centermost ring of the garden's concentric circles, and approached the stables and training yard where they knew Laudan would be serving his punishment. As they turned the northwest corner of the stable, they were met with an unexpected sight.

Laudan was there, but so were all the instructor knights and sergeants-at-arms. And Laudan wasn't marching with a spear as he had been for the last two days. Instead, he was standing in the middle of a circle of the sergeants, with his arms extended straight out from his body and parallel to the ground. He was holding a small rock, about the size of an apple, in each hand. Even at seventeen years old, he was equal in height to many of the men surrounding him, and taller than some. But he still looked all the boy in the presence of such a rough and hardened group of soldiers. Beyond the ring of sergeants, three knights stood in a small cluster, conversing among themselves. And a fourth knight walked slowly around the circle, occasionally issuing words to the sergeants, or perhaps Laudan—Breeden couldn't be sure.

Breeden and the others had stopped when they realized that something unusual was occurring, and they were still about thirty yards away. Kestrel whistled low. "He's in a world of it!"

Breeden looked around and could see no other squires, or anyone else for that matter. "Can we go closer?" He felt he knew the answer was no, but maybe Kestrel might think it okay.

But Kestrel confirmed his opinion. "I'd say not. That doesn't look like a welcoming committee."

Breeden gestured toward the pavilion, and Kestrel considered for a moment before finally shrugging his shoulders. "I suppose they can always tell us to leave." And the three of them changed their course and angled toward the jousting lists and the wooden spectators' platform that straddled both fields.

Once perched above the field, Kestrel, Oskar, and Breeden were slightly closer to their friend than they had been a moment before, but they were now less conspicuous and also had a better view of the proceedings.

Laudan was obviously exhausted, and his arms kept trying to drop from the weight of the stones he held. He would hold steady for a while, perhaps as long as half a minute, and then his arms would lower ever so slowly, twitching back into position when he realized he was slipping. Breeden didn't know how long Laudan had been charged with holding the position, but he was obviously at a point where he was losing the battle. And each time his arms did drop, one of the sergeants would lean into the boy's face and scream at him to resume his position.

And then, a handful of minutes after Breeden and the others had arrived, Laudan's arms began to shake. The shaking was somewhat subtle at first but grew to a pronounced and spasmodic jerking of his arms. He was trying to raise his arms back to their original position, but he couldn't do it. The sergeants could clearly see that he was failing at last and closed in around him even tighter. They joined together in screaming at him, in telling him to hold his position, and asking him where his fabled strength had gone. The ferocity of their assault on his friend made Breeden nearly weep out of pity. And Laudan's normally stoic expression had turned to one of defeat, and of disappointment in himself. Oddly, Breeden didn't see fear in his friend's eyes. Breeden knew that had it been him standing in the middle of those men, he would be cowering on the ground before them, huddled in a heap and hoping they would leave him be. But Breeden would swear that Laudan was more disappointed than fearful. The normally quiet boy held on to something inside himself and weathered the abuse being thrown at him from every side.

The sergeants were not letting up and took turns putting their faces as close to his as they could, screaming for him to raise his arms, howling that he dared disobey their orders. But he could no longer raise his arms. They hung limply at his sides, useless to him.

Breeden saw movement among the knights, and one of them dismissed the sergeants-at-arms. All the sergeants stopped yelling and obeyed instantly, stepping back from Laudan into a rough line. The knight who had called off the sergeants approached Laudan alone, in the midst of the almost eerie silence that followed the raucous chorus of cursing and abuse.

Kestrel interrupted his thoughts. "The giant knight that's walking over to him is Knight-Captain Jenlyns, from Arlon. He's one of the most fearsome fighters in the King's Army. They say he once killed two trolls with a single blow of his sword!"

When the knight got closer to their friend, Breeden realized that Kestrel wasn't exaggerating about the man being big. He was easily a good handspan taller than Laudan, and much broader of shoulder. He stood back from Laudan about an arm's length away and said something Breeden couldn't hear. Laudan raised his head and met the man's eye. The knight spoke again. He appeared to be talking in a conversational voice. Breeden guessed that the other knights and sergeants probably couldn't hear what he was saying any better than he and his friends could from the pavilion.

He talked for a long time. And as he spoke, Breeden could see Laudan's expression change. Breeden saw his friend slowly lose his defiance, and what looked more like anger was replaced by what looked to be genuine shame. The knight kept talking with him for another few minutes. And when he finally turned about and walked off, Laudan's chin dropped toward his chest.

The departing knight made a gesture as he walked away, and one of the sergeants snapped upright and barked out to Laudan that he should return to the barracks and dress for a final inspection before his punishment was deemed to be over. Laudan, looking defeated for the first time Breeden could recall, marched away to the northwest toward the barracks.

Kestrel, Oskar, and Breeden shared a long look, and Oskar queried, "What do you suppose the knight said to him?"

"If he didn't tell him he was sending him home, I'm not sure what he could have said to make Laudan so upset." Kestrel looked discomfited by his own words.

What Breeden had assumed would be another afternoon of trying to distract their friend from his marching in squares turned out to be a far sight less fun. "Let's go to the market and get something to eat. My bread and cheese won't serve today."

Kestrel grunted his agreement and headed off toward the outer bailey. Oskar lingered for a moment until Laudan had disappeared from sight. And then he followed along too.

20

OSKAR

Oskar had a secret. And it was a big one. The thing is, Oskar wasn't really a boy. But she had pretended to be one for so long that she didn't know how or when—or if—she could ever stop being a boy.

Her reasons for acting like a boy were solid. She figured nobody would fault her for it. Because girls on the streets did things much worse than the things she had been forced to do as a boy: picking pockets, robbing merchants, pretending to be crippled and begging for alms, etc. Oskar's street father had known she was a girl, of course. There was no way she would've been able to keep that from Huw. He had even given her her name. She knew that she owed Huw her life many times over. She also knew how lucky she was that he wasn't a man of appetites—as he described the deviants he had helped her avoid since he'd found her wandering the market when she was about five or so.

Oskar had been abandoned by her mother . . . or father . . . or both. She held images in her memory of two people who could have been her parents. But their faces wouldn't hold still in her mind's eye so she could get a good look. So, anyway, she wasn't exactly clear on the who—or even exactly the when, never mind the why—of her abandonment. Huw said that people's minds had a way of protecting them from the bad things that happened to them. 'The lucky among us, anyway!' She didn't even remember her real name. So maybe she was better off not knowing what had happened to her parents.

She suspected Cedric also knew the truth about her. He never said anything about it. But it was just a sense she had. And she had gotten pretty good at reading people and knowing when they were lying or telling the truth. But even as she grew older, Oskar knew that it was still safer to remain a boy. She didn't know how people would react to her if she revealed her secret. For that matter, she still didn't know if her chest was ever going to get any bigger—which would be exciting, of course, but it could also complicate matters for her. So far, a baggy shirt had been all she'd needed to disguise herself. In any event, she'd never thought for too long about letting herself be a girl. Until that friend of Cedric's had found her at the breadline, she had figured she'd spend the rest of her days on the streets of Arlon—as a boy.

On the streets, Oskar had never had the guts to tell anyone the truth. She'd even kissed a few girls over the years—to prove she was just another normal boy, that is. It didn't make her feel much of anything when she did, though she didn't have a problem with it either. She guessed her feelings about such things might grow as she got older. There was something about Laudan, though—and the princess—that stirred the faintest of feelings inside her. The pair of them. As mean as the princess was sometimes, they were both so beautiful. And so strong. And yet even as strong as Laudan was, he was smitten with the princess. He made Oskar believe that dedication like that couldn't possibly be weak. If someone so strong as Laudan could devote himself to another—against all odds and seemingly against reason—maybe Oskar could justify doing the same.

For about the hundredth time, Oskar considered telling her friends the truth. What would they say? Would they treat her differently? She wasn't foolish enough to think that any of the boys would be interested in her. But whenever she thought about having the truth out there, she imagined she would breathe easier. So long as that falsehood existed between her and her friends, she would never be able to get any closer to them.

21

SQUIRE'S RETURN

Breeden and Janelle would sometimes walk together to class. It wasn't planned. And even when Breeden had wanted to, and tried to predict when Janelle would be leaving her house, he often missed her. But they had fallen into the loose habit of walking together whenever the timing worked out. Most often she would shout ahead to him to wait for her, and he would linger until she caught up. But once it had been announced Janelle would be joining the princess in the morning, and she would not be completing his walks with him, Breeden decided there was no need to wait for her, and he began to keep his own schedule. It was a weird feeling, walking past her house without intentionally slowing down in the hopes she might catch up. He realized he had grown accustomed to having Janelle join him for the last part of his walk.

But without Janelle to occupy his time this day, he showed up for classes early. And when he arrived at the side door to the monastery, only Laudan was there to greet him. He was still and quiet, as he always was, and his posture was erect, but there was something else about the way he was holding himself that made

Breeden feel he had changed. He seemed more fidgety. And less . . . something. Not cocky. He was never Kestrel to begin with. And Breeden would never have thought to call him cocky before. What was the change though? Was he less confident? Less solid? Perhaps it was simply the fact that the wind had been taken from his sails during the activities of the last few days.

Breeden didn't want to upset him, but he couldn't think of anything else to say and couldn't help himself. "Good morning! So, what did Captain Jenlyns say to you, anyway?"

Laudan looked mildly shocked for a moment by the question, but then he slowly smiled. "I suppose I can't avoid that one, eh?"

Breeden was glad he hadn't made Laudan upset or angry with the question. He felt that his relationship with Laudan was much less established than what he had with Kestrel or Oskar. And he didn't want to disrupt what goodwill they did have for each other. But the words had left his mouth before he realized they might be taken badly.

"Well, he basically told me that, at my size and as a knight in training, I was obligated to be a protector of the king's subjects and holdings. And that I needed to obey my superiors without question and without emotion before I could ever hope to wear the king's badge. There was more, but I'd rather not talk about it."

Breeden nodded his head. "That's fair. It did seem like he was being pretty hard on you."

Laudan nodded his head slowly in reply. "That he did."

"Well, it's good to have you back!"

"Good to be back. Let me tell you!"

"So, did you hear that the princess was asking after you?"

Laudan's demeanor changed in an instant, all joviality fleeing and his attention focusing on Breeden. "What?" His voice cracked, the word loud but unsteady.

"Kestrel didn't tell you already?" Breeden couldn't keep the surprise from his voice.

"I slept in the south end of the barracks, by myself, as I have for the last few nights. They didn't want me talking to anyone while I was being punished. And last night they wanted me to spend one more night alone, thinking on what I'd done. But wait, the princess asked about me?"

"She did. We saw her talking to one of the sergeants while you were walking the box. She gestured toward you as they talked. Kestrel stopped the sergeant later on and asked him what they'd talked about. Supposedly, she asked what you'd done wrong and smiled when she heard the story. Is she crazy or what? Smiling that you nearly split Ranald in half! And then, of course, there's that bit with the girl stepping on her dress!"

Laudan frowned briefly at the reference to his hurting the squire, but then his mind seemed to spin through a cycle of thoughts and emotions. He looked like he wanted to be happy with the news but hadn't yet figured out whether he should be. Breeden laughed. "She's not the crazy one! You're the one who thinks he can marry the future queen!"

Laudan looked suddenly like his old self again and reached across the space between them, seemingly ready to give Breeden one of the slaps or punches he typically reserved for Kestrel. Then he caught himself. Breeden couldn't tell whether he slowed his punch because he realized it was Breeden before him, not Kestrel, or whether he did so because he had learned a lesson over the past few days. But then he finished his swing and popped Breeden gently on the shoulder. "Who says I can't? She asked about me!"

And Breeden laughed, just as Kestrel and Derek appeared from around the corner.

22

THE PRINCESS

Princess Lorelei sat at a low table, brushing her long blond hair and idly gazing out of the north-facing window of Ridderzaal's royal suite, situated at the top of one of the castle's four main towers. The view was a stunning one that overlooked the entire city, down to the deepwater piers, and afforded a sweeping view of Long Lake and the surrounding countryside. To the west of the lake were a series of low bluffs and steep hills dotted with vineyards as far to the north as she could see. To the east, she could just make out the southern range of the dwarven mountains, their tops shrouded in dark clouds that looked to be trapped against the mountains' shoulders. And of the lake itself, Lorelei could see for so many leagues to the north it was beyond her ability to put the distance in practical terms, such as the number of days by boat or carriage.

She was pensive. And the one thing she couldn't get from her mind was the image she had of the young knight in training who had been punished for not checking his blows. She knew how he felt. She didn't believe in holding back. She thought that letting someone else win something they didn't deserve taught weakness. She felt it was only through establishing her dominance among all people that she could promote in them the healthy degree of fear and respect she needed to be an effective ruler. Despite her father's desire to protect her, she didn't believe she could afford to waste time the way he would have her do. "Let yourself be a child, Lorelei! Cherish this time while you don't carry the burden of the kingdom upon your shoulders!" he would admonish her.

To meet that end, her father was trying to cloister her away from the intrigues and temptations of court by secreting her in this literal backwater of a town. She knew what had been asked of Cedric as well. She knew that her father was concerned about her moral and spiritual growth. It was so obvious to her that her own father didn't trust her, and so frustrating that he didn't think she was capable of ruling! She would be a great and powerful queen. Her father would be deemed weak by comparison. He needn't worry about her.

But even more than her father, it was the other nobles at court and her father's advisers in Arlon who made her furious. Their glances told Lorelei all she needed to know about their faith and trust. They saw the decline of a great line of kings— arguably one of the greatest Erda had ever seen. And they saw a frail girl as his sole heir. Lorelei knew, and her father constantly sought to reassure her, that if her father should die, most would serve her out of loyalty, despite the disappointment that their favorite king was gone. But Lorelei needed no one to tell her that some would also see her father's death as an opportunity.

She saw this young knight as another way she might strengthen her position against that day. While her original attraction to him had been a somewhat detached admiration and sympathy—and admittedly somewhat physical as well— she later learned that his father was Odilon Marchant, Duke of Guéret and third in line behind her and her father for the throne of Hyrde and all of its kingdom states. She had been stunned that he should be hidden away here, as she was. But then she learned that he had an older brother ahead of him in succession to his father's duchy, and the potential succession to king should something happen to Lorelei's line. But still, the potential was there. And not so far removed as to be insignificant.

Lorelei had been considering that potential for a few days now and had finally decided to pursue it. And she was ready to start putting other plans into action as well.

Her plans for cementing her rule had become extensive, and her network of agents and spies was growing. But she had had trouble gaining her father's assistance in taking such steps as she felt would assure an easy transition upon his death. He had constantly reminded her that temperance was called for, that his trusted advisers would remain loyal to her, and that she didn't need to scheme and plot.

She had watched him earn the trust of his charges only with great difficulty over the years. She saw how he was frequently distracted by having to bend his will to some compromise with a minor noble or even a merchant. To her eyes, he was capering before those who owed their obeisance to his crown. Lorelei didn't see why power—her power and her father's power—shouldn't be used to enforce and inspire loyalty. She felt that to have power and not use it was a waste of that power and a sign of weakness. She would often argue with her father on this point. And she wasn't unreasonable or childish in her arguments. Rather, she felt she was circumspect and thoughtful when she argued that an extraordinary exertion of might was a useful tool in and of itself. But her father would frown and dismiss her proposals as youthful enthusiasm whenever she shared them with him.

It was in this way she had come to believe her father was weak, despite the many victories he had won in battle and politics over the years of his long reign.

Her brush caught a snarl in her hair, and pulled her head

downward before she could stop herself. She swore and the reverie was broken. She was back in the castle tower, thoughts of her father and her past debates with him vanished.

Looking out over Long Lake, the princess noticed that it had begun to rain.

23

LADY-IN-WAITING

Janelle was nearly at the top of the long, winding stairway when she heard the princess curse. She picked up her pace, and in a handful of heartbeats, she was at the chamber door, knocking softly.

The princess barked, "What is it?"

Janelle was torn between answering and scurrying away. Best not to hesitate. When she spoke, she had to steel herself to ensure her voice came out firmly and strong. "It is Janelle, Your Highness, here to attend to your matins."

"Well, come in, then." There had been a slight pause. And Janelle hoped she had heard a softening of the princess's tone, but she couldn't be sure.

Janelle sighed beneath hearing as she took in the scene before her, of the beautiful young princess seated in front of a window overlooking the world. The morning sun was not visible, but an orange glow stained the distant sky and cast an odd warmth against the bottoms of the low black and grey rain clouds. The earthy smell of the rain felt cleaner up here at the heights of the castle's tower.

To Janelle, the moment captured perfectly the feel of one of the stories she had heard as a child, of a fair princess trapped in a tower by an unreasonable father. Janelle briefly imagined that a brave young knight who loved her—like Laudan—would have to rescue her so they could run away together. Not for the first time, Janelle wondered if that might not be closer to the truth than she knew. But she was not yet familiar enough with the young princess, and might never be so familiar as to ask about her relationship with her father and the reasons for her presence at Ridderzaal.

Janelle stood inside the doorway for some time, patiently waiting for the princess to instruct her. After a week of learning the princess's routine, Janelle well understood what the princess expected of her. And the first lesson she had learned was never to assume that things should be done in the same order or in the same way as the day before. A simple enough lesson, thought Janelle, and one her own more capricious side could appreciate.

Lorelei brushed her hair in silence.

The moment grew longer, and Janelle kept herself as still as she could. To fill the void and keep her visage from showing any impatience, she allowed her mind to wander. Briefly she thought about Breeden and wondered what her friends were learning about in class. She cracked a smile. Breeden was such an odd boy. Most of the time, he was quiet and unassuming, and even serious. But other times, he was almost ferocious in his response to an argument or debate in class, and then there were the fights with Derek. It was clear to Janelle that Breeden was no sheep, though Derek obviously couldn't help but think of him that way. Janelle smiled again, despite herself.

Lorelei appeared to realize that Janelle was not uncomfortable waiting for the long minutes she required, and she frowned. When she spoke, it seemed she was trying to let Janelle know that she had felt rushed. "All right, enough fidgeting. I need you to untangle my hair—here." The words were impatiently but not necessarily unkindly or harshly spoken. Janelle responded immediately, picking up a slender ivory comb with three long teeth.

The princess had managed to make the knot worse by her own ministrations, but Janelle made short work of the knot and soon shifted from the comb to the princess's fine horsehair brush. She couldn't help but admire the princess's hair as she brushed. It truly was like spun gold. Her mooning friends would find this one reality, at least, not to be the letdown their other ideals of the princess might prove to be.

Over the past week since she had been serving the future queen, Janelle had come to establish something of a friendship with the girl, and even liked her, she supposed. But most of the shine of serving the crown princess had dulled when Janelle had borne witness to enough of the girl's petulance and unpredictability. Fortunately for Janelle, she had yet to make more than the simplest of mistakes in treating with the princess and had therefore earned a rare affection from her. But other members of the household staff were not so confidently well-mannered as Janelle, and therefore not so well received by the princess.

Some mistakes were unforgivable. Those who made such mistakes were dismissed, and it was well understood that they should never again come within sight of the princess. Janelle's position, of course, was the result of just such a series of dismissals. Janelle told herself that the future queen didn't care about nobility so much as ability. But she guessed the likelier reality was that Ridderzaal had run out of young girls of noble blood. Janelle had to admit that she'd probably been, if not the only option, certainly the one option within many leagues with a chance of succeeding where the others before her had failed.

Janelle's pride kept her mind from casting aside the last thin curtain, which would reveal the truth: she was tolerated for her competence, and the most this would ever serve to gain for her was the princess's grudging satisfaction with her work. But today her pride would hang a second curtain across that threshold, as the princess surprised her by asking that she accompany her to church for her morning prayers. And even more remarkably, accompany her afterward for her morning walk!

24

CRAFTING

It was Sunday, and as such, Breeden had no lessons. He was in his father's workshop, and everything had been cleared away from the center of the room except for several heavy wooden pegs that were driven into holes to form a wide arc in the floor. And of course, there was also the fitfully steaming wooden box that ran the length of the room.

From out of the seams, and from several thumb-size holes cut along the length of the box on both sides, steam was issuing forth in jets as if a dozen tiny dragons were trapped inside. Breeden was smiling broadly at the back of the room in admiration of the spectacle. His gloved hand was on the door of a small brick oven boiling the water that fed steam to the box through an awkward-looking rectangular "pipe" made of wood. He was increasing and decreasing the amount of air he allowed into the oven, following periodic instructions from his father.

His father was waiting expectantly at the opposite end of the box, hands and arms covered to the armpit by heavy leather blacksmith's gloves. Breeden wasn't sure why his father's expression was so intense as he stared at the box. Breeden knew he couldn't be looking at the wood inside, because it was obscured by the gouts of white that issued forth in an endless flow from within the box's confines.

Then, for no reason apparent to Breeden beyond some inner chronometer or intuition, and with only a garbled "Now!" his father grabbed a loop of rope at the end of the box and pulled free the end panel to which it was attached. More startlingly, even knowing what his father was about, Breeden watched him reach into the box and begin to withdraw a heavy ironwood timber from the steam. As he had been instructed, Breeden closed the oven door and raced over to help his father. Breeden's gloves weren't nearly as long as his father's, and he traded places at the free end of the timber, allowing his father to take the end still emerging from the box. It was all Breeden could do not to drop the wood. Ironwood was one of the denser woods in the land, and this piece was huge.

When the entire length of wood had been removed from the box, they shuffled sideways a few steps, and Breeden dropped his end between two pegs set closely together at one end of the room. *Not a moment too soon*, thought Breeden. He wasn't sure he could have held on to it for another second.

"Now we slow down just a bit. Can't bend it too fast, or we may splinter it." His father's voice was thin as he gasped for breath from the exertion.

Together they maneuvered and carefully bent the steam-softened timber into the oversized jig without mishap. Once it was in place, Breeden's father took off his gloves and grabbed a mallet and a small box of pegs, and drove them into additional holes in the floor to round out the arc of the rapidly cooling keel of Aegir's boat.

Breeden's father stood up when he was satisfied, and allowed himself a small smile. "That's far and away the biggest bit of bending I've ever done. I wasn't sure we'd get it in place before it cooled."

Breeden wore a detached look and was scanning the product of their labor. A second later he had returned, and he smiled back at his father. "No splintering or cracking. It's incredible! And the strength of the wood is returning already. I never would have thought you could bend something so rigid. What you did with the steam is sort of like what I did with the hinges in the old armory that time. Only I just broke the 'grain' of the metal. You changed the grain of the wood." Breeden's heart dropped, and he realized immediately that his father didn't know about his visit to the cellars of the keep. He realized just as quickly that there was no way for him to take back the words.

Breeden's father was still smiling, still admiring his work, and his son's words didn't register with him right away. But then he seemed to hear them echo in his head, and he turned to face his son, a look of concern visible on his face. "Old armory? What hinges? What happened?"

Breeden kept nothing from his parents, and he wasn't sure why he hadn't yet told his father about the incident under the castle. He lowered his head and apologized. "I'm sorry. I didn't mean to keep it from you. I just never had the chance, and then . . ."

His father appeared to gain control of his emotions in response to the obvious remorse of his son. "It's okay, son. Go ahead and tell me what happened."

Breeden related the story of his breaking loose the hinges, and even told his father about Kestrel's brief interrogation. His father wasn't happy to hear that the noble likely wouldn't let it go. Breeden also mentioned the armor Laudan had found, and how the patterns he saw on the armor's discs had made him dizzy. His father's eyebrows raised at this, and he seemed to consider interrupting but kept his thoughts to himself. Finally, Breeden told him about Tavish Ranald's injury, and how he'd helped the sergeant set the bone. When Breeden was finished, his father remained quiet for a moment, as if considering how to respond.

"That's . . . a lot to take in. You've been busy."

"I'm sorry, Da, for not telling you sooner."

"It's okay. No need to apologize. I can only imagine how I would feel about all of this if it were happening to me."

His father stood still a moment and rested the mallet against his thigh before continuing.

"So . . . in most of these incidents, you've only talked about having a kind of sight. But the story about the old armory door sounded different. So, you think you broke these bonds by willing them to break?"

Breeden nodded. "I'm sure of it. After the first one, I was so surprised I guess it didn't register, but looking back, I think some part of me always knew I could do it. And then when I went to free the second hinge and it broke free too, I knew it for sure."

His father shook his head in disbelief. "Have you considered the fact that you have control of some kind of magic?"

Breeden nodded. He had thought about that. Many times. And even Cedric's lesson on the nature of God so long ago had remained with him and had him wondering whether Cedric's "magic"—or God's essence—wasn't the "stuff" coursing through the bonds of his visions. But he really couldn't say. "I don't know, Dad. I've thought about it, but I don't remember ever hearing anything about magicians seeing inside things."

"No, and I haven't either. But then I guess they keep their own secrets, son. You know, I've been thinking about this for some time now. And I think maybe we should try to find someone other than Cedric to talk with about this."

Now Breeden was curious, thinking his father must have a particular person in mind. "Who?"

"Well, I don't know whom myself, but I think Aegir might."

Breeden smiled. "And he can get his new boat while he's here!"

"I'll write a letter tomorrow and take it down to the deep-water docks. The harbormaster will know who's bound for Ath."

25

OLD TALES

Cedric carefully flattened out the scroll to give it another read. It was a unique piece of writing. Monks of the One God were not known for forbearance in acknowledging the old gods. Most references to them were to be found in private libraries, or in histories commissioned by royalty over the centuries. Only a few of these documents had been discovered outside of family collections. And fewer still could be found inside the walls of a building of the One God.

What was so interesting about these few pages was that they purported to relay an interview between the writer and Mirren the Traveler. The problem was that the piece read as a story. Cedric frowned. He hated it when monks did that. It was one thing to write an allegorical tale to inform and instruct. But when used to capture the essence of words actually spoken, presenting a conversation in the form of a story made one question the veracity of the information the author was trying to convey.

Yes, it was possible Mirren uttered the story to the scribe essentially as presented. After all, Cedric himself had met

Mirren, and the god had been somewhat chatty. But even if the writer had been especially careful not to take liberties, it was impossible to know where the speaker's words, Mirren's words, left off and the listener's words, in writing them down, began. For that matter, there was the question of whether Mirren himself could be trusted to be impartial in his narrative. But if the words were written in earnest, and recorded in good faith, it was likely there were truths to be found within the manuscript. As always, it was the truth Cedric was seeking. The rumors he had heard—about Mirgul returning—were too potentially cataclysmic to ignore. He read the document one more time.

THE OLD GODS *took many forms. Some appeared as humans when they walked among the land. Others appeared as dwarf, elf, or gnome. Still others took as many forms as there were creatures in the world. But those who walked upright, and spoke the common tongue, would sometimes hold council.*

The councils were informal things, a gathering of equals with no leader and no set agenda. They had begun many thousands of years ago, while the gods were vying with each other for power and establishing their domains, and had been used as a forum for grievances, as well as a means of maintaining social contact with their peers.

In a practical sense, the gods were forced to associate with one another because most found that companionship with mortals would lead to despair—the life of mortals being so insignificantly brief. Some gods, like the goddess Mikele, found an easy way around this problem by not limiting their affections to one mortal at a time. Many more saw mortals as pets more than companions and became protective over the legions of followers who organized to worship them. But most understood the advantages of finding companionship, where possible, from among their own kind.

There were also gods who did not attend council. But over thou-

sands of years, their numbers had diminished. Many believed that those who went off on their own may have lost their will to exist. Those remaining came to find that spending time together was important lest they, too, fall prey to isolation and despair.

AMONG THE GODS who appeared as humans, the brothers Mirren and Mirgul were powerful above all others. They were strong of will, strong of ability, and strong of charisma. Together they had defeated many powerful foes, rival gods, demons, and other ancient and fearsome creatures that roamed the world so long ago.

Of the female gods, there remained two in form like Mirren and Mirgul. There was Mikele, the exotic and flighty goddess the humans had come to identify with fertility, bounty, and abandon. And there was Birghid. Birghid the Wise, or Birghid the Serene, as her human worshippers variously called her—the ideal of grace and beauty in the human form.

Mikele was beautiful as well and, like Birghid and the other gods, could change her form to make herself appeal to her choice of partners. She would spend time with Mirren and Mirgul as it struck her fancy. But the brothers found her too unpredictable and directed their true affections toward Birghid. At first, being brothers and caring deeply for one another, they were willing to share her affections. And Birghid, caring for them both, was content to share of herself.

But over time, Birghid became less interested in Mirgul and more attached to Mirren. It happened slowly, over many, many years, but in time, Mirgul came to resent his brother, and to resent Birghid as well. Mirgul became rude with Birghid. Where before he would have won her over with words of love, he began to demand that she spend time with him. Birghid resisted, and her love for Mirgul diminished with each demand. After one such rejection, Mirgul threw a tantrum, toppling trees and splitting boulders until the area surrounding Birghid's favorite spring was laid to waste. Realizing what he had done, he looked back at Birghid's stricken face one last time and disappeared.

Years passed, and Mirren and Birghid became closer than ever before. They came to discover that life together was richer than life apart. And, as unlikely a thing as one might expect from gods, they committed themselves to each other and forswore the attentions of others.

More years passed. And one day Mirgul returned. He had been watching his brother and Birghid, and waited until his brother was away—honoring his worshippers to the north. Mirgul tried to rekindle Birghid's affections with honeyed words. But despite the passing of years, she had seen his darker side before and would not forget. She spurned him once again. He surprised her then and got down on his knees to beg for her forgiveness and affections. She pitied him and raised him from his knees to kiss him on the forehead. But as she kissed him, he drew her to him, and before she knew what he was doing, he had drawn her life's essence into himself. One moment she stood before him, and the next she had faded from sight. Now, he thought, no one can ever keep us apart, as we are one. But though he had captured her life's force, her spirit and her presence had fled. He sought her spirit within himself and cried her name to the air, but the deed was done. Birghid was no more. He had misjudged the effects of his actions, and he had destroyed the one most precious to him. Realizing the finality of his actions, and suddenly fearing the arrival of his brother, Mirgul sped from the place where Birghid's pity had brought about her undoing.

WHEN MIRREN RETURNED HOME, he was surprised that he could not feel Birghid's presence nearby. And he was somewhat saddened by her discourtesy. She had always before told him when she was planning to travel. But as he did not perceive the possibility of any threat to her well-being, it was only when she did not return after many *days that he considered something might be wrong. The date of council arrived two weeks later, and Mikele and a distracted Mirgul arrived, but Birghid was still missing. Mirren was happy to see his long-absent brother but was very upset about Birghid. Mirgul fidgeted but said nothing, relieved that his brother did not suspect him. But Mikele had seen Mirgul talking with Birghid shortly before she disappeared. And in front of his brother, she asked Mirgul if Birghid had not told him where she was going.*

Mirgul looked at his brother with wide eyes and panicked, running from the mountaintop where they had gathered. Mirren, still not aware of what had happened, nonetheless chased after his fleeing brother. His wits having left him in his moment of distress, Mirgul failed to use any of the powers at his disposal and continued to run on foot as he left the mountaintop. Mirren, however, assumed the form of a falcon and flew ahead of him, assumed human form once again, and waited in his path. Mirgul stumbled around a corner and ran into his brother, both toppling to the ground. Without think-ing, Mirgul lashed out and tried to draw his brother's essence into himself—as he had done to Birghid. But his brother had not opened himself up the way Birghid had, had not made himself vulnerable. And Mirren's powers, always greater in strength and more cleverly wielded than those of his brother, allowed him to withstand his brother's frenzied attack and strike out himself. He immobilized the still-bemused Mirgul and neutralized his magic after a brief struggle.

MIRREN FELT pity for his clearly bedeviled brother but wanted to know why he had run away when asked about Birghid, and why he had lashed out at his own brother in such a deadly way. The now sobbing Mirgul, sprawled in the dirt of the mountain path, told him the entire story, described Birghid's pity, and confessed to having destroyed her. Mirren froze. Mirgul had tried to do the same to him. As the gravity of his brother's crimes became clear to him, Mirren flew into a rage, and his heart turned to ice. Knowing there was no way to cause his brother physical pain, he resolved to punish him in whatever way he could, and an idea was born in his mind. He assumed the form of a dragon, picked up the motionless form of his brother in his talons, and flew off to the southeast, toward the home of his friend the king of the dwarves.

His vast winged form was spotted far away from the top of the mountain, and when he landed at the entrance to the King's Hall, a squad of heavily armed and seasoned dwarf soldiers were there to greet him. He resumed his natural form lest the dwarves question his draconic intent. The soldiers, now recognizing a frequent visitor, and one of the most powerful of the gods, parted to let him pass through their ranks. Mirgul's body lifted off the ground and floated behind Mirren as he entered the hall of the dwarven king.

The king descended from his throne at Mirren's approach and bowed his head in respect and greeting. Without ceremony, Mirren asked a boon, and a commission, of his long-time friend. "I wish for you to forge a cage for a serpent, and I wish to lend my magic to its making." The dwarf king looked at the still form lying in the rushes on the floor behind his old and powerful friend, and upon recognizing Mirgul, he lifted an eyebrow. But the eyebrow was all the question he would raise to the undertaking, and he nodded without further hesitation. "By your will."

So it was that for the full cycle of a moon, a score of the finest dwarven craftsmen the king could assemble worked under Mirren the Crafter's direction. Mirgul was bound in a cage that fit tightly about his still-immobile body and placed in a dark and distant mine the dwarves had long ago abandoned. At the end of the mine, where the diligent dwarves had deemed no more ore could be gleaned, they placed Mirgul in his cage against the rock wall and fixed it in place with many and strong bolts of dwarven steel, using the greatest of their arts in binding metal to rock. Then, because Mirren feared he might one day have pity on his brother, he hid him from sight. In front of the cage, they erected a wall of stone and steel, etched with glyphs infused with the magic of Mirren, and hardened by the art of the dwarven smiths, sealing away Mirren's brother for all time.

CEDRIC SIGHED. If only Mirren had followed the One God's enjoinment to forgive.

26

PORTENTS

"The king is dead." Six weeks had passed since Laudan's punishment and Janelle's elevation. And Kestrel had just returned from an excursion to the market.

Breeden was stunned. "But he's younger than my father. What happened?"

Kestrel had too much energy, more even than he usually did, and he couldn't stand still. "Where are the others? It's nearly two bells, and here it is just you and me."

Breeden could see that Kestrel didn't know what to do with himself. "What happened to the king?"

Kestrel's eyes settled on Breeden's own, and he seemed to hear again the words Breeden had spoken. His lips moved without uttering a sound, and then the words came. "He fell from his horse. Nothing more than an afternoon ride. Not even in battle!"

They became silent then, each lost in his own thoughts.

Kestrel broke the silence again. "I met him once. He came to Culuden to visit my father's land, enfeoffed to him, for a renewal of his vassals' oaths. All the nobles of our country came together at moot for the same purpose."

"I remember my father having words with several of the other nobles of our clan. Beyond the oaths, the moot was supposed to be a festival—I even ran in a foot race! But many of our clan leaders saw the gathering as a painful reminder of their oaths to a foreign ruler. My father felt that way, to be sure, but he was more practical than most. He met with the men who were unhappy about giving the oath—some for the first time in their lives—and quieted their voices.

"Even so, I was worried on the day the king was supposed to arrive. But he was a subtle man. He showed respect to even the lowest clan chief. He stopped the wagging tongues, and he won them over to be his own men.

"I was close to him at one point, in the crush of people. I was standing on something—a barrel, I think. I could see over everyone's heads, and I watched him approach. He came right up to me. No more than an arm lengths away. And as he swept the crowd, his eyes locked onto mine and he nodded slightly, acknowledging not just my existence but also my worth in a glance.

"There was a power and a courage in those eyes I will never forget. He was standing among an entire city full of men who, to be kind, didn't exactly wish him well, and he acted as though he had not a care in the world but to meet the worthy men who surrounded him. It was something I will never forget. He was a rare man and a good king."

Kestrel remained silent for a moment, musing. "Now that I think on it, the princess's own eyes have some of his fire, though hers burns more darkly."

As if mention of the princess had summoned her servant, Janelle entered the room then, sobbing uncontrollably.

Breeden's eyes widened. "Janelle? . . . Oh. Lorelei . . ."

Kestrel snapped out of his trance somewhat at the sight of Janelle in tears and at Breeden's exclamation. "That's right. I'd not thought what this might mean to you, Janelle. I'm very sorry."

Janelle raised her head to look at both boys, the tears streaming down her reddened face in bright rivulets, and she wobbled slightly. Breeden reached for her, and she fell awkwardly into his outstretched arms. She remained that way for several minutes, and Breeden continued to hold her even as the sobs dwindled. She remained in his arms when Derek and Laudan came into the room. And finally, when at last her strength seemed to fail her, she spoke.

"I was with her when Cedric came to give her the news. She became as a statue when he told her—it chilled me to see her so. Then she demanded to be brought to Arlon immediately to be by his side. Cedric told her she should stay here until arrangements could be made for the funeral and a safe transition of power. When I left, they were still arguing. She's the queen now, or will be soon. I think she will not listen to what Cedric has to say."

All the boys in the room were clustered around their now quiet female companion. They exchanged uncertain looks. Breeden, Derek, and Kestrel appeared not to know what the death of the king would mean to them. Only one seemed sure of himself. And Laudan was resolute. "I will go with her."

Now all eyes, including Janelle's, turned to look at their friend. He seemed a man standing before them, and not the child the rest of them appeared to be in their frail uncertainty of the moment. His words were deep, nearly bass in tone, and his conviction was that of a man.

Janelle was touched by Laudan's words. She squeezed Breeden against her in thanks and then gingerly released herself from his arms to walk over to the giant boy. "You cannot go with her, Laudan. It will not be allowed. Even now the plans are well underway. And I'm sorry to say it, but they cannot include you."

Laudan looked unconcerned by her words. "Then I will follow her caravan, or if she goes by water, then I will hire a ship to follow her up the lake."

Janelle looked pained, but continued. "Laudan, I'm sorry. I just can't even imagine how it would be possible."

Despite Janelle's certainty that it wouldn't be possible, Laudan's conviction and the emotion of the moment sent them into a flurry of discussion then as to how they could arrange for Laudan to be with the princess. It seemed as though all were willing, for the moment, to forgive the princess her weaknesses and think of her as a girl who had just lost her father. It united them all—even Derek—to try to come up with a workable plan.

Laudan suggested he might pose as a page, but that was shot down when all considered the fact that he was larger than most men and would look the unlikeliest of characters in tight hose and a dandy's hat. Kestrel remained apart as the others schemed, staring out of the window.

Breeden thought that if the princess left by water, he himself could sail Laudan up the lake in his father's boat. "It's faster than anything else on the water," he claimed. When everyone got excited about the idea, Derek reminded them that Laudan would still not be *with* the princess when she arrived in Arlon. They would need an excuse to put him in her train, or better yet, arrange for him to become part of her retinue.

Janelle voiced what Breeden realized was probably her chief fear then. "I don't even know if I'm going to be part of the princess's retinue myself!"

Cedric's voice came from the doorway. "You will not be attending the princess once she leaves Ridderzaal, I'm afraid."

Everyone was startled, not having heard him enter the room.

Laudan further surprised everyone by nearly pouncing on

their instructor, who looked wan, and older than usual. "I need to go with her, brother! Tell me how I can!"

Cedric's attention shifted from Janelle to the unlikely Laudan Marchant. He blinked his eyes and looked up, as if noticing his oversize charge for the first time.

Laudan leaned over his teacher. "How can I go with her, Brother Cedric? She'll need me to keep her safe!"

And then Cedric nodded and mumbled almost below hearing, "I see. Yes. I suppose I knew that on some level. If I weren't already so preoccupied . . . Does she share these feelings, then?"

Laudan glanced at Kestrel, and Kestrel shrugged before answering. "She certainly knows he's alive. She spied him walking the box one day when she was on a stroll, and she stopped to ask the sergeant about him. If required to wager on the matter, I'd say that she was interested, yes."

Laudan didn't smile at the confirmation. If anything, he became even more serious than before. "What can you do to help me?"

Breeden had never seen his friend so focused and unshakable—except perhaps for the incident Kestrel had just referred to indirectly, the time Laudan had nearly killed his fellow squire Tavish Ranald.

Cedric allowed a moment of silence to linger while he considered how best to respond. "I'm afraid, my dear student Laudan, that I would not try to arrange for that even if it were in my power. It is an ill enough thing that the princess will not be able to complete her schooling here with me. I'd not permit that to happen to two of my most aspiring students at once— not without a fight, anyway."

Breeden couldn't be sure, but he almost heard something of a threat in Cedric's words. If it had been anyone but Cedric using the tone, Breeden would have sworn his use of the phrase *not without a fight* was more than using words to make a point.

Laudan didn't respond visibly—to the words or to the

threat behind them—at least as far as Breeden could tell. He seemed to be thinking about what he would say next, and he allowed an even longer silence to hang uncomfortably in the air.

"Besides," Cedric continued as if there had been no pause, "what would you do? Do you think you'd be allowed to follow her about like a puppy?"

Laudan's reserve appeared to crack, just a little, and a worried frown creased his brow. "Why, I'd watch over her, of course. And keep her safe. There will be many who wish her ill."

It was as if Cedric had been awaiting the words, as if Laudan had just made a chess move Cedric had been expecting. "Yes, Laudan. But don't forget that many would think that of you. The son of a line that proves to win the kingship should anything happen to the princess. Your father, I don't think I need to remind you, is next in line behind our Lorelei. Even if something should befall her that is not by your hand, your proximity would be cited by those who seek to gain by neither Lorelei nor your own family inheriting the throne. After your family, Laudan, the line of succession is much muddier. And the opportunity for someone exploiting this fact has never been riper. Though not your father's oldest son, you cannot forget who you are. And all you are, to many in this kingdom, is fourth in line for the throne."

Breeden had had no idea Laudan and his family were so close to the throne, though, as he looked around the room, he realized he might be the only one who did not. Derek was nodding sagely, as if the points Cedric had raised had been apparent to him all along. Kestrel was back from the window and didn't look surprised by the words but was more focused on seeing how his friend was reacting to them. Even Janelle seemed to know. *I am such a commoner*, thought Breeden, for what felt like the hundredth time since he'd begun classes with the former knight and his fold of noble children.

Oskar arrived then. And it was apparent to Breeden that he had been crying. His face was red and splotchy, and his eyelids were swollen. Without saying a word, he walked over to a chair by the window and sat, facing away from his friends and teacher, and looked out over the southern fields, which fell away from the monastery toward the Woodfall's seaward run.

Breeden looked away from Oskar and took in his friends. It was obvious Laudan was still unconvinced about why he could not accompany the princess. His mood was dark. And while he was physically still, he carried an air of impatience about him. Kestrel was visibly upset and was fidgeting with a clasp on the front of his cloak and shifting his weight back and forth from one foot to the other. Derek seemed somber and respectful, but Breeden found he couldn't gauge the boy's true feelings beneath. Janelle looked hollow and empty. But her shuddering and weeping were now past, and strangely, Breeden thought, she appeared the most composed of them all.

Breeden looked at his mentor and saw a struggle taking place on the old man's features. Whatever he wrestled with, thought Breeden, it weighed heavily upon him. Cedric called off the day's lessons and bid them all go their own way to mourn the king's passing with their loved ones.

27

WINDS OF CHANGE

The next morning, Breeden stopped at Janelle's house on his walk to classes. But he didn't have the heart to knock on her door when she didn't immediately appear. Instead, he sat on the bottommost step of her front stairway.

He was confused by the feelings that threatened to overwhelm him right now. He'd never met the king, never even seen him from a distance. But he'd grown up on the stories his father had told about the king's wisdom and his justness. And that the poor princess—his own age—had lost not simply the king but her father was difficult to grasp.

As Breeden had said to Kestrel when he'd first heard the news, his own father was older than the king. What would Breeden himself do should he lose his father? How would he react? The future, as uncertain as it was without such thoughts, felt even more bleak and frightening when envisioned without his father's strength and guidance. And how would his mother handle it? He wanted to imagine her as one of those stubborn widows who became merchants or craftspeople—taking over their husband's business. But his mother didn't know the first thing about being a boatwright. And the doubts within him couldn't shake the image of the widow at the edge of town who begged a meager supply of food from the goodwill of her neighbors, and who rarely crossed the threshold of her humble cottage to walk among other humans. Breeden recalled the time the village men had fixed her roof when someone noticed a gaping hole in it, as wide as a man's arm is long. His father had commented afterward that she'd no doubt had a leaky roof for months, maybe longer, and had never had the courage, or will, to ask for help.

Breeden's mind shifted back to consider what Janelle must be feeling. She had become, if not fast friends, at least friendly with the princess. And now a tragedy that would have brought her to the princess's side to offer her comfort—if their stations in life had been different—instead had become a wedge that drove them apart. In all likelihood, now that Lorelei was to be queen, Janelle would never be close to her again.

Lorelei. Janelle. Laudan! And the king!

Breeden wondered what fate the gods held in store for *him*, if such a depressing mess should have befallen his friends and his king. The cracked paving stone under his foot held no answers. And while the thyme that laced between the stone's two halves smelled fragrant as he crushed a stem of it under his boot, even that sweet distraction was carried away too quickly by the morning breeze.

The door creaked open behind him, and he turned to see Janelle looking somewhat recovered and sporting the faintest of smiles. "Good morning, Breeden. Thank you for waiting for me."

Breeden stood, and they began the walk together toward the monastery in silence. Breeden's sturdy boots hit the street with a slow, repetitive clop like that of an unshod horse, and Janelle's finer winter footwear sounded a faster and more delicate staccato in counterpoint as they went. Breeden couldn't recall having ever heard the sounds of footsteps so loudly and crisply. No other noise broke the mournful silence. None of the baker's laughter, the fruit seller's hawking, or the arguing fish-wives carried on the wind from the next street over.

Janelle reached for his hand. He felt her fingers fumble into his own, and after a moment's adjustment, they were twined together. Breeden squeezed once and Janelle's smile grew. As they passed around a corner, not yet quite in view of the keep's main gate, Janelle stretched up and kissed Breeden on the cheek.

"Thank you for yesterday. For holding me. I'm not sure I'd be going to class today if you hadn't. Thank you."

Breeden felt his heart race, and a lump grew in his throat, making it impossible for him to speak. His face must have shown his difficulty, because when Janelle threw him a quick glance, she saw something that made her laugh, a quick, bright thing that leapt into the air and then was gone.

Her laugh eased the lump enough that he managed, "You're welcome." And then the silence took over again.

THAT MORNING, they had seen new uniforms in the streets. A mustard-yellow tabard with the red lion of the king of Hyrde. They must have traveled by night. And there were more than a score of them spread out, it seemed, to cover all entrances to the keep.

There were other strangers moving about the keep as well. Breeden recognized a handful as being not of Ridderzaal. Some went about their business as if they were right at home. Breeden guessed these were legitimate retainers. Others, however, were trying too hard to fit in and act like they belonged. Breeden spotted them easily. He had no idea what purpose they served for the king—or now the princess. But he suspected they might be there for her protection.

. . .

CLASSES THAT MORNING were not quite real to Breeden. A feeling of floating in his head and stomach had replaced the lump in his throat. The sensation remained with him throughout the day, from the morning's prayer, to the instruction Cedric offered on the etiquette and ceremony associated with a king's death, to the afternoon's funeral mass for the passed monarch—at which Breeden was surprised not to see Cedric or the princess.

Since Cedric still had much to attend to, there were no afternoon classes again. Laudan wanted to approach the altar and add his own prayers to those already shared by the Brothers of the Faith. Derek began to follow him, but when Oskar indicated he would also like to pray with them, Derek changed his mind and casually joined the crowd of people leaving the church. Oskar appeared to take the insult in stride, better than Breeden, who felt himself scowl involuntarily.

Kestrel looked from Derek's slow and measured retreat, to Laudan and Oskar's penitent poses in the sanctuary, to Janelle and Breeden standing close by one another, and then he nodded once to Breeden and slipped away. Breeden watched him disappear into the throng with misgivings. His normally capable friend looked as aimless as a cork caught in the eddies where Long Lake met the Woodfall.

BREEDEN AND JANELLE spent the rest of the day walking about the city. They spoke about themselves, revealing more in that afternoon than they'd learned of each other in the nine months they'd attended Cedric's lessons together. They walked through the market, bought themselves sweetmeats, and then they walked back to the monastery, where they strolled the grounds and discovered the beauty of a spring still ripening toward summer. Green sunlight filtered through the thickening canopies of oak and elm. Bushes and lush decorative grasses were already concealing many of the statues, plinths, and fountains. Birds and squirrels flitted and jumped about with what looked like genuine joy at the bounty surrounding them.

It was in the quiet of the monastery where Janelle once again took Breeden's hand in her own. This time it was she who squeezed his hand first. Breeden felt a thank-you in the squeeze —for the day before, he supposed. He was surprised at how cold her hands were on such a beautiful day. They stood that way for some time in silence before they began the walk home, and she didn't release her grip when they did. But her hand warmed up during the walk, and after a little while, he realized he could no longer tell where his fingers stopped and hers began.

Breeden's cheeks were flushed and his lips dry when they found themselves standing in front of Janelle's door. Back where they'd begun the day together. They'd had an amazing day, thought Breeden. And the time had passed so slowly! She was so smart and funny. And it had been as easy to talk with her as it would have been to talk with his mother or father. Then, just like that, the rising lump was back in his throat, and it threatened to cut off his supply of air. He felt the urge to kiss her then. But just as he couldn't speak that morning, when the lump held his voice, so he found he could not even lean over to kiss her cheek.

She seemed to read the struggle that had taken over his face, and she laughed again. The laugh was not as it had been that morning: bright and quick. It was warmer and softer, and hung in the still air a moment before echoing in his head. She kissed him then, and on the lips this time. Then she opened the door and was gone.

28

REFLECTIONS

The next day was warmer still. Breeden and his parents were on the balcony built out over the Woodfall's waters at the back of their house. They had just finished dinner and were seated on bentwood chairs crafted by his father, quietly admiring the clarity of the night. Despite the warmth, his mother had a light blanket draped over her legs. Grasshoppers, tree frogs, and peepers filled the air with their murmuring song. The black backdrop of the moonless sky was deeper and darker than Breeden could remember. And the stars were spectacular: clear and so bright it almost hurt to look at one too closely.

Breeden's father sat next to his mother, in the chair that was typically downwind from them both, and smoked his pipe. He drew deeply, and Breeden could hear the wet crackle of tobacco being consumed by the ember that also lit up his face with a warm orange glow. He released a large puff of blue-white smoke from his mouth, the cloud roiling outward from its center. The night was so still the smoke lingered long before dispersing on its own, no errant breeze to carry it away.

No one was making an attempt to speak, and Breeden's

mind wandered in the silence. He thought about Laudan's loss of control, the king's death, the princess, Janelle, and even about Derek. It must have driven Derek crazy to hear that the princess had selected a commoner to be her lady-in-waiting.

Breeden thought about his gift, as his father had taken to calling it, struggling with the fact that no one else could do, or even conceive of doing, what he could—at least, as far as he'd always understood magic from the stories he'd heard. And he thought about the silence his father had asked him to maintain about his abilities. He wondered, too, when Kestrel would confront him about it again. He knew it was not a matter of *if*— Kestrel was too persistent and too curious. And this thought led him to consider his friends Kestrel and Oskar, and what they meant to him.

He had never had real friends before—none he saw regularly, anyway, and none he connected with so well as Kestrel and Oskar. He got along well with Tom Conkle, the carpenter's son, and some of the boys who lived a few doors down. But his neighbors were a few years younger than him, and Tom was a few years older. In fact, he realized he was friendlier with his father's friends, and with his neighbors who were his parents' age, than with the boys he had known before meeting Kestrel and Oskar. Without having known it all this time, he realized he had been missing out on something important by not having friends his own age.

He reflected on what it was about his new friends he valued so much more than his other friendships. Maybe it was because Kestrel and Oskar, and to a lesser extent Laudan, were less serious and less careful about saying and doing the proper thing than his adult friends were. And they were willing to test their boundaries and to push the limits of rules and proprieties. Breeden had always been led to believe that such rules were not flexible, but fixed standards of behavior. And he had learned young from his parents that lapses weren't acceptable.

He realized that what he was entertaining might point to Kestrel and Oskar as bad influences, but he knew in his heart that that was anything but true. What his friends gave to him now was just as important as the discipline and respect taught to him by his parents. They were teaching him to believe in himself, in his own judgment, and in his own opinions—not by telling him to do so, as his parents had done so often, but by acting as models for him through their actions.

Could he have put it in precisely these words? Maybe not. He had a sense of it all, but an imperfect one. To him, the recognition of what he gained from his friendship was less analytical and more emotional. Put simply, he felt good when he was around them. He felt confident. And he felt a genuine bond of friendship with these boys. One was an orphan and one was noble-born, but they were still his friends and his peers. And that they were his age, and they shared a common experience day in and day out—the lessons of Brother Cedric —made their relationship closer than any he'd ever had outside of the one with his mother and father.

A thought occurred to Breeden, and he spoke almost before he realized it. "Dad? How often do you see Aegir?"

His father stirred from his reverie, took a deep draw on his pipe, and then released it slowly before responding. "Not often enough, son. He's a good man. Or a good giant at any event. Why do you ask?"

"I was wondering when you'd have his boat completed, and I was thinking that maybe, if I helped you more than I have been, we could finish it sooner."

His father nodded. "His project is well along. The ribs are all cut and ready for bending. You helped me bend the spine, of course. And I've still got to cut the wales. Perhaps a few days more? And then I'll need your help. But for now, I'll manage fine while you're studying with Brother Cedric."

Breeden nodded. He thought again about Aegir and was

saddened at the prospect of having to wait before seeing him again. His mother and father had acted so differently when Aegir was around. And they all three seemed to share a friendship Breeden likened to his own with Kestrel and Oskar. There was no mummery in the way they talked with one another. And there was no sense about the conversation that one had to watch what they said. His parents didn't have this kind of relationship with anyone else—at least not that Breeden had ever observed. And besides, Breeden missed Aegir's stories and the way he could feel the giant's voice when he talked.

"Okay. If there's anything I can do in the meantime, just let me know."

Breeden's mother watched the exchange with a tightened mouth and then reached over and laid her hand on his arm. "Is there anything else you want to talk about, Breeden?"

Breeden wasn't sure he knew exactly what he wanted to talk about. But he was pretty sure that what he wanted to know was whether his parents were happy. And he was wondering why every day couldn't be more like the day they all had when Aegir visited.

"No. There's nothing else."

She tightened her grip on his arm and tried to get him to look at her. "Come on, now, sweetie. What is it?"

Breeden feared his mother's intuition, because it had uncovered more half-truths and broken crockery than he cared to admit. As a result, he had learned that his best bet was to come clean as soon as possible whenever she turned her attention his way.

"I guess I just wonder whether you and Dad are happy. I don't mean together. I know you don't fight very often, at least in front of me. And you hold hands and do that kind of stuff in front of me too. But what I really mean is just happy, you know, with life and everything."

The look his mother gave him let him know he'd caught her

somewhat off guard. But she was a smart woman, and it only took her a moment to recover. "You asked about Aegir because we had so much fun when he was here?" Her words were something like a question but not quite. Her famous intuition had struck at the crux of the matter once again.

Breeden nodded, resigned to the fact that he could hide nothing from the woman who had raised him.

"We aren't frivolous people, Breeden. We don't seek beyond our walls for what we need. We have each other. And we have a comfortable, quiet place to live. I think you know how deeply your father cares for the work he does. And I hope you know how much I enjoy keeping you and your dad honest." She smiled at her own mild jest, obviously hoping to nudge Breeden out of his funk.

Breeden nodded once again, but he still wasn't so sure. "But when Aegir was here, you were laughing late into the night, and you seemed to be having more fun than I can ever remember. Why don't you have that much fun all the time?"

His mother tried a different tack. "But we do have fun—every day. And that we enjoy simpler pleasures more often than nights like the one we had with Aegir doesn't mean we don't enjoy our life. It might be hard for you to understand, Breeden, but nights like that one are so much fun because they don't come along that often. If Aegir had stayed two nights, we might have had just as much fun the second night. And maybe through a third night. But too long in anyone's company, and the spell of reunion fades far more quickly than you might think.

"Do you understand what I'm saying?"

Breeden sort of understood what she meant, but he didn't believe it had to be that way.

She looked at him searchingly, her hand still squeezing his arm. Breeden could tell by her look that she knew he wasn't sure. But she appeared to accept that she couldn't convince him. "I love you, Breeden. We are happy. But it seems you may need to learn this one on your own."

The conversation trailed off again, and each of them was left to contemplate the night. The river was so calm that even the outflow of Long Lake's waters was not enough to disturb the illusion of two vast expanses of stars spread out before them, one beneath the River Woodfall's waters, and the other overhead.

29

LOSS

A week had passed since the king had died, and a pall had been cast over the castle, affecting Breeden and his friends, and spilling out into the city.

Classes had resumed, after a fashion. Sometimes they would meet only in the morning. Sometimes Cedric would dismiss them right away. And Janelle was often called away to help the princess prepare for her trip north.

Laudan projected his voice as soon as he entered the room. "Kestrel is missing. He never came back to the barracks last night. Nobody's seen any sign of him since dinner." The words were calm, as Breeden would have expected from Laudan. But they bore a trace of fear he'd never heard in his friend.

"Has he ever done that before?" Janelle seemed more comfortable with herself today, thought Breeden. It wasn't often she was the first one in on a conversation.

Laudan shook his head. "Never. He's come in late enough plenty of times—most times when he's been with a maid. Er . . ." Laudan stumbled, looking embarrassed that he'd said such a thing to a girl.

Janelle smiled coyly. "I've heard of such things before, Laudan!"

Breeden's ears turned red, and he wondered to himself what experience Janelle might have. Suddenly her boldness felt less refreshing and more intimidating. But he put those thoughts aside and recalled again the misgivings he'd been having about the way his Pretani friend had been acting since the king had died.

"I feel like he's been up to something." Breeden spoke the words at half volume, as if uncommitted to sharing his fears with his friends.

Laudan grabbed his arm—actually causing Breeden some pain—and locked eyes with him. "What was that?"

Breeden winced. "Easy, Laudan. I don't know. It's just something about how he's been acting. He's kept to himself and gone off on his own more than usual this past week. And he's seemed . . . lost. I'm not sure I can offer more than that."

Laudan lessened his grip, too little to Breeden's thinking, though helpful just the same. "Everyone's been down since the king died. What makes you think it's anything more than that?"

Breeden was stumped. Just as he'd had trouble explaining to his father what he'd done with the door to the armory, he wasn't sure he could make someone understand the way his intuition often helped him to see things others couldn't see.

"I can't say, Laudan. All I know is that ever since he found out about the king's death, he's been acting strangely. At first it looked like he couldn't sit still—even more than usual. Then I think it went further than that. It was as if he decided he needed to do something and was mustering his courage to do it. Does that make any sense to you?"

Breeden was relieved when Laudan released his grip and nodded. "Yes. I think I do know what you mean. He seemed upset. I had thought it was me—because I had decided to go with the princess. But I think maybe you're right."

"So, he obviously didn't say anything to you about what might have been bothering him, then." Breeden was discouraged at the thought. "Well," Breeden suggested, "perhaps we could go looking for him after class. Maybe check the market and see if anyone saw him yesterday. Or we could check with one of the girls he's been keeping company with? Do you know who they are?"

Laudan glanced at Janelle again before nodding. "Aye."

"Well, let's get moving and see if we can find out where he went."

Breeden had another thought. "Actually, you should go. But I'll wait here for Cedric—or try to track him down. It's not like him to be late like this. But anyway, Kestrel wouldn't have left Ridderzaal without letting him know. And let's plan to meet here again at noon and see if anyone's found anything by then."

All agreed, and the search began in earnest.

WHEN THEY MET AGAIN, they hadn't been able to find Cedric. And Oskar was the only one to have learned anything. "The steward told me there was a message from Kestrel's father, asking that he return home at once. That's all anyone knows."

Breeden thought about it for a moment and supposed that Kestrel's mood of late could have been due to a letter from his father. But why would he not have shared the news with his friends? And what could be so important it would call Kestrel back home before he had completed his studies and earned his knighthood?

Those thoughts ran through Breeden's head as he considered Oskar's words. But outwardly all he could muster was a disbelieving "Really?"

Janelle appeared to share Breeden's sentiment. "What? No, that can't be. He'd never have left without saying goodbye!" Fire flashed in her eyes, and she seemed ready to challenge Oskar for even suggesting it.

Laudan looked thoughtful. And Derek nodded his head. "I agree with the commoners. It wasn't his way. He'd have told Laudan at least—even if not the rest of us."

"I'd like to think you're right." The tall boy looked unsure. "We haven't exactly spoken much lately. I've been a bit occupied with the princess, and he's been leaving me more and more to myself and going off on his own. I think he tired of hearing me speak of her eyes like precious stones, and her hair like the golden fields of wheat back home." Laudan tried a laugh. But his smile didn't touch his eyes.

Oskar mused aloud. "Maybe the steward knows more than he told me. After all, I didn't really ask him about anything once he'd told me Kestrel had gone home. Huw would have cursed me a fool for not pinning the weasel down. It didn't even occur to me to ask when he left exactly, or by what road, or if he left in anyone's company or by himself." Breeden could see that Oskar was not happy with himself.

Oskar kicked the floor in frustration. "I'll see him again this afternoon and find out whether he knows anything more."

Laudan spoke on the tail of Oskar's words. "Well, I find it very hard to believe he'd have left without telling one of us." Breeden heard the unspoken words: *especially me!* And then Laudan finished. "Let's split up and continue our search. And let's meet here again tomorrow morning as we did today, as if we had class. I would like to see if the sergeant-at-arms has heard anything. He was gone all morning and should be back this afternoon. It would have been impossible for Kestrel to leave without seeking his approval—letter from home or not."

Laudan left the room then. And Derek and Oskar followed after him.

Breeden watched them leave. He felt entirely useless. He could do nothing to help his friends. Even if he could think of someone of authority who might know what had happened to his friend, he was nobody they'd discuss the matter with. He was no nobleman's son.

He looked over at Janelle and took her hand.

She gave him a sympathetic look. "I'm afraid I need to help the princess get her affairs in order. It's only a matter of time before she overrules Cedric and decides she is going to Arlon."

Breeden squeezed her hand. "It's okay. I understand. I'm sorry . . ."

Janelle squeezed him back and gave him a quick peck on the cheek. "I'll talk to you tomorrow." And then she was gone.

Breeden's mind was swimming. He could barely keep his steps straight as he left the inner bailey and walked into the city. Then a thought struck him, and he changed his course, heading toward the market.

He found the satje vendor Kestrel was so crazy about and asked the man when he'd last seen his friend. "Not since two days ago—and my business has suffered!" The hawker was a Mahjar, and the accent that came through his dark-stained smile was heavy with the man's desert home. "But you'll send him back here if you see him, won't you?"

Breeden nodded his head, as much an internal confirmation that his suspicion had been borne out as an acknowledgment of the man's request. "I will. So, tell me, if you would, sir, what did he usually buy from you, and how much of it would he buy at a time?"

The man responded immediately. "He would buy the stick meat, sometimes two, about this time every day. And on Fridays he would buy an entire parcel of my satje as well—and a good-sized bundle when he did."

Breeden had never tried satje. He asked for a bundle the size Kestrel would normally buy. The man loaded about a score of the thickly cut spiced and dried meat strips, each about two hands in length, into a clean rag and tied it into a small parcel.

"This is what he would buy. And sometimes, when he took a trip, he would buy this much three times over."

The words were precisely the ones Breeden had been hoping to hear. "Thank you so much. And one last question: when you saw him last, how much satje did he buy?" Breeden paid the man and gave him an extra copper in thanks.

"He bought only a single stick. He has not bought any parcels in more than a week." The man nodded, and bowed slightly. "Thank you, young master. That is what your young friend would pay me as well."

Breeden smiled grimly to himself and headed back for the barracks, hoping to find Laudan and tell him what he had discovered.

HE CAUGHT up with Laudan little more than half an hour later at the barracks. When Breeden saw him, he couldn't hold back and blurted out, "He didn't go home. I don't know where he is, but he didn't go anywhere."

Laudan looked around to see if anyone could hear them and then ushered Breeden into the barracks themselves. It was Breeden's first time in the building. Normally, he would have been gazing about wide-eyed at the arms and armor stored neatly on racks, hanging on the walls, and strewn about on the cots where the squires and soldiers slept. But he was too excited to notice much of anything.

Laudan held up his hand to indicate Breeden should keep his voice low, and Breeden began again. "He didn't buy any satje. And hasn't bought any in two days. There's no way he'd have gone on a trip home without stopping to buy some satje first!"

Laudan wasn't known among his friends for being the first to arrive at a conclusion, but Breeden knew the boy was a quick enough study when someone else was there to coach him along. "I see. You're confident, then?"

Breeden nodded his head vigorously. "The vendor said he normally saw Kestrel every day—every single day!"

Laudan shook his head. "Well, someone wants us to think he's gone home. But it wasn't the castle steward. It was the princess's minister who put the word out that Kestrel has gone home. I asked the sergeant-at-arms about it. He said that the princess's minister received the missive as part of a confidential letter he'd received on behalf of the princess. And he couldn't share more than that Kestrel was needed at home."

Breeden was confused. "What? I got the impression from Oskar that it was the steward himself who received the message."

Laudan shook his head. "I don't understand either. I'm thinking about asking the princess for an audience, to see if she knows anything about him." He paused for a long moment, but Breeden waited, since it seemed he had more to say. "And I was going to see if there was a place for me on the trip north as well."

Breeden didn't respond. He was surprised Laudan could be thinking of following the princess when his best friend was missing. But he wasn't sure his tenuous relationship with the boy would survive saying as much. Neither boy spoke, and the silence grew between them.

When Breeden did break the silence, it was in a feeble attempt to make Laudan feel guilty. "Could you write to Kestrel's father?"

Laudan nodded. "I was thinking of that this morning. Normally, I wouldn't think twice about him going missing for a few hours. But he missed muster this morning. And if he hadn't been acting so strangely of late . . ."

Breeden nodded. He understood just what Laudan meant.

· · ·

When Breeden and Oskar finally tracked down their teacher, he had known nothing about the boy's departure, and he appeared as concerned as they were. He had frowned at mention of the princess's minister but made no further judgment or comment, and he regretfully told them that the death of a monarch was no mean event and that, for the time being, he would have to rely on them to figure out where Kestrel may have gone. In fact, he told them, they would have no more classes until the princess had left for Arlon.

But Cedric's not knowing about Kestrel's departure was the final nail in the coffin for Breeden and his friends. They were now fairly confident he hadn't gone home and the princess's minister knew something about it. But how would they ever find the boy?

30

CAPTURED

The cell was beyond dark. No matter how many times Kestrel waved his hand in front of his face, he couldn't even sense movement. He was usually comfortable crawling through dark, cramped spaces, and he had even gotten stuck in a tunnel once before and been trapped for hours. But until now he'd never been locked in a cell. And he had never been so terrified in all his life.

The worst thing about the darkness was that he had no way of telling how long he'd been locked up. That ate at him more than anything, because the news he carried could not wait. But the darkness obscured time as effectively as it did the hand he waved in front of his face. He had slept a handful of times already—three or four times at least—so he guessed he'd been in the cell for at least two or three days. But it easily could have been a single day, or a week for his lack of certainty.

After the darkness was the cold. He knew it wasn't cold enough that he should be shivering, but he'd only worn a light tunic when he'd come down to the cellars, and the stones of his cell were ever so slowly sucking the warmth from his body. The shivering had begun right before the last time he'd slept, and he'd had a hard time falling asleep because of it.

After the cold, he supposed the thirst was the worst. He'd gotten over the hunger a long time ago—though the ache would come back occasionally, each time duller than the last. But the thirst was ever present. His lips were cracking. And his nose would bleed if he so much as touched it.

Of growing concern, but still not at a level to cause him too much worry, was the fact that he had started seeing ghostly shapes floating in the air. He tried hard to convince himself that it was just the darkness and his eyes playing tricks on him. But then he'd heard whispers. There were no words he could understand. And they weren't speaking the common tongue. But he was certain that the voices at least were not summoned by his imagination. They were too subtle. And they moved around him with a purpose, as if they were examining him and deciding what they should do about him.

Kestrel tried to reach out toward one of the voices with his manacled hands—and it shrank away from him, still talking but fading backward in the room. He spoke. "What is it? What do you want? Who are you?"

The voices paused while he spoke but then resumed again. He assumed they'd not understood him, or had chosen to ignore his questions. On a whim, he spoke a phrase in elvish he'd learned from the hunt master.

The words he had spoken meant "Are you friend or foe?"

The voices went silent then.

Time passed, and Kestrel struggled to remember other words in the elvish tongue. At first he tried to think of something to say that would mean "Come back," or "I am friend," or "Who are you?"—but the words escaped him. Instead, he spoke what elvish words he hoped would not intimidate the ghosts and might even bring them back, "Friend. Home. Friend."

He stopped talking and strained his ears. The shapes were

gone, and the voices with them. He sat in silence. Nothing. He must have scared them away or angered them or done something else—offended them, perhaps—to make them want to stay away. The silence grew. Kestrel shivered.

And then he heard something. But it wasn't the ghosts—it sounded like footsteps. His heart raced. He sat up straight, his back flat against the stone wall. He tried to bring up some saliva, something to swallow to clear the rising lump in his throat.

It was more than one person. Booted feet. Two people, he thought. And walking with purpose. They knew where they were going. He quailed then, fearing the worst. If someone were searching for him, they'd not be so deliberate. They would be hunting for him, not marching straight for his cell. The darkness was lightening around him, he noticed with an odd mix of joy and fear. He could see his hands. He could see the cell around him. And then the light was bright—like the sun—shining through the small window near the top of the heavy door that held him in.

The torch had been thrust up into the window so whoever had come could see him. It didn't remain there long before he heard the latch being raised and the door gliding open, almost without a sound. They'd oiled the hinges. He remembered smelling the oil when he'd first been imprisoned, but the smell had faded. It was back now, and along with the scent of oil, he could smell the sour sweat of the two men who entered.

He couldn't make out much more than their silhouettes. One was of average build and height. He stood closest to Kestrel. And he appeared to be leaning over and examining him. The other, much larger, stood back in the doorway.

The shorter one grunted, "A boy. They call me from Arlon to question a boy?" Kestrel thought the man sounded annoyed. But after another moment's pause, he continued.

"Very well. Dura! Go fetch me a chair or something to sit on from one of these other rooms."

He held the torch casually, with the butt against his thigh, and he watched Kestrel in silence until the other man had returned with a chair. Then he pulled the chair right in front of Kestrel and sat down—putting his face within a handspan of Kestrel's.

"What do you know, boy? What did you hear, eh? Look me in the eye, boy!"

Kestrel complied, blinking against the light, his eyes nearly squinted shut so he could focus on the man's face. "I can't see very well. I've been in the dark for so long." His voice cracked as he spoke the word *dark*.

The man before him made a pronounced nod, and as his features became clearer, Kestrel saw that he was very old and wore a grim, fixed smile. "You'll not be coming out today either, son. In fact, you'll not be seeing the sun again. The two things you've got to think about now are how much longer you want to be down here and how quickly you want your end to come when it most assuredly does come."

Kestrel's instincts had been right. He was going to be killed. And the man before him spoke of torture. Distractedly Kestrel recalled that the Torturers' Guild had been disbanded by the king. Cedric had mentioned it in one of their lessons on the ethical responsibilities of being a member of royalty.

Kestrel realized the man was waiting for a response. But he didn't know what to offer, what he could possibly say to avoid being killed.

"I don't know what you think I've done, sir."

The fixed smile broadened. "Ah, you see! And I had figured you for one who would boldly tell me straight off what you'd done wrong! Better this way, then. I'd hate to forgo the usual ministrations. Will you show me some spirit, then, son?"

Kestrel's stomach contracted. The hunger cramps had been

dormant for so long, but the man's words brought his guts back to life. He could taste the bile rising in his throat.

"I would hope it doesn't have to come to that, sir."

The man barked a laugh. "So you would hope that I might be convinced of your innocence and that I might choose to set you free? Now, that I really didn't expect from you. I thought I saw a spark of intelligence when I looked in your eyes."

Kestrel merely stared at the man. What could he possibly offer? But the man seemed bent on talking, and he continued after a slight pause.

"There are two kinds I treat with—almost exclusively. First, there's the bold and unapologetic. Then there's the groveling and pitiful. Most are innocent—in their own minds, anyway. But the reality is that all—every last one of them—have been guilty. Not necessarily of the thing I'm supposed to extract, I'll admit. But you'd be disgusted by the things they tell me when I ply my art. The worst are the mad ones, with no motive or reason for what they do, such as the ones that killed—or did worse with—their brothers or sisters or children. Many do it for spite from some trifling offense. And many do things simply for pleasure.

"I understand the darkness in a person who revels in blood and filth. It's why I'm so good at my job, after all. But most who like the darker side of things are undisciplined. And one needs to be disciplined to master the art of inflicting pain.

"Which brings me to my chief point, boy. And that is this: I am a rare man, in that I enjoy this work, but I am also very careful and disciplined in how I go about it. What does that mean for you? It means you can expect your pain to be exquisite. It means I'll push the limits of your ability to bear it.

"I am not boasting, son. You'll see that soon enough. So, the one thing you've got going for you is that you can cooperate and tell me what I want to hear, and I promise I'll keep the sessions short. Because if you don't, well, then I can promise you the last few weeks of your life will feel as long as the life you've already led!"

Kestrel said nothing. And the man allowed the moment to linger.

"Understand what I'm saying, son? I hope for your sake you do. I'll be back when I'm back." With that, the man rose from the chair, and pulled it with him out of the cell. Kestrel heard the latch rattle, and the clunk of a heavy timber falling in place. He had been returned to darkness.

Kestrel could hear the men as they walked down the hall. They weren't trying to mask their words at all. And he caught snippets of their conversation.

"He's nothing but a young eavesdropper. Probably peeps on the ladies' chambers too, I'd wager."

"He's a scared little boy, for sure. I suspect he'll go quickly."

Kestrel realized that the men had made no mention of him being of royalty, or being a squire. And he smiled with a rare glimmer of hope when he remembered he'd worn an old set of clothes down to the cellars. They were worn thin from long use and had holes in both knees of the trousers and one elbow, and his family crest had been removed some time ago to use again on a newer shirt he'd had made. Maybe the man didn't know who he was. Maybe he didn't know that Kestrel was capable of understanding the conversation he'd overheard. There had to be some reason to celebrate that.

But his satisfaction was brief, because he knew that when the man came back, he would have little reason to be happy. Not knowing he was a squire might shorten the torture—and allow Kestrel to protect what he'd heard—but he now knew that it wouldn't save him from being killed down here. And besides, what good would it do him to know about the princess's plans? He hadn't had a chance to tell anyone—not even Laudan! And he knew he couldn't escape. The knowledge would die with him.

31

REVELATIONS

It had been two days since Kestrel had gone missing. And so far they hadn't been able to discover more than the fact that the minister was probably lying. Janelle was spending much of her time helping the princess with her preparations to leave. And Laudan was trying to figure out how he might arrange to go with her. It felt like Oskar and Breeden were the only ones trying to find their missing friend.

Breeden returned home, exhausted from another day's failed search, to discover that Aegir the giant was once again in his kitchen.

But the visit was an altogether different one from the previous spring. It had been more than a year since the giant's last visit. And Breeden had grown. He also had one too many reasons not to be very happy right now.

Oddly, a somehow solemn smile was all the giant was able to muster as well. And Breeden hadn't even noticed the look on his parents' faces right away. But when he did, his own sadness and concern vanished in a moment. "What's wrong? Why are you all so sad?"

Breeden could tell his mother was trying to hold herself

together, but she was failing. Instinctively he ran into her arms to comfort her. As he held her, he turned to his father and the giant. "Why is she so sad? What's happened?"

Breeden's father put his hand on his son's back and gently rubbed it in a circling motion. The unconscious act, a calming ritual he'd used to quiet a young boy having nightmares in his bed, had its effect. Breeden's rising panic held for a moment. "Son, we need to have a talk. Just you and me."

Breeden understood that the conversation likely wouldn't be an enjoyable one, but he nodded his acceptance, squeezed his mother one last time, and turned toward the home's front door. After bending over to give his wife a kiss on the head, his father joined Breeden outside.

They walked in the direction of the deepwater piers, and Breeden's father removed his pipe and a pouch of tobacco from his pocket. He stuffed the pipe full to the top, tamped it down gently so none of the tobacco was visible above the rim of the pipe's scarred and blackened bowl, and then he stopped to light a taper from a lantern hanging next to his neighbor's door.

Breeden understood the comfort and clarity the pipe brought to his father, and despite his impatience, he allowed his father the time to expel his first blue cloud before saying another word. "Dad, please tell me what's going on."

His father glanced at him and agreed. "Yes. Soon enough, my son."

Breeden realized that his father was not sad, as his mother was, but was masking some other emotion. And then his father began to talk.

"When I was a young man, not much older than you are now, I sailed in King Raulin's navy. While I had a few patrols along the southern coasts, I mostly traveled in the northern and eastern waters. We constantly patrolled the edges of the king's domain to remind the Krigares we were there—just in case they might happen to forget their treaties."

Breeden had heard as much from his father before and was wondering why any of this was so important right now. But he also knew his father was not a man of words, and that if he was telling a tale from the past, there was likely a good reason for it.

"Not all among the Krigares were savage. Many among them were good and just men. And I befriended some of them. As you know, too—though you may not know the whole story of how we met—I encountered Aegir on these same travels. He was . . . *is* a rarity among his kind in that he enjoys traveling about, meeting people, and seeing new sights. And he doesn't carry the same fear and distrust of humans most of his kind bear. I can't say I agree with his opinion more than that of the rest of his kin, but that's a discussion for another time.

"Anyway, Aegir was particularly fond of exploring the archipelago, and the waters among them, to the north of his people. Of interest to this story is the fact that within a small cluster of islands he favored, he met a wizard and his young Krigare wife. They were an odd pair. He was not a Krigare. He was a good deal older than she—though apparently still quite strong and healthy. And they had mostly removed themselves from the affairs of her homeland, and from the world at large, really.

"Aegir became attached to these two humans. He appreciated how they lived alone together out on the edges of the world. And he communicated with them in much the same way he stays in touch with me and your mother. Well, as anyone who works on the sea knows can happen, they were killed in one of the raging northeastern storms that make the region infamous. By some miracle, their newborn child was spared by the storm gods, and Aegir himself found the child floating among the wreckage of their sailboat.

"As it turns out, Aegir happened to know another couple—though far to the south. And this second couple were not capable of having children of their own. The woman had proven barren and, more, had even passed beyond the years when a healthy woman can bear a child without risking her life. And Aegir knew how much this second couple desperately wished they could have a child of their own."

Breeden was silent, his mind leaping ahead of his father's tale to draw fearful conclusions.

"And while I can see that you suspect the end of the story, but are not ready to commit to the realization, I will confirm your suspicions: Yes, Breeden. You are that child. And your mother and I, who have raised you, are not your mother and father by blood.

"I'm sorry, my son. You must know I love you no less for your knowing the truth. And it's my hope you feel the same way about your mother and me."

As his father had guessed, Breeden had jumped to the story's conclusion as soon as he mentioned the infant child's survival. Instinctively Breeden realized that the knowledge would have no effect on his relationship with his parents—as far as he was concerned, anyway. And he let his father know as much. "You will always be my da, Dad. And mother will always be mother to me as well. But what does all of this matter, and why the telling now?"

Breeden's father laughed, and he hugged his son, welled tears spilling from the corners of his eyes. "Indeed, you are my son as sure as the stars spin about the earth! I wish your mother were here to hear your answer!" The explosion of mirth was followed by a pronounced sigh and a prolonged inhalation as Breeden's father appeared to draw in strength from the very air around him. "In fact, now the hard part's out, shall we return home and tell her, and perhaps share a cup? Aegir can better tell you the next part of the story, anyway."

Breeden agreed, and they walked the short distance home in silence as he ran the matter of his true heritage again and again through his thoughts.

By the time they entered their kitchen again, Breeden was reassured by the fact that he still felt no change in how he felt about his parents. If anything, he had a new admiration for them in raising another's child as their own. But in essence, the news changed nothing.

He embraced his mother and held her for a long, long moment—reminded, oddly, of the hug he'd shared with Janelle upon her learning of the king's death a week earlier.

And then the floor was given to Aegir, to finish the tale that had begun with the revelation of Breeden's true birth.

"Your father was a wizard. But he was not just any wizard, I'm afraid. He was—and still is—one of the greatest of his kind ever to walk the earth. That's right, Holt, Marlene, and Breeden: Breeden's father still lives. And it is he who has sent me to ask for Breeden's help with a matter that concerns the fate of the world."

Breeden's mother gasped. His father showed no outward change. And Breeden became suddenly angry and confused. "Not dead? But if he's not dead, then why did he abandon me? And why has he not come to visit me?"

It was a rare outburst for Breeden. And he realized, as soon as he'd raised his voice, that Aegir was merely the messenger, and not responsible for his blood father's actions.

Aegir gently interjected. "But he has visited you—a handful of times since the year you were born and I brought you here."

Breeden's eyes widened. And he thought for a moment. *The old man?* When he was unloading fish? Regardless . . . He continued in a more moderate tone. "Well, what need could he possibly have for me, anyway? I hardly even know what my powers can do—never mind how to control them really."

Breeden's mother made a small sound, as though she'd swallowed something unintentionally. He turned to look at her, seeking forgiveness for keeping things from her with his glance. But it was clear from the look she returned that she already knew about his powers. His father must have decided to tell her after all.

Aegir brought them back. "I cannot tell you exactly what part you will play in these events, but your father and his powers are of a nature that would allow him to do things no other could. He believes you might share some of these abilities with him. And he has reason to believe that these unique powers of yours could make a difference in battling against the agents of evil that are gathering even now."

"Agents of evil?" It was Breeden's mother, clearly concerned.

Aegir nodded his massive head. "Yes. Agents of Mirgul, the Dark Lord."

Breeden's father spit on the floor and then mixed it with a small pile of sawdust using the tip of his boot.

Aegir nodded again. "This is no vacation I propose to take your son on. Make no mistake. It may be a hard road. But another reason why Breeden's father hopes to involve you, my young friend, is that he does not believe Mirgul knows you even exist. It is your father's belief, Breeden, that your anonymity will keep you safe."

Breeden surprised them all with his next question. "What is my father's name?"

Aegir responded without hesitation. "He is known by many names. But to your mother, he was known as Einar."

"Einar." Breeden tasted the word. He listened to it echo in his head. He believed that Aegir spoke the truth, that his mother had called his father by this name. But he also sensed that the giant was holding something back, not revealing something important about his father. But the stony face that regarded him revealed no further secrets, and Breeden let the matter drop. He could always raise the question later if his suspicions should grow.

"And my mother? Is she really dead? Or is she alive, too?"

Aegir frowned. "I'm afraid that part of the tale is true, young Breeden. She was truly killed in a storm."

Breeden allowed himself a moment to imagine this woman he would never meet. But his anger came back quickly.

"Who are these agents of the Dark Lord? Humans?"

The giant nodded, as if out of respect for the keenness of the young man's mind. "Yes, for now. Though he also finds it simple enough to exercise his will on weaker races when he chooses to do so. Before it is over, it will likely involve gnomes at the least. And perhaps worse."

Again Breeden had the sense that the giant was failing to reveal some important piece of information. But the giant remained silent. And Breeden didn't care anyway. He would be going with the giant to meet his father. That much was plain.

"When does he need me, and when would we leave?"

Aegir placed his hands firmly on the table. "Tonight. Tomorrow morning at the latest. There is a meeting of the council of wizards at the dwarf city of Ekszer Hegy. He needs us now."

"Tomorrow, then." Breeden wanted to say goodbye to Janelle. And to the rest of his friends if he could manage it.

32

FAREWELL

Breeden knew it was late to be knocking at a girl's door. And he feared a tongue-lashing from her mother or father when the door finally opened. But it was Janelle who answered. She must have seen him from the window. She was wearing a night shift and bore a look of mild alarm. "What is it?"

Breeden was his father's son and knew no other way than to come right out with it. "I have to leave."

"Leave? What? Why?"

Breeden shook his head and reached out for her hand. She took it, and he stepped inside her home so she could close the door. As he passed over the threshold, he could see her father watching from the end of the hallway.

On the walk over, he'd thought about what he would tell her. Especially her, among all of his friends. But he clearly couldn't tell her the truth. At least not all of it. Whether her father was listening or no.

"I learned something tonight."

She squeezed his hand in encouragement and gestured

toward a bench by the door. He gratefully accepted, and they sat down beside each other. She turned toward him and grabbed both of his hands in hers.

"What is it? What did you learn?"

Out with it now. "I learned that I was adopted. And my birth father needs me."

Breeden had been looking down as he spoke. But he lifted his gaze to see how she would process his words. She looked relieved. Then perhaps a little angry. And then something else he couldn't identify.

"But where are you going? And why is it so urgent? Can't you finish the school year with us?"

"No. It's far from here. I'm actually not sure exactly where. But a . . . man has come to take me there. And he tells me it is urgent I see my father as soon as possible."

"Is he dying?"

Breeden shook his head. "No." But then he reconsidered. "Well, perhaps. I'm not sure, to be honest. He did tell me it was a matter of life and death. So, maybe. I'm sorry . . ."

She leaned over and hugged him then. And she clung to him even more tightly after hearing her father's cough. "I will miss you." She whispered the words in his ear.

Breeden breathed in deeply the intoxicating smell of her hair, and his nose brushed her neck as he whispered back. "I will surely miss you too. We were only just . . ."

Janelle's father coughed again, and Breeden pulled away. "I will be leaving very early in the morning. And I don't know when I'll be back. I am so sorry, Janelle."

He stood then, not wishing to prolong his agony. Or Janelle's. But her father be damned . . . he kissed her then, right on the lips. And then he quickly pulled away. "Goodbye, Janelle." And then he was out the door.

He thought about trying to find Laudan and Oskar then.

But he didn't think he had the heart for it. He turned around one last time to look back at Janelle's door. He thought he could make out a shadowy figure through the thick glass sidelight. And then he hung his head and turned toward home.

33

JOURNEY BEGUN

The morning came quickly. And the day looked to be a hot one. But as his goodbyes had been with Janelle the night before, it was a tear-filled goodbye with his mother and father. Their only child—not even a man yet—was off on his first trip away from home. And it was not just any trip but one fraught with danger. His untested abilities, and the might of a giant at his side, were all they could count on to see him safely returned to them.

Breeden had never seen his mother look so miserable and helpless as she did when he released her from the last of their many parting hugs.

"I'll be back, Ma. I promise. And Aegir will keep me safe. I love you, Ma." They were his final words as he left the house. His mother had decided she could not see him off at the pier and that she'd save her worrying and tears for the privacy of their home. Besides, Aegir had enjoined them that the trip should not appear to be an unusual one, lest they draw the notice of one of Mirgul's agents. Breeden carried only a small rucksack on his back, and that was filled almost entirely with food—and was devoid of any possessions beyond spare clothes, rope, a whetstone, and his favorite whittling blade as a backup for the stout workman's blade he wore at his belt. Of course, Breeden's father couldn't help but remark that in the village of Woodfall, a giant's involvement hardly lent to the event a sense of normalcy.

AEGIR CAST off the lines that held his unusual sailboat against the shallow-water pier closest to their family's home. The current was sluggish, but it began turning the boat's nose south almost immediately. Breeden could see that the hull was not very deep, and while the boat turning so easily in the Wood-fall's current had him admiring its nimbleness, it also concerned him that they would have a rough and unpleasant journey once they'd reached the ocean.

The boat itself had a round aspect with a nearly square stern. Attached at the stern was an ingenious removable tiller Breeden saw Aegir putting in place with the ease with which he might fasten his own belt. *Clever!* He looked around more carefully at the boat's contents. The boat was large enough that there was room for the giant to move about, and a good deal of storage space too. Tucked away under the seats were about a dozen long oiled-canvas bags, which Breeden expected would contain extra sails, rope, and material for underway repairs. He also spied a long wooden blade that could have been a tooth extracted from a giant wooden whale. But before he could comment on the oddity and ask Aegir what it was for, he realized that the giant was still allowing the boat to turn south.

"Um, Aegir? Were you planning to turn north?"

The giant smiled again. "No. I thought we'd brave the southern route and pick up a few days on our voyage."

The giant's words upset Breeden, who'd explored the river south on a handful of occasions and had never been able to go more than a few furlongs due to the water's depth, or lack thereof, and the high volume of obstacles in the form of numerous deadfalls. Most notably, there was a massive logjam that had become a permanent part of the river's terrain.

Breeden was silent a moment. "Do you know what lies to the south? Have you traveled this river before?"

Aegir wobbled his head in neither a nod nor a shake. "I have heard tales of what lies to the south, but no, I have never navigated it before. My understanding, however, is that it will get us to where we need to go much faster—a good four or five days faster, in fact. And even if we need to carry the boat around the deadfalls and logjam, we might still gain a few days on the northern route."

Breeden was skeptical. "The first jam has to be two or three furlongs, you know."

Aegir made his odd wobbling-head movement again, which Breeden interpreted to mean he was not yet prepared to agree or disagree.

As they talked, Aegir had been efficiently preparing the boat for sail and had raised a light cloth sail on a taut rope that ran at an angle from the bow of the boat up to the top of the single mast. Breeden had seen these rigs before, though not often, and he'd never sailed on a boat that used one. The light sail proved to be much larger than he'd thought it would—or should—be when it filled with air. And rather than being held flat and taut, as he'd expected, the sail billowed outward from the front of the boat like a cloud pulling them forward. Aegir made no move to raise the mainsail, obviously counting on this odd front sail to do the job of moving them downriver. The wind was coming from just north of west, and Aegir was able to easily maneuver the boat so they reached the first logjam within about a quarter of an hour.

Breeden's mood was sour. And as they approached the jam, he became embarrassed for his father's friend.

"It's okay if we turn around," he offered. "We haven't lost much time at all."

Aegir smiled and steered the boat steadily toward the river's eastern shore. When they had bumped gently against the embankment, he handed a line to Breeden and asked him to secure the boat to a sapling nearby. Breeden stepped ashore and lashed the line as instructed. When he turned back, Aegir had begun to systematically take apart the boat. Or that was how it appeared to Breeden. He lowered the front sail, then removed pins from the base of the mast and lowered the mast as well. Breeden had never seen anything like it. In a matter of minutes, the giant had secured everything to the top of the boat and had attached a stout frame to the boat's stern with two large and heavy wheels close set to one another.

Despite the efficiency with which the giant had disassembled the boat and prepared it for a land voyage, Breeden was still skeptical as to how they would transport this boat two or three furlongs downriver, when the only trail was a footpath hardly wider than a game trail. Aegir answered the unasked question by removing a large axe that, in his hands, would have sent chills down the spine of the stoutest heart. "You can stay here, if you'd like. Or you can join me. I'm not sure how long it will take."

He walked south, along the river's eastern bank, and remained on the game trail that hugged the riverbank.

Breeden opted to follow. After just about the distance he had promised the giant, they reached a point in the path where the logjam ended. Aegir stopped and stood silent for a long moment. Breeden could tell he was thinking, and guessed he was considering the effort that would be required to transport the boat such a distance. The moment lingered. And still Breeden waited for the giant to make some indication he'd reached a decision. Finally Aegir nodded. "It will do. We should be on our way by lunchtime the day after tomorrow at the latest."

Breeden was flabbergasted. The giant was so matter-of-fact. He described accomplishing a feat in two days that Breeden thought would require ten men and a week's work as casually as Breeden's father might give an estimate for a simple repair to a customer.

Aegir wasted no more time chatting with Breeden and began swinging his axe to clear a launch area down to the water's edge. He chose a spot where the embankment had been washed out and the launch would be as smooth as possible. The work went quickly. The giant would crouch down to his knees and swing the axe parallel to the ground, shearing off most saplings and smaller trees in a single blow. Clearing a wide area of all trees for the launch took the giant no more than a handful of minutes.

He paused briefly to survey whether the work would serve, and then he picked up the saplings and smaller trees he'd cut, and he laid them out flat, removing branches as he went and butting them roughly against one another. Breeden thought it looked as though the giant was going to build a raft out of the tiny trees.

When Aegir was done with this last bit of work, a wide area, easily big enough to accommodate the boat, was cleared and covered with a flat makeshift wooden "flooring." He looked at Breeden quizzically. Breeden was unsure what the look signified, but he thought the giant might be offering Breeden a chance to ask a question. So Breeden spoke. "You're going to drag the boat across trees, as you've laid out here, the entire way?"

The giant nodded. "They will roll somewhat and slide a bit, though not as well as the dry-docking logs we use in the north. But they will roll enough that the boat will not simply drag across the wood."

Breeden nodded. "Yes. I've seen my father do this to move a boat a few feet out of the water. But the logs were quite round and smooth, and it was still hard for the men to haul out the boat across them."

Aegir agreed. "Easy it's not. But it will serve. And we should be on our way the day after tomorrow."

And then he resumed the work he'd begun by clearing a small swath to either side of the footpath they had walked. He would clear a few yards and then set the axe down to go back and lay down the saplings on either side of the path. Breeden was amazed at how quickly the giant accomplished so much. And the work on the path went much more quickly than that to prepare the launch.

It was soon sunset at the end of the first day, and the giant had cleared at least a hundred yards in this way. Breeden was hungry, and he guessed the giant had to be ravenous. So he suggested they go back to the boat to eat something. Aegir told Breeden to go back and eat, and indicated he would be along shortly, after doing just a bit more work while the fading sunlight still provided enough illumination to do so. Breeden agreed, wondering what supplies the giant had brought along.

Along with being hungry, Breeden was also very tired. And hot. He was dripping sweat from simply standing in the day's heat and watching the giant work. He couldn't even imagine how hot the giant must be. He walked back toward the boat even less sure of himself—and the voyage he had hardly had a chance to begin—than he had been the night before. It was not a lack of faith in the giant. On the contrary, the giant had more than proven he would be a formidable force in confronting the "dark agents" of an evil god. But Breeden himself had done nothing—the entire day—but watch the giant do everything he could to move the journey forward.

Too, Breeden admired the giant's relentlessness, and his conviction. He had taken on a task that would have foiled

Breeden at the first obstacle—an obstacle Breeden had known his whole life, in fact, and had always assumed to be insurmountable. Not only was it possible to get around the jam, but the giant claimed he would do it in a matter of not much more than two days!

Even knowing that only through muscle and sweat could they overcome this obstacle, and that, according to the giant, time was of such essence that these efforts were necessary due to the great peril facing the world, Breeden still did nothing but watch. Granted, he didn't have an axe, and even if he did, his efforts would have paled alongside those of his father's friend. Regardless, he was humbled by the giant—and at least as much so by his spirit as by his physical might. The giant obviously believed Breeden's father and believed that the threat to the world was real. Further, he must have believed Breeden himself was worth the effort it might take to bring him to his father for the battle ahead.

It was beyond intimidating to Breeden. It was a terrifyingly heavy burden to consider. All of this to bring him along. As if Breeden's meager abilities were worth the effort. As if the powers Breeden didn't understand and couldn't fully control, but seemed more often to take him over and control him, could make a difference in a battle against a god!

Breeden felt unworthy. And as his steps took him near to the landing where they had left the boat, he even considered walking back home. It wasn't far. Another great irony. One bend in the river closer to Ridderzaal, and Breeden could have seen the turrets of the castle.

Thoughts of the castle reminded him that he hadn't had a chance to say goodbye to his mentor, Cedric. Arriving at the boat at last, Breeden leaned against the hull and considered the events that had brought him here.

He regretted not speaking with Cedric, not apologizing for missing the rest of his lessons, and not thanking him for what he had learned so far. But Aegir hadn't given him much opportunity. At least Janelle could tell Cedric what had happened—as best as she understood it, anyway. Breeden had regrets there as well. He had been too evasive with Janelle. He wished he'd had time to confide in her fully before he left. His words had sounded so flat and feeble to his own ears. But Janelle had been in no condition to catch on to what he wasn't telling her. She was too sad and confused and uncertain to pick up on what she normally would have.

Then he thought of how sad his parents had been at his departure, of how difficult saying goodbye to his mother had been. He considered the fact that he was abandoning the search for Kestrel. And that the king was dead. It was overwhelming. It felt as though Breeden's whole world were crashing about him. How could he leave everyone while all of those things were going on? And all because a giant he had met only once before in his life had told his parents he was needed. How could it be? How was there any chance he could actually help? How badly did it speak of their chances that they were hoping to rely on him to help save the world? The world? Him?

How much better a choice Laudan would have been! Laudan could have been swinging an axe alongside the giant. He couldn't have matched the giant physically, of course, but then if any human could come close, Laudan would have to be the only one Breeden knew. Or Kestrel. Kestrel was a hunter, a tracker, a scout. And he was much cleverer than Breeden. He would have been a far better companion for the giant than Breeden. Even Oskar, who had demonstrated time and again his appreciation of the subtleties of politics and human nature, would have been a better choice than him.

Unwilling to entertain the thoughts that jumbled around in his head any longer, Breeden realized he needed to occupy himself. He looked for something to cook with, rummaging through the many canvas bags within the boat.

He found a sack of potatoes, another of carrots, and a hard block of something like bacon among the giant's store of food-stuffs. And in an adjacent sack, he found a set of enormous cookware, which for some inexplicable reason made him smile in amusement. There was a stock pot in which Breeden could nearly have taken a bath! Chuckling to himself, Breeden kept looking for a pot of a more manageable size. The smallest pot still looked huge to Breeden and made him realize that he likely needed to prepare more carrots and potatoes than he'd originally estimated.

It was more than an hour before Breeden had sufficient water, drawn from the river in multiple trips using a large wooden bowl, boiling on a makeshift campfire. And it was another hour after that before Breeden had a fish stew ready to eat. Breeden was now ravenous. And he wondered how the giant could possibly still be working. The moon had been low on the horizon as night came on, and had disappeared a few minutes earlier. And the stars were hardly bright enough for the giant to follow the path. With the moon gone, Breeden became more and more concerned as the minutes slipped away. And it was nearly half an hour before he felt the thump of the giant's approaching footsteps. Or so he hoped that was the source of the noise.

Breeden was making a show of sharpening his workman's knife when the giant stepped into the firelight. And at sight of the giant, he allowed a low sigh to escape his lips. "I wasn't sure you weren't going to work through the night!" Breeden tried to make his voice light and remove all trace of urgency and fear.

Aegir appeared to understand the situation, and he apologized. "Young master, I am very sorry to have left you so long. I became somewhat caught up in my work. I will not let it happen again."

Breeden was grateful for the words, though ashamed at the same time for being so. "It's okay. I had my knife. And we're really not all that far from my home. If I had to, I could have swum across the river. I made you some stew. I . . . I've already eaten. So you can have as much as you like."

"Thank you, Breeden. A hearty meal is just what I need to restore my strength. It will be an early morning for me, I'm afraid. But before I eat . . ."

The giant surprised Breeden then by walking into the river and dunking his head to his shoulders. His head looked like that of an aurochs as it rose from the river, massive, wet and messy. Water poured down his body. He lowered his face to the water and took a long draught. And another. Then he scooped up a handful of sand and gravel from the river's edge and used it to scrub his hands and arms from his fingers to his elbows. He dunked his arms again to rinse off the sand and then stepped back up onto the riverbank.

"Much better. Now I am suitable company for dinner!" He smiled and reached into the boat, removing a large, heavy towel and wiping his hands and arms dry before giving his head a quick pass as well.

"Better to leave my head mostly wet. It will cool me down faster."

Aegir forwent using a bowl and ate the stew straight from the cooking pot with the ladle. "Delicious. Thank you." And after another bite: "The bacon was a good touch with the fish." And a few moments later: "I have a packet of spices somewhere in the bag of utensils. No offense, mind you, but by the quality of the stew, I judge you likely know their use."

Breeden was pleased—and his mother would have been too. The giant liked his cooking.

In a matter of moments, the entire pot was empty, and the giant had tipped it upside down to get the last few drops into his mouth. "Marvelous. Thank you again."

Seeing how quickly the giant had finished, Breeden felt

bad. "I'm sorry if I didn't cook enough. I've never prepared food for someone as big as you are."

"Oh, no. That was plenty. Really. Just right." Aegir grabbed a woolen blanket from the boat that would have served as a tent for Breeden. And without further ado, and with only a deeply rumbled "Thank you again for supper," the giant lay down in some coarse grass at the river's edge, rolled over, and quickly fell asleep.

Breeden was disappointed. He'd imagined that he would be listening to Aegir's wonderful tales of home by firelight each night of the voyage. But Aegir hardly seemed the same person he had met that night nearly a year before. Or *giant*, Breeden mused, wondering whether it was proper to call a giant a *person*!

In any event, he knew the giant must be exhausted, and he wanted to be understanding. But he couldn't help but feel sorry for himself. He was lonely. He missed his mother and father. His missed the smell of his father's pipe. Once again he considered walking, or swimming, home. But if he truly were needed, as the giant was confident he was, then he'd never be able to look himself in the mirror. And he'd never consider himself worthy of hearing another of the giant's tales again.

Breeden rose from his seat by the fire, still hot and nicely blazing from his efforts, and he began cleaning up the cookware. When he had everything ready to go for breakfast, he thought of one other thing he wanted to do, and he set to it. It would be another hour yet before he finished that task and was ready for sleep. The work exhausted him—more than he'd thought it would.

He finished up, grabbed his bedroll from the bottom of his pack, and prepared a bed for himself within two arm lengths of the sleeping giant. Despite his nervousness, homesickness, and outright fear, he fell asleep quickly.

34

SEARCH

Janelle literally cried herself to sleep the night Breeden said goodbye. She didn't understand why he had to go, but she understood that he and his parents had believed it was important. So she had accepted it. What else could she do?

But would her life ever be the same again? Breeden and the princess had both abandoned her, and with the latter's rise to queen, all hopes Janelle had had to rise above her station were lost. A long tenure with the princess as her handmaiden had been the one chance Janelle had to become more than a merchant's daughter. Had the king still been alive, Janelle might have returned with the princess to Arlon after they completed their studies with the monks. But because Lorelei would become queen so soon, Janelle never had the chance to become indispensable to her.

JANELLE SLEPT in late the next morning. Not uncharacteristically, her mother had had to wake her. But Janelle was even more difficult to rouse than usual. There was nothing for her to do. No classes with Cedric. The princess was leaving—and Janelle had officially been dismissed from helping her any further only the day before. Breeden and Kestrel were gone. Kestrel! It hit her then: she could find out what had happened to Kestrel!

Kestrel had been abandoned, just as she had been. Worse, nobody was there to notice or even care that he was missing.

His parents were back in Pretania. Breeden was gone. Laudan was distracted and unlikely to be of much help. And Derek didn't care. In fact, he was probably pleased Kestrel was gone. Could he have had anything to do with the disappearance? Now that she thought about it, the two had always been at odds. And Derek seemed to be the kind of boy who might torture small animals. Maybe it had been Derek! But no, if it had been Derek, why would the princess's minister have tried to cover up her friend's disappearance?

She couldn't focus, and she realized that in her tattered emotional state, she distrusted everyone.

The only other person Janelle thought of who might be able to assist her was Oskar. He was smart and knew his way around the city. And he had also become friendly with nearly everyone who ran the castle. Maybe one of them had seen something. She would start at the bakery, since Oskar was frequently known to show up to class with a heel of bread or something sweeter he had charmed off the girls who worked the ovens.

With renewed purpose, Janelle got out of her bed.

SHE WAS HEADING past the kitchen to ask for Oskar at the bakery when she saw something that caught her eye. She wasn't sure why the sight was remarkable, but there were two men-at-arms, in the princess's livery, standing as if on duty and awaiting a platter of food from one of the cooks. Something about their carriage was odd. It was as if they were uncomfortable standing there. No, that was not quite it. It was as if they were trying to be nonchalant. That was it.

She stopping walking and decided she would watch them for a moment to see if she might confirm her suspicions or chalk them up to being overly eager to see something that wasn't there. The platter was filled. One guard took the tray, and the other walked beside him. They were headed in the direction of the princess's quarters—as Janelle would have expected. Nothing unusual there. So what was bothering her? That guards were picking up food for someone, and it wasn't a servant doing so? Yes, that could be it. So where were they taking the food? To the princess? Perhaps she feared being poisoned now that she was succeeding to the throne. But what if they were taking the food to Kestrel?

She decided to follow them and ran down the hall toward the kitchen where she had seen them last. She asked one of the scullions which direction they had taken, and they confirmed that the guards had gone through a side door that led toward the princess's wing and tower. She slowed down her pace then and walked through the door they'd taken. The hallway was empty.

She ran ahead again in a burst and then decided she would just pretend she was in a hurry and continue to run past them should she overtake them. She picked up her pace again and continued—straight on toward the stairwell that would take her back up to the main sitting room at the base of the princess's tower. But she never overtook them. She picked up her pace yet again and ran straight up the stairs and into the sitting room.

A startled page was about to walk down the stairs, and she

stopped him. "Did you see two guards come out of this stairwell?"

He looked afraid not to answer and responded quickly, probably thinking she was someone with the authority to ask him such a question. Thankfully, he was not experienced enough to recognize that she was a commoner. "No, ma'am. N-nobody came up the stairs. Just you."

Janelle stood where she was and allowed herself a moment to catch her breath. How could they have lost her? Had they not come up the stairs? They must not have. So where had they gone? Where had they taken the food?

She would have to retrace her steps. So she headed back to the kitchen.

THERE WERE a handful of doors and passages leading from the hallway the men had taken. And Janelle took a few moments to determine that all but two were storage rooms, some full, and one empty. The two passages that did not lead to storage rooms were stairways. One was a narrow stairwell leading up to a small chamber off the keep's main dining hall. Hmm. Maybe the guards had taken the food up to the dining hall. Perhaps some event was occurring there, or they were bringing food to the princess herself, eating in the Great Hall.

But something told Janelle that the guards had not taken this stairway either. She returned, fear grabbing ahold of her heart, to the last door the guards could have taken. She had opened it earlier, but the darkness it exposed had prompted her to investigate the others first. She grabbed a torch from a bracket on the wall and opened the door to reveal an unlit stairwell leading down into the cellars—and hopefully the dungeons below.

She remembered the tales the boys had shared of their adventures in the tunnels below the castle, of how they had discovered an old armory, of rooms full of ancient furniture and artifacts, and of the countless empty rooms they found more often than not. She tried to take heart in the fact that they had never spoken of finding the entrance to the dungeons themselves—which were supposed to be located underneath the storage cellars. But the fear would not let go, and it continued to grow as she descended the ancient stone steps.

The stairs ended at a small landing with a door to either side, and a hallway ahead. Janelle opted for the hallway and continued ahead, not sure what she was looking for, but hoping she would recognize it when she saw it. Then she thought she heard a voice—coming from ahead of her. She panicked, swung the torch around her from side to side, and tore open the door to her right, jumping inside and closing it quietly behind her. She could only pray that whoever was coming didn't notice her light coming from beneath the door. She held her breath and listened, waiting to hear if the voices came closer. They did, and she soon heard the sounds of jingling harness accompanying the voices. Armor, she thought. The voices were just outside her door. They had come up so quickly! But just as quickly, they had passed, moving down the hallway from the direction she had come from herself. She wondered if it was the two guards she had seen earlier.

She waited a little longer as her heart slowed in its racing, and the pumping blood ceased pounding in her wrists and temples. She carefully opened the door and stepped out into the hallway again. This time, she felt better at least knowing she was heading in the right direction. And she felt somewhat safer knowing there was probably a good chance those two guards might be the only ones down here.

She turned the corner and walked another twenty yards before she came to the next door. She had decided she would check every door from here on, since she knew the guards had come from this direction. The first room was small and absent any furniture but for a single empty bookcase in the center of the room.

The next was devoid of even a single item. So, on to the next. And the next. And so on for another dozen rooms. Then she came upon a door that was barred from the outside. It was the first she had seen like it. And there was a small window just above her eye level, with tiny metal bars in the shape of a cross. She tried to hold up the torch to see into the room, but even standing on her tiptoes, she could see only darkness.

Unsure, she knocked on the door and whispered, "Kestrel?"

She heard something move inside the room, and she had to step back from the door. The hair on the back of her neck was tingling. But she had come here for a reason, and she couldn't let her fear keep her from finding her friend. "Kestrel, is that you?"

A muffled "Janelle?" came back to her through the door's window.

"Yes! Yes, it's me!"

"What in Mirgul's darkest pit are you doing down here?"

"I'm here to find you."

Janelle almost laughed when she heard her friend's next words, from out of the darkness. "Enough of the finding. Let's see if you can move along to the rescuing. Can you open the door?"

Janelle did as he had bade her. With all of her strength, she managed to lift the heavy oaken plank off the brackets. Then she released the catch and pulled on the handle. The door swung open almost silently on well-oiled hinges. Sitting against the back wall was her friend, looking all the more pitiful from the fitful flickering of her torch, which had begun to gutter.

His wrists were bound one to each end of a stout wooden board. The same for his ankles. And he was shivering. He looked so uncomfortable!

She didn't know how to release him. "What do I do?"

"Hold up the torch."

She did as instructed, and he examined the mechanism on either end of the board at his wrists. "As I thought—and just as the release operates on the stocks at my feet—though the design prevented me from opening them. There is a latch mechanism on each end. Both have to be released at the same time. Do you see right there?" He gestured with his nose, pointing it at a conspicuous metal bump on top of the mechanism.

She saw it and set the torch on the floor in such a way that it still cast a little light where she was working. She tried to push and pull the little metal knob whichever way she could. It hurt to push against the metal. She discovered that the bump would only move one way—away from the center of the stock. But it required mashing her fingertips in the process to apply sufficient force. She bit her lip, and as Kestrel had predicted, when she pushed both bumps outward from the center simultaneously, the manacles on each wrist fell away.

Kestrel rubbed each wrist for some time before releasing his ankles using the same technique, commenting as he did so.

"Clever. They made the stocks for the feet a good three hands farther apart than the ones for the wrists. So there'd be no way you could release the one on your feet yourself: your hands couldn't possibly work both releases at the same time.

"So how did you find me, anyway?"

"I followed the guards who were bringing you your meal."

Kestrel frowned. "I don't know how long I've been down here but I haven't eaten—or had anything to drink. Nobody brought me any food."

"That doesn't make any sense." At the moment, Janelle knew she wasn't fully registering what he was saying, but she was sure that the torch in her hands might not last long enough to see them out of the cellars.

Despite her excitement at having found—and now at least

partly rescued—her friend, Janelle's fear had returned. And she was eager to leave. "So where do we go now?"

He rubbed his wrists again and then urged her forward by placing his hand at the small of her back. "Out the door. And go right. If you'd like, I can take the torch, and we'll be able to go more quickly."

As much as Janelle didn't want to be lost in the dark without a torch, she handed it over immediately.

He spoke to her calmly, as if she was the one who needed to be comforted. "Okay, now hold my hand, and I'll get us out of here." She felt Kestrel's body shudder and realized that he was shivering. He must have been so cold sitting down here on this cruel stone floor for the last few days!

They picked up their pace and were soon moving at a three-quarter run. Despite the running, it seemed Kestrel couldn't wait to begin asking her questions. "So, what happened when I disappeared? Who knows I'm gone? And how in blazes did you find me down here?" He asked the questions one after another and didn't slow down to give her the breath to respond.

She tried, stumblingly, to answer as she ran, but the effort was difficult. "The p-p-princess's minister told everyone you'd been c-called home by your father."

Kestrel appeared to realize she wouldn't be able to talk while she ran, and he interjected. "No matter. We'll have time to talk about it when we get out of here. Just one thing more it would help me to know: is anyone else looking for me?"

"N-no. J-j-just Oskar and me."

Janelle saw a puzzled look cross her friend's face, but then he seemed to steel himself, and he picked up their pace.

They wended their way in the darkness for what felt an eternity to Janelle, and in the opposite direction from where she had come. Turn after turn, stairways up and stairways down. The torch held on, guttering more and more fitfully but still providing enough light for them to run. It was the torch that told Janelle they hadn't been running for as long as it seemed. If as much time had passed as she imagined, the torch would have been out long ago.

And then Janelle saw light ahead. At the top of a narrow staircase, there was a small window. She nearly let go of Kestrel's hand in her desire to run toward the window, but Kestrel held her hand firmly, and he led her directly toward it anyway.

Outside the window was a thick hedge that blocked the window's view entirely, but that did allow light to filter through its tightly woven branches. Janelle couldn't tell where they were, in what part of the castle. But Kestrel continued to move as if he knew the way by heart.

"Not much farther." Janelle thought his voice sounded frantic. And she wondered if he was just managing to hold himself together. But then, a moment later, they came to a small door unlike any she had seen before. It was banded entirely in iron, with no wood showing. Above the door were two thick chains attached to two large iron rings bolted onto a heavy wooden timber that supported a massive block of stone.

Kestrel caught her examining the mechanism and replied briefly, "You break the timber, or remove it, and the block falls, sealing the entrance against an attacking enemy. Many a castle has been taken by an improperly defended postern door. This castle was obviously built by someone who had learned that lesson."

And then he was lifting an iron bar and releasing the latch on the door and pushing it outward. Janelle was surprised to see that the door opened up at the rear of the monastery. She assumed they would be exiting at the back of the main keep itself. But then she had been so turned around in the tunnels, she couldn't have rightly said where they would come out.

Kestrel stood in the doorway a moment and peered out from its shelter to either side, holding himself at the shallowest angle possible to avoid notice. "It's clear. Follow me. QUICKLY!"

And run she did. She began to outpace Kestrel once she determined that he was heading for one of the small shade gardens the monks maintained. They reached it moments later, and Kestrel immediately crouched down and looked back, scanning all directions to see if anyone had followed. Janelle tried to follow his eyes. Along the roofline. Down the narrow path that ran alongside the monastery. And lastly, over by the barracks, a small corner of which was visible through the dense foliage that formed the shade garden where they had stopped.

"I didn't see anyone. Hopefully, we made it unobserved. I have to get out of here. Damn, I wish I had time to talk with Cedric. But it's just too risky. I have to go."

Janelle was concerned. She'd never seen Kestrel so rattled before. And she didn't think it was his health or a side effect of his captivity. He looked scared. And she couldn't imagine what might have scared him so. "What happened, anyway, Kestrel?"

He looked at her, his eyes half-wild and showing an unnatural amount of white. "No. No, you shouldn't know. If you know, then they'll come after you as well. No. It's better I leave and take it with me. You knowing won't do any good."

Janelle was a little frightened to hear him talk this way. While he was almost still a boy, he had never demonstrated anything but courage—at least that she had seen. This was a new side of him. And without knowing why he was so frightened, she couldn't decide what to think about it.

"Maybe we should find Cedric, then, Kestrel? You said yourself you wished you could talk to him. Why not? I could go get him and bring him here."

He considered for a moment. "No. That won't work. They'll just wonder at your calling him away, especially with him so busy and all. And they'll have him followed. They are probably already having him followed, in fact. He's a threat to them and their plans."

Janelle was getting frustrated that she didn't know what Kestrel knew. "Why won't you tell me what happened?" She had raised her voice without meaning to, and Kestrel froze, held his finger to his lips, and crouched down next to a weeping ash to scan the surroundings. A branch broke behind them. Kestrel spun about, reaching for a dagger at his hip that wasn't there.

"No weapon and no supplies . . . I'm a walking dead man." He muttered the words just above hearing.

"And why would that be, young Starkad?" The voice came from the tree above him. Kestrel bolted. But the man in the tree was faster than thought and leapt to the ground to bar Kestrel's way.

"Calm, Starkad. An honest man has nothing to fear from the castle's hunt master."

Kestrel froze again and looked like nothing other than a ferret backed into a corner. His eyes scanned the area around him, and he appeared to be looking for a way to escape.

"Enough!" The hunt master barked the command like a sergeant-at-arms to a green recruit. "You will stop seeking escape, Kestrel Starkad, and you will answer my questions. If you do not, then you will be brought before the master-at-arms, that he may divine your guilt or innocence. Do you understand me? Good. I see that you realize you cannot escape me." The half-elf's words were matter-of-fact. There was no false modesty in his claim that Kestrel could not escape. To Janelle, it seemed a statement both the boy and man accepted as simple truth.

Kestrel nodded finally, resigned at last, or so it appeared to Janelle, to his own death.

The hunt master did not relent. "Tell me your story,

Starkad. Why were you running from the postern? Who are you running from, and what have you done?"

Janelle could see that Kestrel was struggling to answer. But she couldn't tell whether he was unwilling or just did not know how to begin. She suspected it was some combination of both.

He began quietly and had to clear his throat several times. The hunt master seemed to realize the acuteness of Kestrel's condition and threw him a skin of water. Kestrel took a small draught before he began. "Some days ago . . . I'm not sure how many, I'm afraid, but it was after the king's death, and after his memorial service at the cathedral. I was in the cellars beneath the princess's tower. I'd been there the day before too, exploring and seeing what there was to see—and, well, in this case, to hear.

"The day before, I had heard just the smallest bit of a conversation, and it had gotten me thinking about things. I didn't hear enough that I felt comfortable saying anything to anyone about it. As Cedric would say, 'if you wish to tell a half-heard tale, find yourself a fool.' So I kept it to myself. But it was bothering me something fierce. So I had to go back to listen again, and see if I couldn't hear more, to help me understand if I'd heard right the first time.

"Well, that afternoon, I waited a good long time, and in the same place I'd chanced to overhear the conversation the day before. But the wait paid off."

Janelle could see that Kestrel was having difficulty getting it out. She thought he wanted to build up the story as much as he could to avoid telling the hard part. She recognized this when she saw it, because she knew she was guilty of doing the same herself.

But then Kestrel seemed to tire of carrying the burden of it and just blurted it out. "They've killed the king—and worse is coming." While Janelle gasped and the hunt master's eyes narrowed, she could see that Kestrel was still holding something back. Even through his shivering and his nervousness, Janelle could see that. Then it came.

"It was Princess Lorelei."

Janelle's world finally crashed then. The king's death and Breeden's departure had brought her up to the edge. Kestrel's rescue had begun to bring her back. But even the suspicion that the princess could have been involved in her own father's death was too much for her to bear. She knew the princess. She knew she was emotional and prone to fits of temper. All of that was true. And she knew that she and her father didn't always see things the same way. But this?

Janelle ears rang, and darkness crept in from the sides of her vision. She reached out to a nearby sapling to steady herself and only came out of her daze slowly, for a long moment unaware of what was transpiring around her except on the most basic level.

Aelric continued to look Kestrel in the eyes. And it was unclear to Janelle what he might be thinking—whether he was upset, concerned, or indifferent. His elven composure masked any outward emotion. Then he began to ask questions.

"What else did you hear? You said worse is coming. How could anything be worse than killing one's father?"

Kestrel's shivers were becoming worse. He was like the last oak leaf of autumn, clinging to a branch and fluttering in the wind. With each brush of its touch, the light wind seemed enough to fill him with ice. His teeth chattered when he answered the half-elven hunter. "They plan to rule all the lands of Erda. An army is coming. And the army bears magics that will allow them to defeat even the elves and the dwarves."

Aelric's eyes tightened almost imperceptibly at mention of the elves, but he wasn't going to let Kestrel off the hook. "What else did you hear, Starkad?"

Kestrel went into a spasm of shaking so intense Janelle feared for his health. Tears swelled in her eyes. The poor boy!

And it was clear to her then that he was still a boy. Even if a capable hunter, tactician, and budding diplomat, he was still a boy. And right now he was a boy who had found himself caught up in things that would make grown men blanch. On top of that, he appeared to have picked up a fever from his stay in the dungeons.

As the shaking subsided once again, Kestrel spoke one more time. "They are in league with Mirgul."

It was almost as if Aelric expected the words, as if he had been waiting for Kestrel to speak them. He did not even nod his head in acknowledgment, but upon hearing Kestrel's words, he became a blur of efficiency.

"Miss Fuller, do not go home. We must leave in all haste. On the road, you will be able to write your parents a note explaining that you had to leave. For now, stay here with Kestrel, and feed him these leaves." He had been fishing around in a pouch at his waist and removed a small bag of dried leaves. "They will quell his tremors, and if he has a fever, they will help keep that down as well. Move back among the bushes there." He gestured with his hand toward a thick copse of rhododendrons. "Beneath the branches, you will find more than enough room to be comfortable. I will be back in no more than one bell. Do not be seen."

And then he was gone, disappearing into the foliage at the back of the garden and leaving at the opposite end from which they had come. Janelle did as he told her and ushered the rapidly weakening Kestrel into the bushes. They waited for no more than ten minutes before the hunt master returned, bearing three packs and a long bow with two quivers. Janelle noted that he also bore a sword strapped across his back, beneath his high pack.

Kestrel's condition had improved somewhat in the intervening minutes, and he was able to function again on his own. But Janelle could see that the run from the dungeon had taken its toll on him. She feared he wasn't up for much more. But with only a "Let's go!" Aelric gestured for them to follow him—away from the castle proper once again and toward the barracks and the keep's inner wall.

When they were parallel to the barracks, they reached a pergola where Aelric swiftly shimmied up one of the columns, packs, bow, quivers, and all, as if he were a cat climbing a stair. He reached down to assist Janelle. And Kestrel, reading the situation properly, moved to provide a base for Janelle to stand on so she could reach the hunt master's outstretched hand. Janelle accepted the help, though she was concerned Kestrel might not be able to follow after her. Fortunately, a strong pull from the hunt master was sufficient to help Kestrel up as well.

In moments, they had all climbed the pergola and jumped the short span to the keep's inner wall—about the height of two men standing on each other's shoulders. They were now moving through the city's southwest quarter, where most of the well-to-do merchants and minor nobles lived.

No one was about in this quarter of the city, and Aelric maintained their pace in a hurried, but not frantic, manner.

There was no exit at the south end of the city, and the outer wall was five times the height of the inner. So they moved east toward the main gate. They could only hope that Kestrel's absence had not yet been noted.

Janelle knew that it was through this gate that Breeden entered the city proper every morning, and through which he returned every night. She knew also that he was probably well along on a journey about which she didn't have enough details to judge whether or not he was in danger. Though she had sensed he believed himself to be.

As they approached the gate, a wealthy woman in a dark crimson cloak emerged from the ornately carved wooden door of her city manse, which rose four stories into the dusky sky above the streets. The woman appeared disdainful of the obvious haste Janelle, Aelric, and Kestrel were exhibiting, and she halted in her tracks—many yards away and clearly not in any danger of intersecting their path—to allow them the time and space to continue on their way.

Janelle frowned. How rude! That woman had no idea that Janelle had been, but days before, the chief handmaiden of the woman who would be queen of Hyrde. She wished she had the time to stop and tell her as much. Born a commoner, Janelle would never understand how some people could believe themselves better than one not born into a family of means. But Aelric kept her moving forward, and soon she was through the gate and turning south to move beyond the protection of Ridderzaal's outer wall.

From there the journey became a blur of introspection for Janelle. She followed Aelric's lead but ceased even to notice the details of the ground at her feet, or the landscape around her. The leagues passed. Trees and fields. Night fell, and the world became briefly darker. Janelle assumed they would stop soon. But the sky lightened again after dusk. A full moon rose, and the sky became awash with a thick, cloudy band of stars. More leagues passed, and still they trekked through the night, guided by Aelric's abilities. Hours later Aelric indicated it was past midnight, and they stopped for the night's rest.

Janelle was numb from exhaustion. She had never exerted herself so strenuously as she had done that night. And she had never begun a voyage so unprepared, and so wrought with fear and uncertainty. Her mind was close to empty when Aelric handed her a chunk of hardtack and spoke the simple words "You must eat."

She hardly noticed that Kestrel had laid out her bedroll and guided her to sit upon it. She didn't hear a word her friend shared with the castle's hunt master. She ate the hardtack, and then the cheese, and then drank the tea they fed her. She lay down when they bade her do so. And despite the vortex of thoughts threatening to overwhelm her mind, she remained calm and unconcerned by the events around her, and she found sleep quickly. Her last memories of the evening were of stars so bright they looked like enchanted diamonds cast into the sky. And the last words she heard were of Aelric speaking to Kestrel of the elven queen.

35

SQUIRE LOST

Laudan was torn. Kestrel had been missing for days. He couldn't find Breeden or Janelle anywhere. And the princess would be heading back to Arlon the next day. Cedric had still not returned to teach Derek, Oskar, and himself. And technically, Cedric's classes were the last obstacle to Laudan becoming a knight. But Laudan was ready to be done with classes. And he was past done with Cedric's righteousness.

Laudan set down the oiled rag he was using to rub the rust from his chain mail shirt. He was sitting at a low table in the barracks' mess, somewhat hunched over due to his height. He looked around then, as if to make sure he was alone with his thoughts. The barracks was empty, and he leaned forward onto the table with a heavy sigh.

The king's death had put everything on hold.

Worse, it meant he wouldn't have a chance to get to know the princess before she became queen. She was the most beautiful girl he'd ever seen. And that she knew he existed, and had even asked questions about him, made his stomach churn whenever he let himself think of it. How could he arrange to go with her? And if he couldn't . . . ? How could he win her heart if he were given no chance to do so?

It wasn't about becoming king. That was the last thing he cared about. His father and brother would be much better kings than he ever would. It was about the girl named Lorelei who had stolen his heart from his first sight of her.

She was all he could think about. Before classes had been interrupted by the king's death, it had been all he could do to concentrate. Cedric and his peers may have thought him incapable of learning, he thought wryly. But the truth was he simply couldn't keep his mind on history, politics, or religion. He could think only of the beautiful young girl with eyes the color of a pale morning sky, and hair that would bring shame to spun gold.

Drill and the tactics of warfare had been an exception and a welcome diversion. His curiosity and his hunger to master the arts of war were among the few things that could distract him from his all-consuming thoughts of the princess. And the physical aspects of training helped him release his pent-up energy.

He loved swordplay, loved working with horses, loved the exercises where he was asked to lead the other squires in mock battles against one another. It was one area where he truly excelled. He was so much better than his peers—and even many of his superiors—at nearly all aspects of war that he was constantly asked to lead. That suited him fine. Since he had a much harder time as a follower.

When he was not in charge, he would chomp at the bit to offer the "squire captain" of the moment advice on everything from how to draw his sword, to how to offer mercy to his defeated foes. He would, without even realizing it, issue orders in the heat of the moment. He would rush to the hottest points of a mock battle. And wherever he went, his decisions were good—or the effect of his presence was enough to shore up a weak point in a defense.

It was instinctive for him. And he never felt so alive, and so in charge of his own life, as he did when he was leading others. The rest of his life was his father's to dictate. Or his sergeant-at-arms's. Or Cedric's. But when he was drilling, he was in his element.

So . . . he needed to be knighted as soon as possible. But he couldn't figure out how to manage it. He thought about asking Lorelei to knight him and his stomach turned over at even the thought of it. He tried to smile, but doing so made him lose his concentration. His face flushed with heat, and sweat broke out on his forearms. That plan wouldn't work, he realized. His body would betray him long before he succeeded. There had to be another way. But how? And who else had the power to help him?

It occurred to him that he would normally talk to Kestrel about something like this. Where was Kestrel, anyway? He should have heard something from him by now. But he couldn't let himself think about it. If he dwelled on the possibilities, he would make himself crazy. And there was nothing he could do to help his friend, in any event, since he didn't even know where he was. Kestrel was all right. Some part of him knew the boy would weather whatever storm might have come his way. So, who else could help him, then?

Cedric? He was too busy with the affairs of the princess. Knight-Captain Jenlyns? He had returned to Arlon weeks ago. And how willing would he be to help the boy he'd just chastised for hurting another squire, anyway?

The door to the sleeping quarters of the barracks opened and snapped Laudan out of his moment's reverie. He picked up the rag again and resumed his work. He tried to be casual about glancing over his shoulder at the sergeant walking toward him between the beds of the barracks' long, narrow sleeping quarters.

The sergeant met his eyes and smiled. "Polishing your mail

in the barracks while the weather is trying to decide whether to be spring or full summer, eh? That's not like you, Marchant. You should be outside! I'm sure I can find someone willing to spar with you. Well, maybe not, at that!" And he laughed good-naturedly at his own jest.

Laudan cracked a smile but didn't know how to respond. So he shrugged his shoulders at the sergeant's remark.

"What is it, lad? Thinking of Kestrel? Something tells me he's fine—wherever he is. That boy could squirm his way out of a locked iron maiden! Come on, lad. You know that!"

Laudan nodded. "I do. No, I'm not thinking of Kestrel. Well, not much, anyway. I'm just ready to move on, I guess. The waiting is killing me. I think I'm going to run off to Arlon and beg to be made a knight at once." Laudan laughed, as if trying to pass off his comment as a joke, even though it was at the very heart of what was bothering him.

The sergeant pulled out the chair next to Laudan and pushed it far back from the table so there was a good five feet between them when he sat down and faced him.

"Well, now. I can see that, certainly. Nothing worse in the army, nor more commonplace, I'm afraid, than sitting around with naught to do."

Laudan felt comfortable with the sergeant. Maybe he could chance his question with him. In what he knew was a rare moment for himself, Laudan bolstered his courage and asked, "Could I? Could I become a knight now? Or do I really have to wait until summer's end, when the other squires are knighted?"

The sergeant gave him an appraising look, as if trying to judge his earnestness. He scratched his day's growth of whiskers in thought. "Well, now. If it were anyone else—'cept maybe Ranald—I'd have talked you out of the thought alto-gether and just told you to be patient. But frankly, there's little left for you to learn from me at this point. Only problem I see, really, is finding someone with the authority to knight you. Cap'n Jenlyn's not around. The king's gone and died—God rest his soul. Course, your father could knight you. But I don't know as you can convince him to come up here to do it. And the old king didn't like his men to be knighted by anyone but through his own hand—wanted them loyal to Hyrde first. And then there's the princess. But I suppose she isn't quite queen yet."

Laudan felt the familiar gnawing at his stomach. The sergeant had confirmed what he had suspected all along. "What about Cedric?" The question surprised even himself when Laudan realized he'd given it voice. But then it grew a certain appeal when he'd heard it out loud. Why hadn't he thought of that before? Cedric had been a knight-general! He wondered whether it would be possible.

The sergeant looked confused. "Hmph. I don't know what to think about that one. Sure, he was knight-general at one point. And he still holds the title as an honorary thing. But folks might think it odd you were knighted outside of protocol. You could write to Cap'n Jenlyns and see what he says. Course, by the time you hear back, you'll already be knighted by his own hand!" He laughed again, more of a rough bark. "I guess, all told, the best thing to do is just hold tight. You'll be a knight for sure in two months. What's the rush, anyway? It's got to be more than simple boredom, eh?"

Laudan didn't answer. He was distracted as it was, and he pretended to be so distracted as not to have heard the question. He was grateful the sergeant didn't ask again. "I think I'll talk with Cedric anyway. Maybe he'll be able to think of something we couldn't."

At that, Sergeant Hewrey stood up and pushed the chair back into place. "Oh, I'm sure of that, lad. Cedric may be too old to swing a sword—though I'm not so sure even of that—but I'd wager he could think us both under the table. Ha!" He paused a moment before he left, to rest his hand on Laudan's shoulder. "Whatever it is, son, I hope you come out of it better than Kestrel did, and better than the king. Don't rush into something that's going to get you killed too quickly. I'm looking forward to fighting alongside you someday. Don't deny me that. You hear?" He gave Laudan a final slap on the back of the shoulder and walked back the way he'd come. His heavy boots scuffed the ground as he went, and Laudan sat where he was until the sound passed from hearing.

Laudan hardly noticed that he'd stopped sweating and the heat had gone from his face. He took a deep breath and stood from the table. There had to be something Cedric could do.

LAUDAN HAD NEVER SEEN Cedric so busy. He had tracked him down by talking with one of the girls Kestrel had tumbled back in the autumn. Like most girls Kestrel had been with, she was no less infatuated with the boy than she had been before they'd gotten together. Laudan didn't know anyone else who could manage to do that.

This particular girl's name was Mairwen, and she was able to quickly determine where Cedric could be found. He had taken over one of the small research libraries in the tower opposite the one occupied by the princess and her retinue. The room was scattered with scrolls, missives, and other documents.

Laudan stood in the doorway for a moment and watched his mentor making hashes on a waxed tablet, picking up his quill and making a notation on a piece of parchment, and then flattening the wax and starting over again. After three or four such notations, Laudan knocked on the open door to get the man's attention.

Cedric looked up briefly, then down again to finish whatever calculation he'd just begun. "What is it, then, Laudan?" The cleric continued working as he spoke.

Laudan had no idea what Cedric could be doing. Didn't the old cleric have people to keep track of numbers? And what was it about the princess leaving that required such involved planning? As Laudan wondered how to ask for what he needed, Cedric's scribbling quickened, and he appeared to become more and more agitated.

"By the One God, boy! Out with it! What is it you need?"

Put on the spot as he was, Laudan froze up even more. "I ... That is ..."

And then Cedric exploded—something Laudan had never seen him do. "Laudan Marchant, if you do not state your business immediately, I will call the guards to remove you. These are not trifling times. And I can't be interrupted by such as those who cannot speak their minds. If you have business with me, state it now, or LEAVE!"

The anger in Cedric's voice had shifted from annoyance into something more like a command issued in battle. And it had its desired effect, putting Laudan into a place where he was a soldier speaking to a superior officer. "Sir, I wish to be knighted as soon as possible. I don't wish to wait until summer's end."

"Absolutely not." The answer, and the speed with which it was delivered, surprised Laudan.

"But—"

"What are your reasons, Laudan? To follow the princess to Arlon? To become her protector? I am not unaware of your infatuation with the princess. But your skills would be wasted on such a job, and your proximity to the woman who will be our queen would eventually make you see her as everyone else does. Once you realize what a mistake you've made, it will already be too late. You will have proven yourself to her, and to her advisers, and they'll never let you rejoin the army as a common soldier. You'd become a bodyguard and worse: a painted doll for her to put on display, to intimidate her enemies at court.

"That is no life for you, Laudan. That is not why I've spent the last three years teaching you as much of the world as I could. I will not see you spend your life on such folly!"

Laudan was stunned. On many levels. For Cedric to have ferreted out Laudan's motivations, and even logically carried Laudan's potential actions through to a hypothetical failed ending? Laudan struggled within himself for a moment, and then, to his own great surprise, he felt tears well up in his eyes. He shifted his head to the side so his teacher couldn't see them fall. And he turned around in preparation to leave.

The tears, he knew, were not because of the princess—or not entirely, in any event. But he couldn't be sure what exactly they were from. Was it the loss of the king that had him so unsure of himself, and unsure about life and his place in the world? Or was it that Kestrel's death had finally caught up with him?

His death? What had made Laudan think that? There had been no indication from anyone that he was believed to be dead. But Laudan realized suddenly that he had believed his friend dead all along. That was why he'd stopped looking for him. With the admission, the grief hit him hard.

He grasped the doorframe, still standing with his back to Cedric, and then sank down on one knee as the emotion washed over him. It racked his body. It consumed all of his strength until he felt pain in the muscles of his face and shoulders. The pain reached a point of such intensity that he felt he couldn't bear it any longer. And then, at the first shudder that took him, the tension was lessened. Over the course of another minute or so, the memory of the pain left him feeling strangely renewed and healed.

"Kestrel." Laudan whispered his friend's name. Had it been

Kestrel after all, and not the princess? Was it his inability to do anything about his missing friend that had been tormenting him and making him restless? He wasn't capable of accepting the truth—at least not yet—that his friend may have been lost to him forever. He found himself wondering if he had thrown himself into the idea of following the princess even more completely to keep his mind off Kestrel. But for a moment, at least, the helpless rage and sadness that had warred within him were subdued, spent along with his tears.

But somehow he knew it was a temporary thing. And the void that filled his life would soon bring the pain back. Kestrel was gone. And he would feel no relief until he knew the truth of what had happened to him.

At some point, Cedric had come from behind his desk and was now kneeling beside him, his arm draped across the boy's shoulders. Laudan had not even been aware. The old man's strength was apparent in the squeeze he gave Laudan when he saw him begin to come around.

Laudan turned toward his mentor. "I am useless here, brother. Please, if you cannot see me knighted, see me put to good use somewhere. I cannot stand the idleness. I will go mad."

Cedric replied in a soothing voice. "I will find you something. It would be best, for all concerned, if you were knighted by the new queen. But I will find you something else to do to keep your mind occupied until then. Come back here tomorrow, and I will let you know what I've worked out.

"But you cannot blame yourself, my son. Besides," he continued, "Kestrel is an enterprising fellow. He may yet surprise us all."

"I hope you're right, Cedric. I hope you're right."

As Laudan left his teacher's room, he thought of his friend. And he wondered if he were still alive. He'd heard tales of brothers knowing when their kin had been killed, knowing in a moment—even when separated by country borders and leagues of ocean. He closed his eyes to see if he could sense Kestrel's aliveness but could feel nothing. Nothing foreboding, which reassured him somewhat. But neither did he feel even the smallest glimmer of hope.

36

PRACTICAL MAGIC

B reeden woke up somewhat stiff from sleeping on the hard ground but otherwise well rested and ready to go. A warming yellow glow was forming on the horizon to the southeast. The sun was not yet up. And Aegir was still asleep. So he cooked breakfast. Fish again. And potatoes, but fried this time, in a pan in which he had heated up another thin slice of the bacon—and some water he'd retrieved from the river. He had also found some tea while he was looking for the spices the giant had mentioned the night before. And by the time the giant woke up, he had boiled several cups of a very strong tea he'd never tried before.

Aegir roused somewhat groggily, and Breeden immediately offered him a cup of the strong brew, which he accepted in silence and downed in a single gulp.

He grimaced slightly. "Strong." The word rumbled as deeply in his chest as any word Breeden had ever heard the giant speak. His voice sounded rough—as if he'd been yelling and had nearly lost it. "But needed. Perhaps some honey. There's a jar among my pickled eggs, if you've found those yet. Far back in the bow, wedged between two sacks of flour."

Breeden found the honey and supplied the giant with the jar to help himself. "There's breakfast too."

Aegir smiled. "My young master, you are a worthy companion. And I thank you." He rolled toward the fire, grabbed an empty bowl, and helped himself to some fish and potatoes from the fire's edge, where Breeden had left them to stay warm.

Breeden accepted the words humbly but didn't believe them and knew the truth himself. Cooking for the giant seemed to be the one thing he had done so far that was actually helpful.

But for now, the giant appeared happy enough. He wolfed down the first portion in seconds and went back for more, quickly polishing off the remainder.

"Excellent fare, young Breeden. My thanks again."

The giant had unwrapped his axe and begun to walk back down the path when he stopped and turned back to face Breeden. "My axe! You've gone and put an edge on it!"

Breeden shrugged. In his guilt the night before, he had done just as the giant had guessed, sharpened his axe blade using his whetstone—and his powers as well—to ensure the edge was as perfect as possible. The effort had been difficult just on scale, since he'd never tried to sharpen such a massive blade before. But the work of aligning the metal along the blade's edge had been difficult too. The metal was quite hard, nearly the equal of the chisels he had found at the tinker's stall, and moving the essence-bearing lines within the metal had drained him physically.

"It was the least I could do—and I thought your work would go faster with a sharper blade. Besides, my da always says that using a dull blade when you are tired is a sure way to have an accident."

The giant shook his head and then positioned his eye at a low angle to the axe blade. He held it up to catch the morning sunlight streaming into their clearing through the lowlands to the southeast. "You are a marvel, Breeden. This blade has never been so sharp. Not even on the day it left my father's forge. And on that day, I could have shaved with it. Again, and again, my thanks. I'm not sure how you did it, but I begin to see why your father believed you could help."

Breeden felt pride, and gratitude to the giant for the kind words. But at mention of his father, and Breeden knew which one the giant had meant, Breeden felt doubtful once again. So he could sharpen an axe. And break a rusty iron hinge. And spot a broken wooden spindle. How were these things going to help them against Mirgul?

But he restored his smile anyway, thanked the giant for his praise, and began collecting the cookware he'd used to make breakfast before the giant had even turned to walk back up the trail.

37

FLIGHT

The next day, Janelle awoke and was entirely too aware of where she was. Well, not exactly sure where, but on the road south of Ridderzaal. But while she remembered why she was there, she had also regained the clarity of mind to recognize that she didn't know where she was going. She sat up on her bedroll and saw both of her companions already awake.

Aelric was nosing the morning's light wind as if, she thought in all seriousness, he were determining the direction in which they would be traveling for the day.

And Kestrel was building a fire. He looked much recovered already from his fevered shaking of the night before, and she was pleased to see that he once again seemed a man to her. The thought was comforting. Kestrel had always been so capable and confident. It was good to see *that* Kestrel moving about the morning breakfast fire with efficiency.

Without ceremony, she raised the question that had been haunting her dreams. "Where are we going?"

She didn't direct the question to either man but hoped that by not choosing whom to address, she would be more likely to receive a prompt answer.

Kestrel and Aelric were sharing a look at her question, and while no words were exchanged, she could see that some type of communication occurred. Aelric finally nodded, and Kestrel answered, apparently, for them both. "Aoilfhionn. We've got to warn the elf queen of the princess's plans. And perhaps she can help us as well."

Aelric nodded again, to confirm he agreed with Kestrel's words.

Janelle had never been farther from home than Arlon, to the north, and Miremont, to the south and west. But as much as the thought of visiting the homeland of the elves appealed to her, she was intimidated by the idea of traveling so far from home. She was afraid, too, of what dangers would await them on their journey. If the princess had consorted with people with the capacity to attack the elves, and they had any hope for success, then she wielded far more power—before she had even been crowned—than Janelle had ever imagined.

She wasn't sure she could make it to Aoilfhionn. She feared she might lose her mind, or die from the grief and fear.

Aelric and Kestrel watched Janelle's face contort, shifting between anguish and fear, and shared another look. Aelric shook his head. And Kestrel took control.

"Janelle. Janelle?"

She realized she had been consumed by her thoughts again and had not heard what Kestrel and Aelric had been saying. "I'm sorry. Yes, what is it?"

"Didn't you once tell me you had family in Miremont? An uncle, maybe."

"Yes. My aunt and uncle run a successful business there in cloth—just as my father does in Ridderzaal."

Kestrel nodded. "Good. I thought I'd remembered that. Well, I think it would be a good idea if we went through Miremont on our way to Aoilfhionn. And I was wondering if you thought you might be welcomed to stay there with your uncle for a while."

Janelle was torn. She knew what they were doing. And part of her wanted to lash out and tell them she could make the trip to Aoilfhionn just fine. But the wiser part of her knew that their concerns were well-founded. She was a mess. And perhaps it would be a good idea for her to spend some time away from Ridderzaal and its intrigues. The more she thought about it, the more she clung to the idea. Maybe this change would be just what she needed. If she remained in Ridderzaal, she would be constantly reminded of her losses. But perhaps in Miremont she might even find a new opportunity. Perhaps there was a Laonese noble who would like having in her service a girl who was once handmaiden to the queen. Janelle smiled. Yes, she was sure such a noblewoman would be easily found. Perhaps this was what she needed.

"Yes, I think that would probably be for the best. Thank you, Kestrel. And I'm sorry I've become such a burden for you. It's just all . . . so much to deal with."

Aelric nodded again. "It is decided, then. We head for Miremont after breakfast. We can try to procure some mounts along the way, and if we fail, we will certainly do well with the stock we find in Miremont's stables."

38

SQUIRE'S END

L audan reported to Cedric's room in the tower the next day, as he'd been told to do. The cleric wasn't there. And he had to wait for several long minutes. It was not unprecedented that he should be late, but it was unusual. Laudan grudgingly acknowledged that these were anything but normal times, but as the time drew longer, he became restless. To keep himself occupied, he glanced at the documents on Cedric's desk. Maybe they would help him understand what could possibly be keeping the man so busy.

Among the piles of paper, one bore a seal that looked familiar to him, and he walked around the desk to examine it. He was right. It was Kestrel's family seal. He scanned the letter and realized it was from Kestrel's father. The letter described rumors of Krigare activity to the north of Pretania—and a scarcely believable report of unknown troops moving west through Ath.

But above all, the letter brought home to Laudan the fact that Kestrel's father had no idea about his son and heir's disappearance. Next to the letter appeared to be an unfinished response Cedric was writing to Kestrel's father.

. . .

Dear Lord Starkad,

Your reports of troop movements are deeply concerning and align with reports we have heard ourselves. But before I speak further of those concerns, I must relate to you some ill news of a much more personal nature. Your son, Kestrel, has gone missing. I wish I could tell you it was some youthful escapade. But I'm afraid that in these dark times, it is likely something much more sinister.

I can't begin to tell you what Kestrel's loss means to us, to his peers, and to our countries. He is a young man of great wit and ability.

I myself continue to lead the investigation into his disappearance, and it is only the death of the king and the preparations for the succession of the new queen that have distracted me from my task. These activities will soon be over, and I will be able to refocus my energies and efforts more exclusively to finding your son.

THAT WAS the extent of the letter so far.

Laudan could only imagine how hard writing such a letter must be. And he could understand why Cedric might want to walk away from it.

Laudan also felt sorry for Kestrel's father. He had met the man once, the summer before. He was lean and wiry, like Kestrel, albeit with an old man's paunch. He was also a few inches taller than his son, and his hair had been streaked with grey and white. He had been much more affectionate than Laudan's own father, hugging Laudan upon meeting him for the first time—or at least trying to hug him, anyway, before Laudan had pushed him away. Laudan cracked a gentle smile at the memory.

Footsteps sounded on the stone floor outside the room, and Laudan came around from behind the desk a moment before

Cedric entered. But the monk was looking at the ground as he walked and likely didn't notice Laudan's snooping. It took him a moment even to realize there was someone in his room.

"Ahhh. I had forgotten about our meeting, my son. Well, I have work for you after all. And important work it is. I need you to go to Arlon and carry some messages for me. I can trust no one but you. And you must defend the messages with great care. If they should fall into the wrong hands, it could mean your life, as well as my own. They are messages concerning suspicions that have recently come to my attention. They are in code, and may therefore look innocuous enough, but one talented in cipher could very well unlock their secrets."

He paused a moment, as if to add weight to the words that followed. "Laudan, it has come to me that word was brought to the princess's minister about a captive escaping from the dungeons. To my knowledge, the only person known to be missing within the city is Kestrel. Now, it may be that the prisoner mentioned was not Kestrel. But my sources also referred to the one who escaped as 'the boy' and 'the westerner.' I think it all far too coincidental to consider that the prisoner could be anyone else. And how is it that I didn't know someone was being held in the keep's dungeons? No. If the prisoner had been one of the minister's own retinue, then there would have been no need for secrecy. And a suitable place could have been found on the main floors of the keep."

Laudan felt a lump rise in his throat and a weight lift from his shoulders. Kestrel might be alive!

"I have already spoken with the princess's minister about you accompanying her retinue when they leave the castle at noon today. He has no reason to suspect that I know anything. But listen carefully to me. I said nothing about your carrying messages. He could just as easily have had one of his own runners carry them for me. I told him you were to see Knight-Captain Jenlyns as part of your training. I indicated we had high hopes for your abilities and believed that some time under his tutelage would give him the chance to see your potential for himself.

"One of the messages you are to carry will be for him. And it will say just what I have told you—or near to it, in any event. Bring it to Captain Jenlyns, along with the rest of the messages you will carry. And tell him this when you are alone, and away from prying ears. Tell him what I told you about the prisoner, that I believe it to have been Kestrel, and that Kestrel may know something he should not. You need say no more than that, and he should understand what you mean.

"These messages are of the gravest import, Laudan. You must protect them and handle them with the greatest care. Do you have any questions for me?"

Impulsively Laudan thought of the armor he'd found so many months earlier.

"I'm sure you'll think this is odd, but many months ago, Kestrel and I were in the tunnels beneath the castle when we found an old armory. There was a suit of studded leather armor. I left it behind, and I assume it is still there, but I was hoping that, if it's not too much to presume, I might have it—or use it, at the least, on my trip to Arlon."

Cedric looked at him strangely, and Laudan cursed himself for even suggesting such a thing. Cedric clearly thought him a fool and was now second-guessing himself for even considering sending him on such an important mission. He had been given everything he could have wanted—including traveling with the princess to Arlon—and now he had ruined the whole thing. His face fell as he waited for Cedric to speak and pronounce him unfit for the task at hand.

But Cedric surprised him. "An old armory in the cellars? How often did you go down there? And what was the extent of your exploration?"

Laudan answered without understanding quite what the

old man was getting at. "Yes. Not often—as a group. Perhaps three or four times, though Kestrel would often explore on his own."

Cedric didn't answer for some time and even turned away from Laudan to pace the room in the small space behind the writing desk. "I wonder . . ." He spoke in such a low voice that Laudan wasn't sure if the older man had trailed off or just left the sentence unfinished.

And then he seemed to snap out of his reverie. "Yes, Laudan. I am sure you could take a suit of armor from an old armory in the cellar. Have you checked with the sergeant-at-arms? Is it an active armory?"

Laudan answered at once, elated that he had been permitted to wear the ancient armor. It was a rare day indeed! "No, sir, I have not checked with the sergeant-at-arms. But it is no active armory. The arms and armor are all extremely old. Everything is covered in dust. And, well, I had to break open the door with my shoulder, since the hinges had rusted fast."

Cedric nodded, his eyebrows raised at the last admission. "Very well. Then I see no problem with you using it. If we should discover your opinion of the armor's status is incorrect, you will simply have to forfeit it to whoever lays claim upon it. Does that seem fair to you?"

"Yes, sir. Of course I would, sir." And just like that, Laudan was off, moving toward the door to retrieve the armor.

But he didn't get far. "Laudan?"

Laudan stopped in his tracks. "Yes, brother. What is it?"

"You should return here in one hour's time. I will have the letters prepared for you then and will take you down to meet the princess's minister."

Laudan was abashed. He had been so eager to retrieve the armor that he'd not let his mentor finish. "Yes, sir. I'm sorry, sir."

Cedric looked him in the eye and held his gaze for a long

moment. Laudan felt as though he were being weighed and measured.

"You may go now. But collect everything you plan to take with you, and meet me here again in one hour's time. Go."

And just like that, Laudan had been told he could have everything he wanted.

Once in the hallway, he began to run, a strange sensation of lightness making him feel he was capable of running faster than ever before. He didn't overdo it, knowing that in the sometimes-narrow hallways of the keep, he might easily run down an unsuspecting servant if he were not careful.

He would head for the kitchens and then into the cellars beneath the keep to retrieve the armor first. Then he would head back to the barracks to collect his other things.

In a few minutes, he was back in the old armory. The door was closed, as they had left it, but this time it opened with relative ease. The rust had not had time to reclaim the room's contents for itself.

It was just as he remembered it. The surfaces of hundreds of weapons and pieces of armor reflected back his torchlight as he entered. He walked straight over to the stand where he'd left the armor. He noticed, with minor annoyance, that he hadn't straightened the armor when he'd put it back on the dummy. It was twisted somewhat. The thought raised sensations of discomfort as he thought back to when he had first worn a chain mail shirt as a boy.

He remembered being unhorsed by his older brother and falling in a heap of metal links onto the ground. When he'd gotten up, the metal shirt had twisted on him, and it took several agonizing moments to straighten it out. His brother had, of course, given him no time for such adjustments and had dismounted and come at him with his sparring sword. It had been all Laudan could do to find his own blade and defend himself. And he had fought the remainder of the match hampered by the slightly oversize armor, which still hadn't been settled properly on his shoulders. His brother had drubbed him.

But such a thing would never happen were he wearing such a shirt as this one. As lightweight to one accustomed to wearing chain mail as wearing no armor at all, with short sleeves extending to just above his elbow, and leather straps to snug it tight against him. He had the armor off the dummy and couldn't help but throw it over his head, to try it on and see if it fit him any better now than it had those many months earlier. Even without a gambeson underneath, it fit well enough that he could probably wear it into battle as is—with the straps pulled as tightly as they would allow. He hadn't realized he'd grown so much in such a short time.

He considered taking it off before heading back to the barracks but thought it would be easier to carry if he just left it on. On a day of impulses, Laudan surprised himself once more by deciding he should look for a suitable sword while he was down here. Most he saw were the short broadswords popular during a period in the distant past—likely the same time as that of the armor he wore.

And then he noticed a rack of weapons that, while still old, appeared to have been made more recently than those filling the rest of the room. Among them was a large hand-and-a-half sword—or so it would be to Laudan, though he realized it may have been more of a two-handed weapon for its original owner. He hefted it in one hand, and the balance was slightly heavier at the tip than felt natural. He snugged his right hand up against the guard and his left hand rested neatly between his right hand and the pommel. A perfect fit for both hands, if a tiny bit crowded. But with both hands on the grip the weapon became much easier for him to control. Lighter than the two-handed swords he'd used before, and something he was sure he could wield with one hand if he practiced with it enough.

Yes, this sword would work nicely. And Cedric's approval of the armor had come easily enough that he didn't think anyone would have a problem with him taking a sword too. But he couldn't allow himself time to be any greedier, so he looked around the room one last time and left. He jogged back toward the kitchens and then to the barracks to gather the rest of his gear.

LAUDAN WAS BACK in Cedric's room in a little more than the hour his teacher had given him. He could see by the look Cedric gave him that he'd pushed his luck. But there was no helping it now. As his father would say, "you can't call back the arrow." Cedric sprang up from his writing table with a large tome in his hand, and a rolled and sealed parchment in the other.

"The book is for Knight-Captain Jenlyns and bears messages in cipher. The scroll is a decoy, and also contains a cipher. But the scroll's hidden message is false. Or at least it tells nothing of import."

Laudan and the others had learned the art of cipher under Cedric's tutelage, and it had been one of the very few of the more scholarly lessons he taught that Laudan had enjoyed. He and Kestrel had made a game of ciphering simple coded messages. And they had even made up their own list of phrases to expand on the handful Cedric had taught them. He smiled at the memory.

"Further . . . Laudan! Please listen to me!" Laudan's thoughts had wandered again. *What was wrong with him?* He couldn't stay focused.

Cedric held his eyes then. "Are you sure you can do this, Laudan? This is no ride in the country you take here. Do you understand that the danger your foe represents cannot be met with a sword on the field of battle?"

He gestured then toward one of the bronze discs on Laudan's armor. "This protection will serve you naught. Do you understand?"

Laudan nodded. "I do, brother."

Cedric continued to hold his gaze. Laudan felt as though the man were searching his thoughts and emotions, and looking for weakness and doubt. Well, he would find none of those things there. Laudan didn't know what to expect. He truly didn't. But he knew it would be better than what he faced by remaining in Ridderzaal with idle hands and wandering thoughts. As if to reassure the former knight of his confidence, Laudan asserted, "I am ready, Brother Cedric. There is nothing left for me here."

To Laudan, the statement was a fact he had long recognized but had yet to utter out loud. And as he spoke the words, and steeled his resolve, a light sparked in his eyes.

Cedric appeared to sense the change in his student's demeanor. And his own expression shifted to one of mild relief. "Perhaps you are, my son. Perhaps you are at that."

He raised the book and the scroll once again, from where they had been hanging at his sides. "Remember, now, share nothing of what we have discussed with anyone but Captain Jenlyns. My network in Arlon has dwindled. I do not nurture it as I once did. As a consequence, I cannot vouch for anyone else with certainty. Give him the book—and the scroll. And trust in his guidance as my own.

"Now, let us go down to the north gate to join the princess's train. It could leave at any time now."

39
___

TO ARLON

The princess was impatient. She squirmed in her seat as she awaited the lurch that would mean her exquisitely carved and gilded carriage had begun the journey back to Arlon. There would be so much to do when she returned home. And while she had demonstrably moved things along from her exile in Ridderzaal, she still felt she hadn't yet achieved enough control over the kingdom and the people she had left behind in Arlon. Using couriers and having whispered conversations in secret meetings beneath the keep had been burdensome.

But then, that boy had overheard her despite the precautions. And before she had discovered exactly what he had heard, or more precisely, before her inquisitor had been given a chance to ply his arts upon the boy, he had escaped. It mattered little, she supposed, since her plans were already well underway, and less for the fact that she had learned this morning that her spies had picked up the boy's trail heading south.

But it irked her still that she hadn't had the comfort and protections offered by the royal palace's honeycomb of secret rooms and passages. She had played in them as a child. She knew of the room where one could eavesdrop on a conversation by standing in a secret passage. And if she were the one in that room and not wanting to be overheard, she knew that the counterweights in the floor of the passage behind the wall would cause one of the pictures on the wall to dip at a slight angle, alerting one who knew the room's secret that she was being overheard.

It was her favorite room in the royal palace. The profound sense of security and isolation it offered could be found nowhere else she had ever been. There she could be alone with her thoughts. And there she would never be surprised. She would put the room to heavy use when she returned. There were many agents in need of questioning and instruction, and many allies with whom she needed to catch up.

The carriage lurched, surprising her as it always did and causing her to stretch her hands out to either side to catch her balance. But she smiled anyway, despite the annoyance. She was going home. She was going back to Arlon.

40

RUNNING RIVER

The sound of Aegir's axe in the distance reminded Breeden, oddly enough, of his mother chopping vegetables on her wooden cutting board. *Shhhck. Shhhck. Shhhck.* Most of the time, he could discern a pattern in the rhythm of the strokes, as if Aegir were timing his blows to a song that only he knew, and that only his axe could give voice to.

As the giant worked his way toward him, Breeden could see that it was the effort of downing a particularly large tree or tearing up a stubborn root or moving a boulder that was slowing him down at times and breaking his rhythm. But even these obstacles, some fairly impressive, hardly slowed him down this morning. And his axe flew faster and faster the closer he came to Breeden and the boat.

As Breeden watched, Aegir looked up one last time at three saplings still blocking his way. As quick as a glance, each fell in three rapid blows, and he had completed his trail. Breeden couldn't believe how easy the giant had made it look. The giant kissed the axe and walked over to the boat to wrap it up and put it away. But before he did so, he looked it over once more and grunted.

"Nearly unmarked! In fact, I think it's all sap and dirt. There isn't even a scratch on the edge of the blade! Hmph. Well, I'm not sure what you did to my axe, young master, but I thank you."

Breeden said nothing in response. He was embarrassed by the praise and still didn't feel his contributions to the trip were anywhere near what the giant's had already been in their time traveling together. His musings were only reinforced as he watched Aegir put away the axe, secure a harness to the bow of his boat and to his shoulders, and begin to haul it across the rolling wooden "floor" he'd built as he had cleared the saplings that bordered the path. He stopped only infrequently to clear minor snags as the wheel assembly became caught up, but for the most part, the hull of the boat slid and rolled along the bed of saplings with little obstruction, and the effort went fairly quickly.

Not two hours later, Aegir was removing the wheels, replacing the mast and stays, and pushing the boat back into the water—the "insurmountable" obstacle bypassed after all.

Once Breeden boarded, Aegir pushed off with his massive legs and climbed over the gunwale. Like the boat entering the nearly still water below the logjam, the giant's movements were slow. Despite the apparent ease with which the giant had performed the work of the past two and a half days, Breeden could see that the effort had taken its toll. The giant was exhausted, and he sank heavily against the aft gunwale, resting his right arm on the tiller. He sat there for a long moment to catch his breath before he made any effort to adjust the sails and move them downriver. So Breeden collected the sheets for the mainsail and brought them back to his companion, laying them within easy reach of his off hand. Then he rummaged around in his pack of supplies and pulled out one of the unopened bundles of Kestrel's satje, handing it to the giant along with a skin of water so large it required both of Breeden's hands even to lift it.

Aegir muttered a low, raspy thanks and drew a long pull from the skin—drinking on one breath of air enough water to last Breeden a week or more on their voyage. The giant then popped the entire package of satje, which Breeden had removed from its sticks, into his mouth and began to chew. "Mmm. Mmm." The noise sounded like a bull in rut—only louder and deeper—and Breeden couldn't help but laugh. His giant companion opened his eyes and smiled as he looked at Breeden. "Yes, that is very good. Very good indeed. And a fine fare that would make for a long sea voyage too!"

Breeden's laughing trailed off, and he decided he needed to know more about their trip. He started out haltingly. "We left so quickly I didn't really get much of a chance to ask questions. And now we've gone a few days, I feel more than ever that the trip is important. Or at least it's obvious you think it so. But I really don't understand why I am so important, and why you are going to such lengths to bring me back to this wizards' council. I suppose I won't know the answer to 'Why me?' until I meet my father and he explains to me what he expects I can do to help. But the 'What?' and the 'Why so quickly?' are still unanswered as well. What is it they want me to do?"

Aegir's smile softened but remained in place as he responded, adjusting his seat and checking their progress downstream before doing so. "You are the son of a wizard with great powers. I have said to your father before that you were in need of a proper teacher. And while Cedric is renowned as a scholar and statesman, he could not teach you the practical art and use of magic.

"But even knowing that this trip might have been made sooner, and should have been made sooner—if your parents had been willing to part with you—I don't fault them. They love you very much. And I can understand that they did not want to see you go. But while all parents know that someday they must wish their children well and send them out into the world alone, your parents have known that someday their parting with you would be different. They knew you were born of a wielder of magic. And they were warned you might be special as a result of your birth.

"I wrote regular letters to your parents, to check on you and see how you were doing. I tried to determine if you had exhibited any unusual capabilities. And I asked regularly if they would let me take you to Ekszer Hegy to have you evaluated. They always said no. They always demurred for another time. But your true father, through me, was persistent. And it finally came down to your father who raised you—Holt, that is—promising that if you ever exhibited powers beyond your ken, they would contact me, and they would let you go—to study with the wizards and help you master your abilities.

"The last time I came, you had begun to show your powers. Whether you were aware that your parents knew or not, I don't know, but they had seen little things they couldn't explain. A chair that had been broken for weeks and that you had mended with glue. Or so you said, though your father could not, for all his skill, find a break or crack that had been glued in the leg of any chair he examined afterward. Your selection of wood stock for projects. Your rejection of other stock, which seemed sound. It added up. Your father figured it out first—probably because you appeared to have a particular affinity for wood. And your mother had not fully pieced it together until your father told her just a few days ago. Apparently, she was relieved—that so many strange occurrences had been neatly wrapped up with a tidy explanation. But then the more she thought about it, the harder it was for her to accept.

"Nearly a year ago, your father and I fought over your fate. I wanted to take you back with me, and your father would not allow it. I even sank low enough to call him on his promise, and threatened to hold him to it by his honor. He acceded then—in principle, anyway—though he asked for one more year to school you in letters and history. But, to be clear, I don't think he ever intended to break his promise. I just think he wanted more time with you—more time to prepare himself for the day you would leave him. I was not proud of doing that to your father. He is a man of rare integrity. But your true father had convinced me of the importance of you mastering your powers. I'm not sure how he knew that such a day as this would come, but then, he can often see things others cannot.

"It may have seemed a quick decision three nights ago, when your parents gave in to my pleadings. And it may have hurt you that they did not fight harder to keep you in Woodfall. But in truth, it has been a long battle. And that battle began at your birth.

"Most importantly of all of that, Breeden, there is no more time to waste. It is not that there is little time, Breeden. There is no more time. The ships of the enemy are under sail even as we speak. I am sorry to have been the harbinger, young master. But your childhood is over. And this journey marks the beginning of a new life for you. We must prepare to battle Mirgul for the fate of all Erda."

Breeden had listened quietly. And the words of the giant had almost wrapped him in a spell as they did when he spun tales of his home. But this was no faerie tale. This was Breeden's life. It almost felt like whatever had passed for his life so far had been just a temporary arrangement. Breeden's parents had known all along that this time would come. And Breeden could do nothing about it. He frowned upon hearing the giant's concluding remarks. But he couldn't respond. He didn't know what he might be expected to say, so he allowed a silence to grow in the space that followed the giant's answer.

The part of him that recognized the unfairness to his parents of the whole thing wanted to rebel. What if he didn't want to return to his blood father? He couldn't stand the phrase "true father," because he believed no man could be a truer father than Holt Andehar had been to him. What if he wanted to live out his life simply, the son of a boatwright and his wife? And who was this wizard, this stranger who had abandoned him? All pity aside for a man who, in his grief at losing his wife, may have made a hasty decision in handing over his son to be raised by others. But as sad as the thought was that he would never know his birth mother—who had not abandoned him after all—and that her death had weighed heavily on his father, Breeden still felt forsaken. Usually respectful and obedient, Breeden wanted to lash out. What was happening was so unfair —to his parents and to him.

He looked about him and saw that their boat was now traveling over a series of gentle rapids. The water level was not much deeper than the draught of the boat they traveled in, and the surface of the water was churning over the bed of rounded, irregular stones that made up the river bottom. He had been thinking he wanted to jump out of the boat. It may have been a whim, and nothing he'd have truly carried out, but the rapids quashed even his ability to pretend he might swim to shore and find his way back home.

But his streak of resistance didn't die with his prospects of immediate escape, and he tried to calm down by reminding himself that he could leave at any time. The giant would never try to stop him. Nonetheless, it still took some doing before he had his emotions back under control.

Aegir, as if reading his mood the entire time, finally queried, "Do you wish to ask me anything more, young master?"

Breeden thought for a moment but shook his head. "No. I just miss my ma and da. And I guess I don't really know what to think about this voyage."

Aegir remained silent, concern evident on the craggy, bark-like features of his face as he waited for the boy to go on. Breeden continued, and some of the fire he felt within him crept into his voice. "I still don't understand how my feeble magics are supposed to help in a fight against a god!"

Aegir's face took on an unusual expression Breeden couldn't quite read. It seemed as if he wanted to say something in response to Breeden's statement, but he couldn't decide how to say it—or perhaps whether to say it at all. When the giant did respond, he spoke slowly and with great care.

"Your father wields magics that have proven effective against Mirgul in the past. And while he fears the Dark Brother's rage, he does not think the world is without hope. He believes Mirgul may be brought down. But he would have you at his side, to lend your craft to his own, to help ensure that the god's defeat this time is final. While I know no more than that of his plans, I know that your father is extremely wise and a man of great compassion. He did not want to pull you away from your parents so he could have you back for himself—though I know that he regrets having to give you up as he did. What he does now he only does out of necessity. And because he values the world above any single life."

Breeden felt somewhat mollified, though not yet convinced. He wasn't sure why, but he believed the giant and put stock in his opinion. He supposed it was the deep affection he saw between Aegir and his parents that made him trust the giant so well.

"You've known my father a long time—my real father, that is. Holt Andehar. How would you compare him with the father who abandoned me as a child?"

Aegir made a sour face. "A strong and heavy word. And one that shows me your heart, if not your mind. But I will answer the question anyway. They are both men of great integrity. They both value the needs of others before their own needs. They both love you very much, though one has been lucky enough to live with you all these many years and the other must be content with the occasional visit, in disguise, to check in on you from a distance. Each loves, or loved, his wife more than anything else in all the world—excepting you, perhaps. Hmph.

"The more I think about it, Breeden, the better a question I think it is. And the more I begin to see what strange fate must have guided my hand in suggesting your parents to raise you. Magical powers and boatbuilding aside, your fathers have many things in common. Both believe in family and sacrifice. Both were travelers in their youth, and became crafters as they grew older. And both possess a rare sense of honor. I suspect they would get along well should they ever meet."

"So they've never met each other, then?" The thought had not even occurred to Breeden.

Aegir shook his head. "No. Your true father has visited, as I said, and he has seen Holt from a distance, perhaps even exchanged a word or two, but they have never met in recognition of who the other truly is."

Breeden pondered the matter. He wondered what his blood father was like. He wondered if he would agree with Aegir and find the men to have as much in common as the giant believed. His mind cast away from him, and he realized he was staring at the passing river water, brown now, but smooth as they passed below the gurgling section of rapids. He had an image flash before his mind then, of an old man with white hair and a close-cropped white beard. Then the image was gone, lost in a swirl of brown water.

"Ho!" It was Aegir. "There's a sandbar ahead. Hold on to something." And just like that, Aegir threw the tiller hard to the other side of the boat, away from his body. The boat careened to the left, and despite the warning, Breeden lost his grip and fumbled for a moment before he grabbed hold of something—one of the ropes that ran alongside the mast and held the boom suspended parallel to the deck. Just as he was settling himself onto the bench seat, the boom came swinging around with the change in wind and threatened to take off his head. Instinctively he ducked and brought his left forearm up to protect his head. The boom connected with his wrist and nearly pulled him with it over the starboard side of the boat.

Breeden landed poorly against the gunwale, his ribs taking the brunt of the fall's force. Pain coursed through him in a wave, as if a fire had been lit upon his side. He crumpled onto the bench, struggling with the decision to protect and cradle his aching wrist or to nurse the pain that raged through his torso, and failing to effectively do either.

Breeden was hardly aware of anything but daggers and fire in his wrist and side. But Aegir acted quickly and moved to release and lower the mainsail so he could attend to his young charge. But as he was doing so, the boat had continued to drift downstream, and Aegir had to leap back to guide the boat onto another sandbar, grabbing the tiller and causing the boat's bow to drive straight into the sand.

The pain and the sudden cessation of movement disoriented Breeden, and it was moments later before he reclaimed his wits and was able to focus his thoughts again on his wrist. Almost without effort he probed the injury with his mind. The bone was not broken, though it certainly felt as though it were. His ribs, too, had escaped serious injury, but when he lifted his shirt, he could see they had already begun to bruise. Breeden told the giant that he had no broken bones and would be fine with some rest.

Aegir was relieved. "I am sorry, Breeden."

But by the tone the giant used and by his expression, Breeden couldn't be sure what the giant was sorry for exactly: the accident at hand or his greater involvement in taking Breeden away from his parents.

"It's not a terribly long journey, young master. But if you're truly okay, we'd best be moving along again."

He got out of the boat then and surveyed the situation. The sandbar extended nearly the entire width of the river. The giant walked it back and forth to look for a likely spot for the boat to pass and ultimately had to use a shovel to dig a shallow trench at its narrowest point. He then pulled and pushed the boat through the small channel he'd dug.

But he made short work of it, and less than an hour had passed before Aegir was climbing back aboard the boat, another obstacle behind them. Once again they were on their way. From there they made good progress, and their trip went more smoothly as the water became deeper and they were carried closer and closer to the ocean. The hours passed quickly.

They traveled in silence for a long while after the encounter with the sandbar. Aegir was tired, and Breeden was focused on nursing his wounds. But Breeden snapped out of his reverie when Aegir made a familiar chest-rattling "Mmm." Breeden looked up and saw that the giant had raised his head to the breeze. "We can't be far. I can smell the tide's offal."

As if the river itself begrudged their progress and their having overcome its obstacles, it threw one more in their path. A massive pine tree had fallen across the river at a narrow point. The tree required the attention, once again, of Aegir's eyebrow-raising axe work. The giant dispatched the huge tree with renewed energy, and in moments, they were under sail again.

Once past the fallen tree, their pace increased yet again. A steady cross breeze had sprung up, and Aegir was using its force to good effect. Not long thereafter, Breeden caught sight of gulls circling in the distance. The trees and bushes of the previous day and a half were gradually being replaced by more gnarled and sparser shrubs, and finally by nothing more than different types of grasses. Rolling dunes replaced the woods. And then the land dropped away.

They had reached the river's mouth. He could see only water on the horizon ahead.

BREEDEN COULDN'T BELIEVE the trip had been made in only three days, or even that it had been possible to make it at all. The determination of the giant had seen them past the logjam, a barrier that had been an insurmountable fact to Breeden, as well as his father and the entire village of Woodfall, for the whole of his life. And the sandbar and downed tree, though insignificant by comparison, would surely have been enough to stop him were he taking this voyage alone.

Only three days had passed, and yet so much had changed. It was at that moment that Breeden first felt he might have some idea of what the princess meant when she called Woodfall and Ridderzaal "backwater" towns. If this giant saw the logjam as nothing more than something to move around, and Breeden's entire village had almost forgotten there was even a river beyond it, then maybe the princess was right. And maybe it would be a good thing for Breeden to see what existed of the world beyond.

The boat entered the chop where the ocean current met the Woodfall's outflow, and a spray of water caught Breeden in the face. It stung his eyes, and he could taste salt on his lips. They had reached the ocean.

EPILOGUE

M irren didn't know where he was.

HE HAD BEEN STANDING with the dwarven king and his army at the head of the northern valley leading into Dvargheim. An unprecedented assemblage of trolls was pouring south out of the Jetningen Mountains toward the dwarves' homeland, and he was preparing to assist them in holding back the snarling horde. And then his brother had appeared beside him. *Mirgul? How?* He was so stunned he forgot all about the trolls. And before he could act, almost before he could think, his vision had narrowed to a pinpoint of light, and he lost consciousness. His last memory was of his brother's febrile eyes and gleaming white teeth. Then everything had gone black.

When his thoughts returned, he tried to feel around him, but his hands wouldn't respond to his will. Nor his feet. Nor any part of him. He felt paralyzed. And blind. And he realized he couldn't hear or feel or smell anything either. Where was he? And what had his brother done to him? Was he . . . wherever

Birghid had gone? Was this void what he could expect of his existence from now on?

Time passed. Or at least he felt that time must be passing. But without the aid of his senses, he wasn't sure.

He tried to calm himself down. But a sense of guilt was growing within him, at the reminder that he had done as much to Mirgul first. Locking him in that cave for decades. Centuries. As time passed, presumably, and Mirren remained alone with his thoughts, part of him acknowledged that he deserved this. If he'd shown his brother mercy, he would never have come to this fate himself. He tried to speak. But he couldn't even feel his mouth. Was he asleep? He didn't feel asleep. He felt far too lucid. Was he somehow trapped in his own mind?

None of this made sense. He couldn't begin to sort it out.

He reached out with his thoughts, cast his mind's voice into the darkness that enveloped him. "Mirgul!"

There was no reply. He hadn't really expected one. But he didn't know what else to do, what else to try. And then, more softly: "Birghid? . . . Birghid, are you there?"

He waited. For a few seconds, he thought. But he realized that his ability to track time depended on his ability to see, or touch, or hear. Without that feedback, he wasn't sure he'd be able to maintain his sense of time. Or perhaps even his sense of identity.

What had he done to Mirgul for all of those years? And how had his brother survived this, never mind survived long enough to escape his cage?

What had he done?

BOOK TWO, The Queen and the Soldier, *will continue the tale of Breeden and his friends. In the meantime . . .*

ALSO BY MATTHEW B. BERG

Available Now!

A Monk's Tale - The first novelette released in the world of The Crafter Chronicles

The Crafter's Son - Book One of the Exciting New Coming of Age Epic Fantasy Series, The Crafter Chronicles

Coming Soon (in 2020)!

The Queen & The Soldier - Book Two of the Exciting New Coming of Age Epic Fantasy Series, The Crafter Chronicles

The Orphan's Plight (working title) - Another novelette in the world of The Crafter Chronicles

Coming in 2021 . . .

The Ranger King - Book Three of the Exciting New Coming of Age Epic Fantasy Series, The Crafter Chronicles

The Lay of Legorel (working title) - Yet another novelette in the world of The Crafter Chronicles

A BRIEF GLOSSARY, WITH
PRONUNCIATIONS

Aegir - (Ā-jeer) - A seafaring giant.

Aelric - (ALE-Rick) - A half-elf ranger.

Andehar - (AN-dǝ-här) - The family/last name of Breeden, and his parents Holt and Marlene.

Aoilfhionn - (Ā-ō-lǝn) - The city of trees. Capital city of Fardach Sidhe, homeland of the elves.

Arlon - (ar-LON) - The capital of Hyrde, and seat of the kingdom.

Ath - (rhymes with bath) - A land comprised of mountains and a fertile river valley. Home of the giants. It occupies the northeast region of Erda.

bailey - (BĀ-lē) - A defensive wall that encloses the land surrounding a castle. Also can refer to the area enclosed by such a wall.

Beltide - (BEL-tide) - A holiday celebrating the arrival of spring.

Bertil - (BURR-til) - A dwarven smith of ancient legend.

Birghid - (burr-3ĒD) - Goddess of wisdom and beauty.

Chavenay - *(shä-və -NĀ)* - *A large family estate in Laon held by the Robinet family.*

Conkle - *(CON-kəl)* - *Last/family name of a Ridderzaal Carpenter and his son.*

Culuden - *(CƏ-lə-den)* - *Capital city of Pretania. Seat of the Pretanian clan chief.*

Dura - *(DÜ-rə)* - *Assistant to the Princess's torturer.*

Dvargheim - *(DVARG-hīm)* - *Mountainous home of the dwarves, occupying the eastern region of Erda.*

Einar - *(Ī-nar)* - *The name of Breeden's father, given to him by Aegir the giant.*

Ekszer Hegy - *(ECK-Zurr HEH-gee)* - *An island off the dwarven coast of Dvargheim. Home to a fortress run by wizards and scholars.*

Erda - *(UR-dä)* - *The continent of known lands where* The Crafter's Son *takes place.*

Fardach Sidhe - *(far-däk SHĒ)* - *Forested homeland of the Elves, occupying the western region of Erda.*

Fuller - *(FƏL-ər)* - *Last/family name of Janelle, daughter of a cloth merchant of Ridderzaal.*

Gaidheal - *(GĀ-ell)* - *The ancient name of the people of the land of Shenn Frith, who are colloquially referred to as Shenn Frith.*

gambeson - *(GAM-bə-sən)* - *A padded shirt worn under armor.*

Geornlice - *(JORN-liss)* - *Southern land known for its swamps and bayous. Inhabited predominantly by gnomes.*

Götar - *(GÖ-tär)* - *Dwarf god of war.*

Guéret - *(GÖ-rā)* - *The land in Laon held by the Marchant family.*

Hewrey - *(HYÜ-rē)* - *Raffe, sergeant at arms at Ridderzaal.*

Hyrde - *(HĒRD)* - *Central region of Erda. Homeland of Cedric.*

Hyrden - *(HĒRDen)* - *The people of Hyrde.*

Jenlyns - *(JEN-linz)* - *A Knight-Captain of Hyrde.*

Jetningen - *(JET-ning-en)* - *Mountainous land to the east of Erda. Inhabited by trolls.*

Keir - *(KAIR)* - *Famous Pretanian King who lived 200 years before The Crafter's Son.*

Krigare - *(CREE-gar)* - *The war-like race of people living in the north.*

Krigsrike - *(KRĒG's-rike)* - *Home of the Krigare. The land occupying the northern-most region of Erda.*

Laon - *(LAY-on)* - *The breadbasket of Erda. A flat land of rich soil where a majority of the grain consumed in Erda is produced. Occupying the southwest corner of Erda, between the forests of Fardach Sidhe and Shenn Frith, and the swamplands of Geornlice.*

Laonese - *(LAY-on-ēz)* - *The people of Laon.*

Long Lake - *A large lake which forms the eastern border of Hyrde. To the east of the lake lie Jetningen and Dvargheim.*

Lorelei - *(LORE-ə -lie)* - *A princess of Hyrde.*

Mahjar - *(MÄ-ʒar)* - *A tribal and nomadic race of humans from the Namur region, famed for their horses. All Mahjars are from Namur. But not all people of Namur are of the race of the Mahjar.*

Mairwen - *(MAIR-wen)* - *A maid of Ridderzaal castle.*

Marchant - *(marsh-AUNT)* - *Laonese family name of Laudan and his father Odilon.*

Mikele - *(mi-KEL-lay) - A goddess and patron/protector of the Gaidheal.*

Miremont - *(MIR-ə-mont) - A large trade city in central Laon.*

Mirgul - *(MEER-gül) - A god. Brother to Mirren.*

Mirren - *(MIR-en) - A god. Brother to Mirgul.*

Mungo - *(Mung-go) - Pretani god of luck.*

Namur - *(NÄ-mur) - A land of rolling hills and wild grassland where the Namur people raise their herds of half-tame horses. It occupies the region between Pretania to the west, Krigsrike to the north, Ath to the east, and Hyrde to the south.*

Oskar - *(OSS-kar) - An orphan who grew up on the streets of Arlon*

Per/Pers - *(Pur/Purz) - Short for Persimmon. A young boy who helped Breeden and Sergeant Hewrey with the binding of Tavish Ranald's injury.*

Pretania - *(pre-TÄN-ya) - A land of high elevation with a challenging terrain composed of bluffs and steep hills, occupying the northwest region of Erda.*

Pretani/Pretanian - *(pre-TÄN-ē/pre-TÄN-ē-ən) - The people of Pretania.*

Ranald - *(RA-nəld) - Last/family name of Tavish, a Hyrden noble.*

Raulin - *(Raw-lin) - The King of Hyrde, Laon, and Pretania.*

Rhonwen - *(RON-wen) - An elven princess and warrior.*

Ridderzaal *(RID-ur-zäl) - The name of the castle, and the city which surrounds it, in the south of Hyrde, on Long Lake.*

Robinet - (rob-i-NĀ) - Family name of Derek, and his father Hugh. Laonese nobles.

satje - (SÄT-jay) - A spicy treat of smoked or dried fish, beef or poultry served on sticks.

seneschal - (SEN-ə-Shəl) - A steward in charge of a lord's estate.

Shenn Frith - (shenn FRITH) - A small region of land located in the western forests of Erda, occupied by the Gaidheal. Also, the name commonly used to describe the people of that land.

Starkad - (STAR-kad) - Family name of Kestrel, and his father Ayres, Pretanian nobles.

tabard - (TA-bard) - An outer tunic worn by a knight over his armor.

Usen - (YÜ-sen) - Prophet of the One God.

Wilham - (WILL-em) - A famous conquering king of Hyrde who consolidated the nations of Pretania, Laon, and Hyrde as a single kingdom.

Woodfall - (WOOD-fall) - River and town on Long Lake where Breeden grew up.

Ydenia - (ē-DĒN-yə) - A journeyman mage, and friend of Cedric.

* Stress/emphasis is shown by word parts in ALL CAPS (non-stressed syllables are in lower case). Where I've used symbols or diacritical marks, here is what they mean!

a - "a" as in bad
ä- "ah" as in ma or father
ā - "ay" as in day
ə - "uh" as in duh or what
e - "e" as in bed

ē- *"ee" as in* feed

i - *"ih" as in* dip

ī– *"ii" as in* wide

ʒ - *"zh" as in* version *or* usual

ö - *"oe" as in* voy**eur**

ō- *"oh" as in* go

ü- *"oo" as in* goose *or* blue

Other:

Knight-Captain - *A commanding officer of an army of knights and accompanying foot soldiers.*

Knight-General - *A commanding officer in charge of a nation's army in times of war.*

Currency:

1 gold crown = 10 silver swans

1 silver swan = 10 copper commons

Join the Crafter's Guild!

This book may have ended. But your journey begins now. Join the guild and become part of the story.

- Members of the guild are always the first to hear about Matthew's new books and publications.
- Members will receive access to free behind-the-scenes content, such as maps, character sheets, and other Crafter artifacts—as we create them.
- Finally, some lucky guild members will have the opportunity to become beta readers for book two (and beyond!).

Join the Crafter's Guild!
http://www.matthewbberg.com/join

Reviews needed!

Like the book? If so, it would mean a lot to me if you would leave a review on Amazon.

Many people won't take a chance on a new writer putting out a first book. So the more positive reviews I can accumulate, the more likely it is for other readers to give my work a chance.

Thanks in advance for your help!

ABOUT THE AUTHOR

Matthew Berg is a Director of IT by day, a dad and husband by night and weekend, and a writer by commute. He loves to travel —though mostly for the food. He's been playing D&D (on and off) since he and his brothers picked up the *Basic Set* at Lauriat's Books in 1977. He is known to attend renaissance fairs in period garb. And he has far, far too many hobbies.

Since this is the initial release of his first book, he doesn't have compelling quotes about his work to share from authors like Terry Brooks and Brandon Sanderson. Yet. But when he does, you can be sure he'll include them here in his author's biography.

Printed in Great Britain
by Amazon

40178481R00177